澄清聲明

親愛的讀者：

倍斯特出版事業有限公司鄭重聲明，大陸中國紡織出版社與本社無業務往來。

近來發現本社之公司Logo，出現於中國紡織出版社之貝斯特英語系列書籍，該出版社自 2012年11月1日起之所有出版品與本社並無任何關係；鑑於此事件，懷疑有人利用本社之商業信譽，藉此誤導大眾，本社予以高度關注。特此聲明，以正視聽。

倍斯特出版事業有限公司　敬啟

倍斯特出版事業有限公司
Best Publishing Ltd.

職場英語
社交力的全盤突破

倍斯特編輯部 ◎著

上班族 開口就會的英語溝通術

WOW~
Just Talk Every Day!

著重美式俚語的表達與學習，文章對白幽默雋永：讓你的表達更加流暢自然，不再有詞無法達意的窘境。

主題式情境對話和精選單字：開會或應答時，不再沉默，本書深知讀者的難處，精選上班族所真正需要的情境用詞，輔以情境對白與句例，對症下藥，職場英語不再怕。

延伸句型：由例句來學習和例句相關的句型，培養英語的紮實基礎，舉一馬上聯想到相關的應答語彙，使你得以靈活運用，溝通有自信，英語交談總是合宜。

100篇商務會話：用老外的邏輯，模擬實況與對策，強化英語表達方式，遇到老外，得以合作無間，深得上司的賞識與老闆的心。

會說英語還不夠，要讓英語表達，適逢其時、源源不絕、字字珠璣！
一旦想不出來怎樣說，馬上參閱本書，讓你的職場英語馬上溜！

特約編輯序

PREFACE

　　相信大家都曾有過相同的經驗，就是在職場上與同事、客戶或者是上司的英文對話中有時會出現 "卡住" 或是 "冷場" 的狀況，這樣除了會造成自己本身對開口說英文的挫敗感，有時也會讓上司覺得自己的英文程度不佳，甚至嚴重一點的，可能會在商業談判當中錯失先機。有鑑於此，在《上班族一開口就會的英語溝通術》這一本書當中，我們設計了50種在職場上最常發生的情境，並以對話的方式呈現。在情境對話當中收錄可能會遇到的問題，以及應對的對策及回答方式，希望能加深讀者的印象，並能更進一步的簡單運用在日常的職場生活上。

　　在本書中，除了有由不同立場角度出發的情境對話之外，還收錄了一些常用的單字、片語以及俚語，並加上例句或是相關的由來解說，讓讀者能在這一些單字、片語及俚語的使用上能夠更加的得心應手。在對話當中，加入一些常用但容易被混淆的文法觀念的句子，以對話的情境加上簡單的文法解釋，讓該文法的使用方式更能簡單易懂，希望讀者在職場中能更清楚明白的表達自己的意見，為自己的表現加分，為自己在職場上的英文社交能力加分！

陳欣慧

　　《上班族一開口就會的英語溝通術》是一本實用又符合職場需求的萬用英語學習書。由於瞭解到，在上班時，需要用英語對話的場面，有時著實讓人心生恐懼，就怕應對的不好或不恰當，讓人不由自主地緊張起來。因應許多上班族和公司行號的需要，本書收納了各式各樣上班族會面對的英語溝通場景，有好的預備，就不怕應用的時候會沒辦法。解決上班時英語溝通的困擾，就是要在許多常用與會用到的工作情境英語的對談的內容上學習如何用英語來表達，本書就是最好的輔助，讓你對於很多常常使用卻又不知道如何用英語說才好的會話、句型、與詞彙，有一個全盤吸收的主題式學習，經由令人感到興趣的辦公室話題與討論，增進讀者的對於學英語的興趣並加深印象，讓學習的動機與成果更加有效與提升。特別是本書讀起來讓人有輕鬆愉快之感，隨著有趣的情境對話，一步步強化職場英語的能力。鼓勵您好好善用本書，您會有意想不到的收穫的。

倍斯特編輯部

SEQUENCE EDITOR

編輯序

目 次
CONTENTS

目　次
CONTENTS

Part Seven 業務絕對成交會話

目 次
CONTENTS

Part Eight | 上班後

Part One

上班前

Before you go to work

Unit 01 詢問確認面試時間

Dialog 1

Annie	Hello!	哈囉！
Leo	Hello, may I speak to Annie Patterson, please?	哈囉！請問Annie Patterson在嗎？
Annie	This is Annie speaking, who's calling, please?	我就是，請問是哪位？
Leo	Hi, Annie, this is Leo Jonas calling from BC Corporation. We had received your resume for applying the position of Sales Superviso. And we would like to invite you to come to our company for interview. Can we make an appointment for Wednesday morning at 10 am?	嗨，Annie，我是BC公司的Leo Jonas。我們有收到妳應徵銷售主任一職的履歷。我們希望妳能到本公司來面試。我們可以約在星期三早上10點鐘嗎？
Annie	Oh, thank you for calling, Mr. Jonas. About the appointment, I have a scheduling conflict, I cannot make it on Wednesday. I will be out of town that day. Is there any possibility that we can make it on Friday?	喔，謝謝您的來電，Jonas先生。關於面試時間，跟我的預定行程有一些衝突，我不能約在星期三，那天我人會在外地。是否能改約在星期五呢？

Leo	Please hold on one second, let me check my schedule. Friday? It looks like I don't have any time available after Thursday within this week. How about Thursday at 10 am?	請等一下，我看一下我的行程表。星期五？看起來在這一週之內從星期四之後我的行程是滿檔的。能約在星期四早上10點嗎？
Leo	I am sorry, but I can't make it that early. Actually, I'll be back on Thursday morning.	我很抱歉，但我沒辦法約那麼早。事實上，我要到星期四早上才能回來。
Leo	If I put you in at a later spot, would that work out?	如果我幫你安排在晚一點的時段，這樣可以嗎？
Annie	That will be great.	那就太好了。
Leo	How about 2 pm?	下午2點？
Annie	Perfect. Thank you, Mr. Jonas. Can I take you phone number, please.	沒問題，謝謝您Jonas先生。可以給我您的聯絡電話嗎？
Leo	Yes, do you have a pen and some paper?	可以，你手邊有紙筆嗎？
Annie	Yes, I have.	有的。
Leo	My office number is ****-**** extension ***. If you have any problem, please feel free to contact me.	我的辦公室電話是****-****分機***。如果有任何問題，隨時方便跟我聯絡。
Annie	I'm sorry, I didn't quite catch that, could you please repeat the number?	不好意思，我沒有聽清楚，可以再跟我說一次電話號碼嗎？
Leo	No problem. My office number is ****-****, extension ***.	沒問題，我的辦公室電話是****-****分機***。

Annie	Sorry, Mr. Jonas, just to confirm, your last name is spelled J-O-N-A-S, is that correct?	不好意思，Jonas先生，跟您確認一下，您的姓氏是拼做J-O-N-A-S，沒錯吧？
Leo	Yes, that's correct.	沒有錯。
Annie	Thank you so much for calling me, Mr. Jonas, and I'll see you on Thursday afternoon at 2 o'clock.	謝謝您的來電通知，Jonas先生，那我們星期四下午2點鐘見。
Leo	You are welcome, see you on Thursday.	不客氣，星期四見。

Dialog 2

Michelle	Good afternoon. How may I help you?	午安，有什麼能為您效勞的嗎？
Annie	Good afternoon. My name is Annie Patterson. I would like to see Mr. Jonas.	午安。我是Annie Patterson。我要找Jonas先生。
Michelle	Mr. Jonas of the Human Resource Department?	人力資源部的Jonas先生嗎？
Annie	Yes.	是的。
Michelle	Do you have an appointment?	請問有預約嗎？
Annie	Yes, I am here for the interview, and we have an appointment at 2 o'clock.	有的，我是來面試的，我們約在2點鐘。
Michelle	Can you please wait here just a moment, I will get Mr. Jonas for you.	可以麻煩您等一下嗎？我馬上為您跟Jonas先生聯絡。
Annie	Sure, thank you very much.	當然可以，謝謝您。

Michelle	Ms. Patterson, I sorry that Mr. Jonas has an emergency meeting this afternoon, and is not expected to be finished before 5 o'clock. Would you please have a seat? And I'll find out if he made any arrangement for someone else to interview you.	不好意思，Patterson小姐。Jonas先生今天下午有一個緊急會議，可能在5點鐘之前都無法結束。您可以先稍坐一下嗎？我問問看他是不是有安排其他人幫您做面試？
Annie	Thank you.	謝謝。
Michelle	You are welcome.	不客氣。
Michelle	Ms. Patterson, I just checked with the Human Resource Department, and Mrs. Bradley will be your interviewer today. She is just finishing up an interview and she will be ready to see you shortly. Would you like to have a cup of tea while you are waiting?	Patterson小姐，我剛與人力資源部聯繫過了，Bradley太太是您今天的面試官。她剛剛才結束一個面試，再等一會兒就可以見您了。要不要先來杯茶呢？
Annie	Yes, please. That would be nice.	好的，那麻煩您了。
Michelle	Here's your tea.	這是您的茶。
Annie	Thanks.	謝謝。
Michelle	You are welcome.	不客氣。
Michelle	Ms. Patterson, Mrs. Bradley is ready to see you. The Human Resource Department is on the fifth floor, and you can take the elevator at the front. Good luck to your interview.	Patterson小姐，Bradley太太可以見您了。人力資源部門在5樓，您可以在前面搭電梯上去。祝您面試順利。
Annie	Thank you so much.	非常謝謝您。

💬 精選單字及片語

1. resume(s) *n.* 履歷表
   We have received your resume.
   我們收到了你的履歷表。

2. apply 不及物動詞應徵，申請，請求 (+for / to) apply for + 欲申請的標的物 （如職務，許可等）
   I want to apply for the position of manager.
   我要應徵經理的職務。

   apply to + 欲申請的對象 （如公司，學校等）
   I want to apply to BC Corporation as a manager.
   我要應徵BC公司經理的職務。

3. make an appointment 相約，預定
   Can we make an appointment at 8 pm?
   我們可以約在晚上八點嗎？

   make an appointment with + (某人) 與某人有約
   I've made an appointment with Johnny.
   我已與和強尼有約。

4. conflict(s) *n.* 衝突，抵觸
   I have a scheduling conflict.
   與我的預定行程有衝突。

5. emergency (emergencies) *n.* 緊急情況，突發事件
   He has to attend an emergency meeting.
   他必須參加一個緊急會議。

6. find out 發現，查明，找出
   Let's find out the difference.
   讓我們來找出不一樣的地方。

7. finish up 結束，完成
   We must finish up this project in day or two.
   我們必須在這1~2天內完成這項計畫。

💬 精選句子與延伸

1. I am sorry, but I can't make it that early.　我很抱歉，但我沒辦法約那麼早。
   在句中 it 是指 appointment。
   也可以 I cannot make it at that time.
   我沒辦法約那個時間。

2. If I put you in at a later spot, would that work out?　如果我幫你安排在晚一點的時段，
   這樣可以嗎？
   put in- (使)在內; 加進，投入; 插話，做補充; 選舉…執政
   They have put in lots of time and effort on that project.
   他們在那企劃上投入了大量的時間及精力。
   "He was a doctor before that."　Annie put in.
   "在那之前，他是個醫生"　安妮插話補充。
   The candidate was put in with an increased majority.
   候選人以多數選票當選。

3. I didn't quite catch that.　我沒有聽清楚。
   I don't get it. / I don't get your point. / I don't quite follow you.
   我不明白你的意思。

4. I just checked with the Human Resource Department.　我剛與人力資源部聯繫過了。
   check with- 與…聯繫。但有些情況可作為跟…相符，
   例如 The shipment does not check with the sample.
   　　　裝船的貨物與其樣品不符。

個人學經歷描述

Mrs. Bradley	Good afternoon, my name is Jami and you must be Annie.	午安,我是Jami,妳一定是Annie吧。
Annie	Yes, I am Annie, very nice to meet you.	是,我是Annie,非常高興能見到妳。
Mrs. Bradley	Very nice to meet you, too. Welcome to our company.	我也是。歡迎到我們的公司來。
Annie	Thank you.	謝謝。
Mrs. Bradley	OK, tell me a little bit about yourself.	OK,跟我聊一聊妳自己。
Annie	I am 26 years old. I have a Master degree with a major in Marketing. I have 4 years work experience and have been worked as a sales supervisor for 1.5 years.	我今年26歲。我有碩士學位主修行銷。我有4年的工作經驗,一年半擔任銷售主任的職位。
Mrs. Bradley	Where did you get your degree?	妳是哪個學校畢業的?
Annie	I was graduated from Durham University.	我畢業於德倫大學。
Mrs. Bradley	Is that in UK?	是在英國嗎?
Annie	Yes, it is.	是的。

Mrs. Bradley	Do you mind to tell me about why you studied in UK?	妳介不介意告訴我為什麼在英國唸書？
Annie	No, not at all. My parents divorced when I was 15. My mom is British, she went back London after divorce, and I lived with her.	不，一點也不。我父母在我15歲時離婚。我媽媽是英國人，在離婚後回到倫敦，而我跟她住。
Mrs. Bradley	Oh, I'm sorry.	喔，不好意思。
Annie	Never mind, actually my parents resumed their marital relationship when I was 18, so my mother moved back to L.A. and lived with my father. I still stayed in UK, because the university had already accepted my enrollment.	沒關係，事實上我父母在我18歲時復婚了，所以我母親搬回洛杉磯與我父親同住。我還待在英國，因為當時學校已經接受我的入學申請了。
Mrs. Bradley	As I know that you worked for your former company for 4 years since your internship, what makes you leave that job?	據我所知，妳在妳之前任職的那家公司工作了四年，從實習時就開始了。什麼原因讓妳離職呢？
Annie	My father had a heart surgery several months ago, and my mother was panic. I'm worried about my father's illness and don't want to live too far away from them, so I quit and moved back.	我父親幾個月前動了一次心臟手術，我母親嚇壞了。我很擔心我父親的病情，不想住的離他們太遠，所以我辭職並搬回來。
Mrs. Bradley	Tell me about your last job.	跟我聊聊你之前的工作。

| Annie | I was the sales supervisor of a mobile devices company. I made sales to telecom companies. I worked with 10 other people in my team, and we helped each other by sharing ideas and experiences. | 我以前是一家行動裝置公司的銷售主任。負責的是電信公司的業務。我的團隊裡有10人，我們會分享意見及經驗來互相幫忙。 |

Dialog 2

Bob	Good morning, welcome to our company. I am your interviewer, my name is Bob.	早安，歡迎來到我們公司。我是你今天的面試官，我叫Bob。
George	Thank you, I am George, very pleased to see you.	謝謝，我是George，非常高興見到你。
Bob	Me, too. OK, can you introduce yourself first?	我也是。OK，可以先介紹你自己嗎？
George	I graduated from New York University last year. I have one year volunteer work experience in Africa.	我去年從紐約大學畢業。我有一年在非洲擔任義工的經驗。
Bob	Can you describe that what kind of volunteer work you did in Africa?	你可以描述一下你在非洲的義務工作性質為何？
George	I participated in the volunteer teaching program, and I taught English and Math to children.	我參與的是義務教育項目，我教孩子們英文及數學。
Bob	What was your major at university?	你在大學裡主修是什麼？

George	I was majoring in the Human Resource Management.	我主修人力資源管理。
Bob	What did you get from the volunteer work?	你從義務工作中得到了些什麼呢？
George	I gained lots of life experiences through that work. I saw war, disease, and poverty there, but they never give up, and always look on the sunnyside, and strive for the better.	我獲得了不少的人生經驗。我在那裡看到了戰爭，疾病及貧窮，但他們從不放棄，總是看好的一面，及努力向上。
Bob	That's a precious experience. Do you know we are actually looking for someone who has at least 1 year work experience in this area?	那是很寶貴的經驗。你知道我們實際上要找的人至少要有一年以上的相關工作經驗嗎？
George	Yes, I know. I think my education background makes me qualified for this job.	是的，我知道。我認為我的教育背景使我能勝任這份工作。
Bob	Do you have any internship experience?	你有實習的經驗嗎？
George	Yes, I have. I had my internship in a small company. I have experience in administration and human resource development.	有，我有。我在一家小公司裡實習。我有行政及人力資源發展的相關經驗。
Bob	That's great. Before we go on for the further interview, here's a survey I need you to fill out. I'll give you 30 minutes.	很好。在我們進行更進一步的面試之前，這裡有一份問卷調查我需要你來完成它。我會給你30分鐘。
George	Okay.	好的。

Bob	If you have any question, just let me know, and I'll be outside.	如果你有任何問題，就讓我知道，我人就在外面。
George	Thank you, Bob.	謝謝你，Bob。
Bob	You are welcome.	不客氣。

💬 精選單字及片語

1. **master** *n.* 碩士；雇主；大師等。在用於指碩士學位時常會以大寫M表示，還有在用於稱呼時也會大寫。
   學位：學士- Bachelor；碩士- Master；博士- Doctor

2. **enrollment** *n.* 註冊；登記；入伍。
   I got the enrollment notice from TsingHua University.
   我收到清華大學的入學通知。

3. **mobile devices** 行動裝置，也稱移動設備，流動裝置等。包含有智慧型手機，平板電腦，筆記型電腦及攜帶型遊樂器等，一般泛指便於攜帶，並可經由網路隨時獲得資訊的設備。
   Apple is a mobile devices company.
   蘋果是一家行動裝置公司。

4. **participate in** 參與，參加
   How many people participated in this campus recruitment fair?
   在這次的校園招募會上共有多少人參與呢？

5. **look on the sunny side** 看到光明的一面，看好的一面，樂觀的。
   We make life much easier and happier by always looking on the sunny side.
   我們總是從好的方面想，使我們的生活變得更簡單也更快樂。

6. **survey(s)** *n.* 調查，問卷。
   They have made a survey of public attitudes.
   他們做了一次民意調查。

🗨 精選句子與延伸

1. My mom is British, she went back London after divorce, and I lived with her.
   我媽媽是英國人，在離婚後回到倫敦，而我跟她住。
   ＝My mother is British, I lived with her in London after she and my father split up.
   British 英國人，英國的。英國 (United Kingdom) 是由4個國家聯合組成的，分別為英格蘭，蘇格蘭，威爾斯及北愛爾蘭，在英文中一般統稱英國人為British，而我們一般常見的English則是專指英格蘭人。蘇格蘭人是Scottish，威爾斯人是Welsh，及北愛爾蘭人是North Irish。

2. My parents resumed their marital relationship when I was 18, so my mother moved back to L.A. and lived with my father. 我父母在我18歲時復婚了，所以我母親搬回洛杉磯與我父親同住。＝My dad remarried my mom when I was 18, and my mom moved back to live with him in L.A.
   resume (v.) 重新開始，繼續。
   move back to 搬回

3. I graduated from New York University last year. I have one year volunteer work experience in Africa. 我去年從紐約大學畢業。我有一年在非洲擔任義工的經驗。
   ＝I was graduated from New York University last year, and have been volunteered in Africa for 1 year.
   我畢業於…有兩種說法：I was graduated …及 I graduated from …，以過去被動式語氣的I was graduated from…曾經為唯一正確的說法，但隨著時代變遷，人們認為畢業是靠自己努力，於是逐漸以過去式的 I graduated from…被人們所接受。常見的錯誤說法則為 I am graduated from…。

Unit 03 個性特質描述（優勢 vs. 劣勢）

Dialog 1

Bob	Did you finish the survey?	你完成問卷調查了嗎？
George	Yes, I did.	是的，我完成了。
Bob	How did you find the survey?	你覺得這個問卷調查如何？
George	It's very interesting. Sort of like the psychological test.	這個還蠻有趣的。有一點像是心理測驗。
Bob	As a matter of fact, it is. It is a personality test. It is used as a typology to gain insights into workplace dynamics.	事實上，你說的沒錯。這是一種性格測驗。常被用在以深入了解職場動態的一種類型學上面。
George	The Enneagram of Personality.	九型人格。
Bob	That's correct. It seems that you've learned a lot from your expertise.	沒錯。看起來你的專業學得很不錯。
George	Our psychology professor is very well-known in this area. I have benefited a lot from her lectures.	我們的心理學教授在這個領域相當有名氣。我在她的課堂上學到了很多。

Bob	That's good. Our boss believes psych tests provide very reliable and wide-ranging of the human assessment. So we use a lot of psych tests for the hiring, and evaluation. Hehe, I've gotten carried away, let's go back to the interview. George, what is your greatest strength? Because we have already had over 20 applicants for this position. What sets you apart from all the other candidates?	這樣很好。我們老闆認為心理測驗能提供非常可靠及範圍相當廣泛的人員評估。所以我們在聘僱及評估上用了很多的心理測驗。嘿嘿，我有點離題了，讓我們回到面試上。George，你最大的優點是什麼？因為我們有超過20位的應徵者在競爭這個職位。什麼使你與其他的應徵者有所不同？
George	My time management skills are excellent and I'm organized, efficient, and take pride in my ability to resolve what could be difficult situations.	我非常善於管理時間，還有我的組織力很強，有效率，並且對我自己解決困難的能力非常有自信。
Bob	Anything else?	還有其他的嗎？
George	I have already passed the PHR exam.	我已經通過人力資源管理專家的考試了。
Bob	Wow, that is a plus for you, so you'll need the working experience to get that license, right?	哇，這對你來說相當有利，所以你需要工作經驗來拿到那張證書？
George	Yes.	是的。
Bob	All right, I will let my boss to do the final decision.	好吧，我會讓我的老闆來做最後的決定。

Dialog 2

A　Please tell me what kind of person you are?

請告訴我妳是什麼樣的人？

B　I am very enthusiastic, especially in my work. I like to take up challenges, and always face challenges with a positive attitude.

我非常的有熱忱，尤其是在工作上。我喜歡接受挑戰，並總是會以正面的態度來面對挑戰。

A　So I can say that you are an optimist?

所以我可以說妳是一個樂觀主義者？

B　Yes, and I think I am not only an optimist, but also a realist. I am optimistic to face my life and every challenge, and realistic in my self-estimation, neither being conceited nor belittling myself.

對的，我認為我不只是個樂觀主義者，同時也是個現實主義者。我樂觀的面對我的生活及每一個挑戰，在自我的衡量上會實事求是，不自滿自大也不會妄自菲薄。

A　What are your strengths and weaknesses?

妳的優點及缺點是什麼呢？

B　My greatest strength is that I am performance-driven, always got my job done with excellent quality by the deadline. As to my weakness, I think I enjoy my work too much. I can't stand leaving my work half-done, so sometimes I put too much time in my work. But I am aware of my tendency to overwork and have been learning to pace myself for optimal.

我最大的優點是我追求卓越的表現，總是能在期限之前完成我的工作並有優良的品質。至於我的缺點則是，我認為我太過喜歡工作了。我無法忍受工作只做到一半，所以我投入太多時間在工作上。但我有意識到我傾向於超時工作，已經在慢慢的學著調整我的自己的步伐以達到最佳狀態。

A So does that mean you don't mind working overtime if that's necessary?

所以這代表如果需要的話妳不介意加班嗎？

B No, not at all. I'm willing to work overtime in order to achieve my progress target.

不，一點也不介意。我願意加班來達成我的進度目標。

A Actually we don't encourage our employees to work overtime, and our boss thinks that working overtime is just "robbing Peter to pay Paul". But you know, sometimes working overtime does necessary.

事實上我們並不鼓勵我們的員工加班，而且我們老闆認為加班是在 "挖東牆補西牆"。但是妳知道的，有時候加班的確是需要的。

B Yes, I do understand. Too much overtime can have negative effect on the employee's performance, however sometimes it does necessary.

是的，我了解。太常加班會造成員工表現不佳，然而有時的確是必須的。

A Is that from your experience?

這是從妳的經驗得來的嗎？

B Yes, and I'm still learning how to get a balance between them.

對，而且我還在學習要如何在兩者間取得平衡。

💬 精選單字及片語

1. **the Enneagram of Personality** 九型人格。又稱為九柱性格學，常被用在職場上員工性格的基本分析，作為分發或是雇用的參考資料。

2. **candidate(s)** *n.* 應徵者，候選人，報考者。
   He stood as a candidate in the local election.
   他作為候選人參加地方上的選舉。

3. **PHR** 人力資源管理專家。這是一種由美國人力資源認證協會所核發的資格證照，PHR是 Professional in Human Resources 的簡寫，為該協會所核發的證照中最初級的，在大學就讀的學生即可報考，但必須在畢業後有相當及相關的工作經驗方可拿到執照。是在人資界中相當有名也受肯定的證照。

4. **performance-driven** 表現、績效導向；產品性能導向。
   We're looking for someone who has good communication capability and team spirit, regard the performance-driven.
   我們要找有良好溝通能力及具團隊精神，能注意績效導向的人。

5. **pace oneself** 調整某人（工作上或是生活中）的步伐或是節奏。通常是指在有個要達成的目標之下，以持續相同的速度來進行。
   You are likely to feel a little rundown if you don't pace yourself.
   你可能會感到有些力不從心如果你沒有好好調整你的節奏的話。

6. **negative** *adj.* 負面的
   This crisis had a negative impact on the company.
   這次的危機對公司造成了負面的衝擊。

精選句子與延伸

1. I've gotten carried away.

   我有點離題了。

   美國俚語，也可以解釋為 "我扯太遠了"，這裡被 carried away（帶走）的是心思或是主題。當要說對方在談話中有心或是無心離題時就可以說 "You have gotten carried away."。

2. What is your greatest strength?

   你最大的優點是什麼？

   在面試當中，一定會聽到的前 10 大問題之一。strength 在這裡當優點，優勢，長處解釋。在回答這類型的問題時，需有自信的回答，以避免造成面試官有不信任的感覺。

3. Neither being conceited nor belittling myself.

   不自滿自大也不會妄自菲薄。

   這個句子為一個否定句，neither 及 nor 都是帶有否定的意思，連在一起使用則是兩者皆非的意思。

   neither… nor… 既不…也不…。

   She likes neither celery nor carrot.

   她不喜歡芹菜也不喜歡胡蘿蔔。

   Neither Dad nor Mom is at home.

   爸媽都不在家。

   如果要將這類型的句子改寫為肯定句的話，可以將 neither… nor… 以both… and…做替換，而在第 2 個例句則要注意 be 動詞的變化，is 要改成 are。

4. Rob Peter to pay Paul.

   挖東牆補西牆。

   英文諺語。這個諺語的起源有一個說法是在 1550 年時，倫敦的聖彼得大教堂在併入倫敦主教區之後，其資金與物資被挪用來修葺聖保羅大教堂，所以有了 "打劫彼得來付錢給保羅" 的有趣說法。但其實據考證，這句諺語早在 1550 年前就已出現，但因為形容的非常貼切及符合史證，因此這個說法被流傳下來。

Part Two

公司內部
In the Office

Unit 04 初次見面，多多指教

 Dialog 1

| Employee 1 | Hey there, you must be new to this company; I have never seen you around before. | 嗨，你一定是新進員工，我之前沒有看過你。 |

Employee 1 Hey there, you must be new to this company; I have never seen you around before.
嗨，你一定是新進員工，我之前沒有看過你。

Employee 2 I just started today, my name is Jason.
我今天剛報到，我叫做Jason。

Employee 1 Nice to meet you Jason, my name is Chris, I am one of the designers for our jewelry company.
非常高興認識你，我是Chris，我是我們珠寶公司的設計師之一。

Employee 2 Very honored to meet one of the designers of such an inspiring company.
非常榮幸能遇上在這樣一間能啟發人心的公司中工作的設計師。

Employee 1 Are you the new designer of our department?
你是我們部門新來的設計師嗎？

Employee 2 Yes, I am very happy that they chose me out of so many worthy competitors!
是的，我非常高興我能在眾多傑出的競爭者中被選上！

Employee 1 I am happy that you can join our team, Jason. Do you live in this city?
Jason，非常高興你能進入我們的團隊。你住在這個城市嗎？

Employee 2 Yes, I recently moved here from Minnesota to look for work.
是的，我為了找工作剛從明尼蘇達搬過來。

Employee 1	Oh, I have relatives in Cambridge, Minnesota.	喔，我有親戚住在明尼蘇達的劍橋市。
Employee 2	What a coincidence, that's where I lived and so does the rest of my family.	真巧，我之前就住在那，我的家人現在也還住在那裡。
Employee 1	I feel a good connection with you and I think that if we work together we will help each other become the designers of this company!	我覺得我們倆很有緣，我想如果我們一起工作的話一定能互相幫助成為這個公司的設計師！
Employee 2	It has always been my dream to design jewelry for this company and I am glad that I have met someone so nice and from my home town, now I don't feel like "a fish out of water".	為這家公司設計珠寶一直是我的夢想，我很高興能遇見這麼好的同鄉，現在我比較沒有那「渾身不自在」的感覺了。
Employee 1	All the employees in the designing department are very friendly; I will introduce them to you in a little bit.	設計部門的同事都很友善，我待會把他們介紹給你認識。
Employee 2	I have already met the head designer, Jessica, she seems very strict.	我已經見過首席設計師Jessica了，她看起來很嚴厲。
Employee 1	Yes, she may seem strict but she is passionate about her work. She is easy to get along with after you get to know her.	對，她或許看起來很嚴格但她對工作卻非常的熱血。你認識她之後會發現其實她很好相處。
Employee 2	Hope she won't be too strict on me.	希望她不會對我太嚴格。
Employee 1	Well, enough chit chat, we have to get back to work now, plenty of time to get to know each other in the future.	好了，先聊到這，我們現在要開始工作了，我們以後有大把的時間可以互相認識。

Employee 2	I am looking forward to working with you and knowing everyone else in the future.	我很期待和你一起工作及認識其他人。
Employee 1	See you later!	待會見！
Employee 2	Talk to you soon.	等一下再聊。

Dialog 2

Employee 1	Hey, so you are the new sales associate in our car company?	嗨，你是我們汽車公司新進的銷售人員嗎？
Employee 2	Yes my name is George, very pleased to meet you.	是的，我叫做George，非常高興認識你。
Employee 1	Where are you from?	你從哪來的？
Employee 2	I have always lived in this city, I just graduated from college.	我一直住在這個城市，我剛從大學畢業。
Employee 1	You are very young, what made you want to be a car salesman?	你年紀這麼輕，為什麼想當汽車銷售人員呢？
Employee 2	Well, my dad is a car mechanic so since I was very young, I have always been very interested in cars and though that I would make a very good salesperson.	嗯，我爸爸是個汽車技工，所以從我小時候，我就對汽車有很大的興趣，而且我覺得我應該可以成為一個不錯的銷售人員。

Employee 1	Sounds like our boss made a good choice hiring you. Well, sales is a tougher job than you think, I have had this job for about 10 years now, you can say I am the one with the most experience here! I have gotten employee of the year 3 years in a row already!	聽起來老闆決定雇用你是對的。嗯，銷售的工作比想像中的難，我在這一行已經做了快10年了，算是公司裡最有經驗的！我已經連續3年都得到年度最佳員工。
Employee 2	Wow, it is my pleasure to work aside such a wise and experience person such as yourself.	哇，我真榮幸能在像你這樣有智慧及經驗的人身邊工作。
Employee 1	Oh, I am very flattered, you don't seem too bad yourself, and once you sell your first car you will get the hang of it real soon. The stall and I will guide you.	你過獎了，你也不錯，當你在賣出你的第一輛車之後就會慢慢上軌道的。營業所和我都會引導你的。
Employee 1	Thank you! Come to think of it I never asked for your name.	謝謝！突然想到還沒請教你的大名是？
Employee 1	Oh, my name is Richard but you can call me Ricky.	喔，我是Richard你可以叫我Ricky。
Employee 2	Nice to meet you Ricky, I feel very comfortable and welcomed here already.	非常高興認識你，Ricky，我已經感受到自在及受歡迎了。
Employee 1	You are now a part of our team; we all treat each other like family.	你現在是我們團隊的一份子了，我們都像是家人一般的相處。
Employee 2	Thank you so much for such a warm welcome.	謝謝你們的熱烈歡迎。

Employee 1	No problem, just let me know if you need any advice, ok?	不客氣，需要建議時儘管問我，知道了嗎？
Employee 2	I will definitely need a lot of help settling in these next few days.	我在接下來的這幾天內穩定之前一定會需要許多協助的。
Employee 1	The entire staff would love to help you out.	所有的員工都會很樂意幫你的。
Employee 2	I hope to make the most out of this job.	我希望能在工作中充分發揮所能。
Employee 1	I am sure you will.	我相信你可以做到的。
Employee 2	Thank you!	謝謝！

精選單字及片語

1. **Inspiring** *adj.* 鼓舞人心的，啟發靈感的，激勵的
   It is an inspiring sight.
   那是個振奮人心的光景。

2. **a fish out of water** 如魚離水，用以形容因環境的改變或是不熟悉而產生的不自在，不舒服的感覺
   I was a fish out of water at his party because I knew no one.
   在他的派對上我感到渾身不自在，因為我一個人也不認識。

3. **get the hang of** 進入狀況，摸到訣竅
   You get the hang of it so quickly.
   你很快就進入狀況了。

4. **stall(s)** *n.* 馬廄，牛棚，貨攤，小隔間
   stall 亦可做動詞使用，有將牲畜關入柵欄中；使進退不得；使停頓；推託，支吾其詞等之意。在名詞的用法上，也有許多含意，如停車位，牧師席或是牧師職位，飛機失速，汽車拋錨熄火，也有做藉口，敷衍或是盜賊扒手同黨的解釋。stall 在本文中意為銷售汽車的營業所。

5. I am flattered.　你過獎了，受寵若驚，深感榮幸
I am flattered by her commendation.
被她誇獎讓我感到十分榮幸。

💬 精選句子與延伸

1. I am very happy that they chose me out of so many worthy competitors!　我非常高
興我能在眾多傑出的競爭者中被選上！
out of 從…中，在…當中
I am going to choose 1 student out of the 15 who have A's to be the mentor for this
class.
我要從15個拿到A的學生中選出一位來當班上的小老師。
worthy *adj.*　傑出的，值得的，足以…的；亦可當名詞使用，如傑出人士，知名人
物，偉人

2. Well, enough chit chat.　好了，先聊到這。
chit chat/chitchat(s) *n./ vi.*　閒聊，談天，哈啦。chit chat指的是在一些社交場合中非
正式的談話。
My sister and I love to chitchat on the phone after work.
我姊姊和我喜歡下班後在電話裡閒聊。

3. Come to think of it I never asked for your name.　突然想到還沒請教你的大名是？
come to think of it 回頭一想，突然想起，這樣一想
Come to think of it, I don't have your address.
這樣一想，我沒有你的地址。

4. I hope to make the most out of this job. 我希望能在工作中充分發揮所能。
＝I will do my best in job.
make the most (out) of
充分利用，最大限度的發揮

Unit 05 同事的升遷 party

Dialog 1

Bill Hey, did you guys hear that Johnny got promoted into our department head?

嘿，大家有沒有聽説Johnny已被晉升成為我們的部門主管？

Kate Yeah! My husband is the best! He's been working so hard for this position for 5 years; he finally has gotten the approval of the Chairman!

耶！我丈夫最棒了。他為了這個職位辛苦工作了5年，他終於得到董事長的認同了！

Nathan I really admire his work ethic, hope one day I will rise to the top like him.

我很敬佩他敬業的態度，希望有一天我也能爬到那麼高的位置。

Kate You are still young Nathan, you will have your chance in the future.

Nathan你還年輕啦，將來一定會有機會的。

Bill Yeah Nathan, you have only been with this company for a year, you still have much to learn. You should go take some advice from Johnny. We should all take advice from Johnny.

對啊，Nathan，你才剛進公司一年，還有許多要學的。你應該多向Johnny請教。我們都應該跟Johnny請教。

Jennifer I was competing against him for that spot! Although I am disappointed I lost, he deserves it. We should celebrate!

我跟他一同競爭那個職位。雖然我輸了我很失望，但那是他應得的。我們應該慶祝。

Kate	I was thinking of throwing a surprise promotion party for him this Friday night at my house. You guys are all invited.	這個星期五在我家，我打算要替他辦個驚喜的升官派對。我邀請大家一起來。
Bill	Let's invite the whole department!	讓我們邀請整個部門！
Nathan	Let's invite the whole company! I bet he would be really surprised if we got the Chairman to go!	讓我們邀請整個公司！我猜如果我們請到董事長的話，他一定會很驚訝的。
Kate	The more the merrier! The point is to surprise him! Now we think of a flawless plan so that he doesn't find out.	愈多人愈好！目的就是要讓他大吃一驚！現在我們來想個完美的計畫不要讓他發現。
Jennifer	How about you take him to a nice restaurant for a romantic dinner first so a few of us can go to your house and decorate before you guys come home?	要不要妳先帶他去高級餐廳來個浪漫的晚餐，我們幾個在你們回來之前到妳家去佈置？
Nathan	Yeah! that way he would think that the dinner was the surprise and would never think that there would be a bunch of people at his house.	對！這樣的話他就會以為晚餐是驚喜了，不會想到有一堆人在他家等著。
Bill	I will tell everyone to park a block away so it doesn't look suspicious.	我會通知所有人將車停在別條街上，這樣才不會看起來可疑。
Jennifer	I will go to the party store after work and get some party decorations as well as cups and plates.	我下班後會到派對商店買些派對裝飾還有杯子及盤子。

| Nathan | I'll grab food and drinks! Can't have a party without those! | 我會帶一些食物和飲料！派對上少不了這些。 |

| Kate | OK, seems like we have everything set, now I'll send an invitation to everyone via e-mail. What time should it start? | OK，看起來我們都分配好工作了，現在我會用email發邀請函給大家。派對要在什麼時候開始呢？ |

| Bill | I think 8 is a good time. | 我想8點好了。 |

| Kate | OK, 8 it is, my house. | OK，就8點，我家。 |

| Jennifer | Can't wait to see his surprised face! | 我等不及要看他那一張驚訝的臉了！ |

| Kate | Thanks everyone, I'll update you guys if anything changes, and please don't let my husband find out! | 謝謝大家，如果有變化的話，我會通知大家，請不要讓我先生發現！ |

Dialog 2

Johnny walks into the house with Kate. | Johnny和Kate一起走進屋內。

| Everyone | Congratulations Johnny! | 恭喜，Johnny！ |

| Johnny | I am so flattered! Did you put this together Kate? | 我真是受寵若驚！Kate這是妳安排的嗎？ |

| Kate | Nathan, Jennifer, and Bill helped as well! | Nathan，Jennifer和Bill也一起幫忙。 |

| Johnny | I better go thank them! Hey Bill! | 我最好去謝謝他們。嘿，Bill！ |

Bill	Congratulations on the promotion Johnny!	恭喜升官，Johnny！
Johnny	Thank you so much for helping to put together all this!	謝謝你協助安排這一切！
Bill	No problem, you deserve it!	不客氣，這是你應得的！
Nathan	You do deserve it and we got a special guest here for you as well! Let's welcome the Chairman!	你是當之無愧的，我們還幫你邀請到一位特別來賓喔！讓我們歡迎董事長！
Chairman	Congrats Johnny, I know I have made the right choice in promoting you. You have worked very hard in the past years to support this company.	恭喜你Johnny，我知道把你升上來是正確的決定。在過去的這幾年來，你一直都為了公司在辛勤的工作。
Johnny	Thank you, sir. I know with more power comes greater responsibilities so I will do my best.	謝謝您，董事長。我知道權力越多責任就越重，我會盡我的全力的。
Chairman	Glad to hear.	非常高興你這麼說。
Jennifer	Well, you are the only person in the world that I am happy about losing.	你是唯一一位在這個世界上讓我輸給了你，我還感到高興的人。
Johnny	Thank you for coming and even helping to make this party happen. I think that you would be just as good of a department head as I am if you were chosen.	謝謝你來參加甚至還幫忙籌辦派對。我認為如果是妳被提拔的話，妳也跟我一樣足以勝任部門主管的位置。
Jennifer	We will be completing again soon, don't think that I have given up!	我們很快會再有競爭的機會，不要以為我會就此放棄！

Johnny	That's the Jennifer I know!	這正是我所認識的Jennifer！
Jennifer	Congratulations again.	再一次恭喜你。
Johnny	I appreciate it, Jennifer.	謝謝你Jennifer。
Nathan	Let's raise a toast to Johnny!	讓我們敬Johnny一杯！
Everyone	To Johnny!	敬Johnny！

💬 精選單字及片語

1. take advice　聽話，徵求意見，請教
   Take advice and listen to other.
   接受建議及傾聽別人的想法。
   Take advice from your mother.
   聽你母親的話。

2. compete against　與…競爭
   Kim was competing against Jim for the position of manager.
   Kim和Jim在爭奪經理這一個職位。

3. the more the merrier＝the more the better　越多越好，多多益善
   Everyone loves money, the more the better.
   每個人都愛錢，越多越好。

4. deserve v.　應得，值得
   You deserve it. 這是你應得的。（在英文中，這一句話同時具有褒貶義，可以作為實至名歸，也可作為活該的解釋，通常需以對話內容及對方語氣來做分別。）

5. congrats n.　口語中的祝賀，恭喜＝congratulations。
   Please accept this gift as a token of my congratulations.
   請接受這一個禮物以聊表我的祝賀之意。

精選句子與延伸

1. Hey, did you guys hear that Johnny got promoted into our department head?
   嘿，大家有沒有聽說Johnny已被晉升成為我們的部門主管？
   ＝Have you ever heard that Johnny was promoted to our department head? 如果在句子中要強調Johnny的升遷是他應得的，句中的Johnny was promoted可以用Jonny earned a promotion來代替，亦可寫作Johnny achieved a promotion to our department head.

2. I was thinking of throwing a surprise promotion party for him this Friday night at my house. You guys are all invited!
   這個星期五在我家，我打算要替他辦個驚喜的升官派對。
   think of 打算，考慮，認為。這個片語是及物動詞，所以在後面需接名詞，於是在句中是接throwing動名詞（動詞+ing），而不是throw。
   I am thinking of investing in real estate. 我考慮投資房地產。
   throw a party 舉辦派對，也可以用hold a party, arrange a party等等。

3. I know with more power comes greater responsibilities so I will do my best.
   我知道權力越多責任就越重，我會盡我的全力的。
   在蜘蛛人電影中，Uncle Ben勉勵男主角 "With great power comes greater responsibilities"（能力越強，責任越大），被選為百大電影經典名句之一。在片中的power指的是男主角的能力。而在Johnny與董事長的對話中，這裡的power則是指Johnny在升官後所得到的更多權力。

Unit 06 下屬跟主管請假

Dialog 1

Employee	Morning Manager, I would like to ask for a day off tomorrow.	早安經理，明天我想要請個假。
Manager	A day off tomorrow? What is the reason that you need to take the day off?	你明天要請假？為什麼要請假呢？
Employee	Well you see, my wife and I are expecting a child and it is getting close to the due date so we are heading into the hospital tomorrow to prepare.	你知道的，我太太懷孕了，而我妻子的預產期就在這幾天了，所以我們明天要到醫院待產。
Manager	OK, well first you need to fill out some forms so that we may document your absence. You know that the company does not cover this and you will not be paid for your absence?	OK，那首先你必需填一些表格，讓公司有你請假的記錄。你知道，公司在你這段請假期間是不付薪水的嗎？
Employee	Yes, I know very well sir. Who do I give the forms to?	是的，我了解這個狀況。那這些請假單要交給誰呢？
Manager	I think there might be a problem because you have to send it up to our payment department as well as the head of the department for approval first. This might take a few days.	我想會有點問題，因為在你送到我們的薪資部門之前必須先經過部門主管的同意。這可能需要幾天的時間。

Employee	I did not know that the process was so lengthy.	我不知道這過程會這麼長。
Manager	Yes, well, if you submit the paperwork now, they might approve it by the afternoon.	對啊,如果你現在呈交這些表格,他們可能可以在這個下午完成批准。
Employee	What if I do not get the approval by this afternoon?	那如果這個下午還沒被批准呢?
Manager	Then I think you might have to wait until it is approved for you to take the day off.	那我想你可能要到被批准之後才能請假。
Employee	But we have an appointment with the doctor tomorrow.	但我們明天已經預約好了醫生。
Manager	You know very well that this company has very strict policies especially regarding absences.	你十分清楚公司有非常嚴格的規定,特別是在請假這方面。
Employee	Is there any way that I can make the approval process faster?	有沒有任何辦法可以讓批准過程快一些?
Manager	I believe if you go into both offices personally and fill out all documents there, they would approve you faster.	我相信如果你親自到這兩間辦公室辦理並當場填妥表格,他們應該會快一點批准的。
Employee	Do you think that would work?	你認為這樣可行?
Manager	It would be better if you fill out all the forms now and bring them in with you. I am sure they will understand your urgency.	如果你現在將這些表格填妥並親自送去。我想他們能了解你的緊急狀況。

Employee	I better get on it now!	我最好現在就去做！
Manager	No problem, hope you get your absence approved.	沒問題，希望你能快點被准假。
Employee	Thank you, sir.	謝謝你，長官。
Manager	Congratulations on the baby!	恭喜你就要當爸爸了！

Dialog 2

Employee	Hey Mr. Smith, I would like to request a day off for tomorrow.	Smith先生，我明天想請一天假。
Manager	So soon? What's the emergency?	這麼快？有什麼緊急狀況嗎？
Employee	You see, it is my birthday today and I am holding a get-together at my apartment. There will be alcoholic beverages and I think that I will be more responsible for me not to come to work with a hangover.	你知道，今天是我的生日，我在我家辦了個聚會，會提供含酒精飲料，我認為不要帶著宿醉來上班是比較負責任的方式。
Manager	Happy birthday! Although not coming to work with a hangover is a responsible thing to do, the better option would be to change the date of the get-together.	生日快樂！雖然宿醉不來上班是負責任的態度，但是更好的選擇是將聚會改期。
Employee	I have been planning this for a long time with many of my friends, it would be inconvenient for everyone.	我已經跟很多朋友計畫好久了，更改日期對大家來說都不方便。

Manager	If you have been planning for a long time, you should have looked into our company's absence policy.	如果你已經計畫很久了，你就更應該有仔細研究過我們公司的請假規定。
Employee	I have never had an absence before so do you think they would overlook it?	我之前從來沒有請過假，你想他們會不會通融？
Manager	I am one of the heads of this department and although I can help approve your absence, our company has rules that we cannot ignore.	我是這個部門的主管之一，雖然我可以批准你的假，但是公司規定是不容疏忽的。
Employee	Please sir, can you help me?	拜託，經理，可以幫幫我嗎？
Manager	I'll see what I can do, but please fill out all the necessary forms first.	我盡力吧，但是先填好所有需要的表格。
Employee	OK.	沒問題。
Manager	Let me go talk to the other heads and I'll come back to you with the results.	讓我先和其他主管討論一下，待會我再過來告訴你結果。
Employee	Thank you sir, I appreciate your help.	謝謝你，經理。非常感謝你的幫忙。
Manager	They said that there will be a penalty fee for submitting forms at the last minute, is that OK?	他們說這麼晚才提出假單要罰款，這樣可以嗎？
Employee	Yes, I accept the penalty.	好的，我接受罰款。
Manager	OK, then they have approved your absence for tomorrow.	好的，那他們准許你明天請假。

Employee	I don't get paid tomorrow and now I have to pay a penalty fee as well…	我這樣少了明天一天的薪資還要加上罰款…
Manager	So don't forget to submit absence documents earlier next time.	所以下次記得要早一點提出假單。
Employee	I will, thank you so much sir.	我會的，非常謝謝你，經理。
Manager	Happy birthday once again.	再一次祝你生日快樂。

精選單字及片語

1. take a day off　請假，休假。與 ask for leave/absence 相同，其中 leave 及 absence 為不可數名詞，所以前面不可加 a。兩個片語有些微的差異，day off 中包含週休二日或是公休日，而 leave 通常是指必須申請的休假，如年假或是事假。
   一般常用的假別如下：
   sick leave- 病假
   personal leave- 事假
   maternity leave- 產假及陪產假，可在maternity leave後加上for female/male employee（女性/男性員工）做區別。
   marital/marriage leave- 婚假
   annual leave- 年假
   official leave- 公假
   parental leave- 育嬰假，有時還會看到paternity leave，這是專指男性員工的育嬰假
   funeral leave- 喪假
   menstrual leave/period leave/sick leave- 生理假
   work related injury leave- 工傷假
   job seeking leave- 謀職假

2. penalty(penalties) *n.*　懲罰，罰款，報應
   Crimes of violence carry heavy penalties.　嚴懲暴力罪行。

💬 精選句子與延伸

1. My wife and I are expecting a child and it is getting close to the due date so we are heading into the hospital tomorrow to prepare. 我太太懷孕了，而我妻子的預產期就在這幾天了，所以我們明天要到醫院待產。
   ＝My wife is pregnant and the baby is due in a few days, so we are going to the hospital tomorrow to prepare.
   be expecting a child/baby 懷孕，期待孩子的誕生。

2. You need to fill out some forms so that we may document your absence. 你必需填一些表格，讓公司有你請假的記錄。
   form 表格，在這裡是指假單，英文是leave request form或是leave absence form。
   fill out 填寫（表格）。用以表示填寫表格的片語還有fill in，但fill in強調的是填寫表格空白的內容，而fill out則是強調完整的填寫。
   e.g. You have to fill out the leave request form and be sure to fill in each blank.
   你必須填好假單，注意每個空格處都要填寫。

3. I have never had an absence before so do you think they would overlook it? 我之前從來沒有請過假，你想他們會不會通融？
   absence(s) (n.) 缺席，缺勤，缺乏，缺少，心不在焉。absence通常指的是缺席或是不在的事實，這時候是不可數名詞。但在指不在場或是缺席的次數時，absence為可數名詞。
   e.g. Absence increased because of the flu. 因為流行性感冒，缺席的人數增加了。
   overlook (vt.) 忽略，不計較，瞭望，檢查。在本文中overlook意為不計較。
   e.g. We decide to overlook her mistake. 我們決定寬容她犯的過失。

Unit 07 團購

Dialog 1

Linda	Hey, everyone! It's almost Christmas! We all know that every year around this time, there will be a giant Gucci bag sale; everyone knows that they sell out really fast but my sister works at a Gucci store and she gets an employee's discount on top of the sale price.	大家注意！就快到耶誕節了！我們都知道每年到了這個時候，都會有Gucci包的大減價。大家都知道它們一下子就賣完了，但是我妹妹在Gucci店裡工作，她可以拿到減價後的價錢再加上員工折扣。
Michelle	Oh, I have been eyeing this purse for the longest time but it's never on sale!	喔，我已經相中一個錢包好久了，但一直都沒有打折。
Linda	They sell items for men too, ties, suits, wallets, and bags!	他們也有賣男士的品項，領帶、西裝、皮夾及包包。
Jason	Oh, I want a Gucci tie to wear at meetings and show off to my colleagues!	喔，我要一條Gucci的領帶，要在開會時在同事面前賣弄一番。
Lara	I want a couple of men wallets and a small purse to give as Christmas gifts to my family.	我要兩個男用皮夾和一個小的錢包做為家人的耶誕節禮物。
Linda	This is the best time to spend, won't get another chance like this until next Christmas.	這是下手購買的最好時機，一直到明年的耶誕節之前都不會有這樣的機會了。

| George | Here is the picture of the laptop bag that I want, if she can't get that one, here is the backup one that I want to get. | 這是我要的電腦包的圖片，如果她拿不到這一個的話，這裡還有一個候補的也可以。 |

| Linda | Oh, that reminds me; make sure you all have 2 to 3 items in case my sister can't find the one you want or if it runs out. | 喔，這倒提醒了我，你們最好都選2到3個商品，免得我妹妹沒找到你們要的或是已經賣完了。 |

| Nolan | Count me in and get me a tie too! I don't want to look bad standing next to Jason! | 算我一份，我也要一條領帶！我不想站在Jason旁邊顯得太難看。 |

| Katie | So when do they arrive and how do we pay? | 所以大概何時可以拿到，還有我們怎麼付錢？ |

| Linda | Once I have written down what everyone wants, I will send an e-mail to my sister; she lives in another state so she will have to ship everything to me. | 只要我們大家都寫下要的商品，我會email給我妹妹，她住在另一州會將大家要的東西寄給我。 |

| Michelle | Do we pay for shipping? | 那我們要付運費嗎？ |

| Linda | Yes, once she's gotten the shipping price, everyone will split even. She is planning to buy everything this weekend. | 要的，在她知道運費多少錢之後，我們大家平分。她預定在這個週末前將所有東西買齊。 |

| George | Can we ask other people who do not work in this company if they want anything? | 我們可以問其他不在這家公司上班的人是否要買些什麼嗎？ |

Linda	Sure, but I don't want too many people!	當然可以，不過我不希望有太多人！
Michelle	You should tell us about this sooner next time so we can look up all the things we want!	你下次應該早點告訴我們，讓我們有時間可以去看我們要的商品。
George	I think a couple of days are enough time for everyone.	我想兩天的時間對大家而言應該足夠了。
Linda	No rush, the sale goes on for the entire weekend so if anyone else wants to add anything I will call her right away.	不急，這個週末都在大減價，所以如果有要追加東西的話，我可以馬上打電話給她。
Michelle	Thanks Linda!	謝囉，Linda！
Jason	The manager is coming!	經理過來了！
Linda	Everyone back to work!	大家回去工作吧！

Dialog 2

Vera	Hey, girls, you guys hear about the new facial mask by Neutrogena that came out last week?	女孩們，有聽說過露得清上星期新出的面膜嗎？
Jean	The one that hydrates your skin really well with cucumber and lavender?	那個含小黃瓜及薰衣草成分，對於皮膚保濕效果很好的面膜嗎？
Vera	No, Jean, that one came out last year. I am talking about the anti-aging, wrinkle and dark circle reducing mask.	不是，Jean，那種是去年出的。我說的是抗老化，及減少皺紋，黑眼圈的面膜。

Mina	Oh, I read about that last night! It's gotten a lot of good reviews.	喔，我昨晚有看到過！它有不少蠻高的評價。
April	I saw a before-and-after video someone posted, I can see why that mask is so expensive, seems like it does wonders.	我有看到有人上傳使用前後對照的影片，難怪那面膜這麼貴，看起來就像是在創造奇蹟。
Vera	Neutrogena has always been an affordable skin care company, but this new product they came out with is definitely pricey. Good thing I have their Golden Membership card that allows be to get a 20% discount on the masks and also buy 5 get 1 free.	露得清一直走的都是平價保養品路線，但這個新產品的價錢卻非常的昂貴。幸虧我有金卡會員可以打8折購買面膜，而且還有買5送1。
Jean	You must get me some!	你一定要幫我買一些！
Vera	Each box comes with three masks and they only sell by boxes.	每一盒中有3片面膜，而且是以盒裝販售的。
Jean	Buy me three boxes then! I am getting old and definitely don't want these wrinkles to get worse.	那我要買3盒！年紀越來越大，我堅決不讓這些皺紋變嚴重。
Mina	I am more worried about my dark circles from this work load so buy me 5 boxes.	我比較在意我因為工作量而產生的黑眼圈，所以幫我買5盒。
April	Can I get a box too? I want to try it out since I have sensitive skin; I never know which products work on me and which don't.	可以也幫我買一盒嗎？我想先試看看，因為我是敏感性肌膚，我總是不知道什麼產品對我有用或是什麼沒用。

Vera	Yeah sure everyone, as this is all done online, I need you guys to write me a check or give me cash.	當然可以囉,各位,這是上網購買的,請你們給我支票或是現金吧。
Jean	Can we transfer money to your account?	可以轉帳到你的戶頭嗎?
Vera	Yes, each box is $30. With the 20% discount, it'll be about $24 per box. I'll cover for shipping.	可以,每一盒是30元。打8折後,每盒是24元。運費我出。
April	Thanks Vera, please tell us when any new products come out and we'll order from you again!	謝了,Vera。下次有新產品的時候,請告訴我們,我們會再跟你一起訂購。
Vera	No problem, I'll order tonight and your masks will be here in 2 days.	沒問題,我今晚就會下單,你們要的面膜大概2天內會到貨。
Jean and Mina	Thanks Vera.	謝了,Vera。
Vera	No problem guys. The next product comes out in a month but if there are any older products you girls need, I have 30% off all older products.	不客氣。下一個新產品在一個月內會出來,如果你們有需要其他以前出的產品的話,我可以拿到7折。
Mina	I'll get back to you on that tomorrow Vera.	我明天再跟你說,Vera。
Vera	OK, glad to help out any time.	OK,隨時都可以。

精選單字及片語

1. sell out *v.* - 賣光；脫手；出售股份；背叛。在作為名詞使用時，寫做 sell-out，指演出或是體育比賽的門票已售完，座無虛席。
   The shirt you want is sold out. 你要的那件襯衫已經銷售一空。
   We have decided to sell out our share of this company. 我們已經決定將我們持有的這間公司的股份讓售出去。
   He was sold out by his best friend. 他被他最好的朋友給背叛了。
   Her world-wide concert tour was a sell-out success. 她的世界巡迴演唱會場場爆滿，座無虛席。

2. show off- 炫耀，賣弄
   She was showing off her diamond ring in the office. 她在辦公室裡四處炫耀她的鑽戒。

3. laptop *n.* 筆記型電腦。desktop 桌上型電腦。
   I want to change my desktop for the laptop. 我要將我的桌上型電腦更換成筆記型電腦。

4. come out- 上市；出版；出現；出獄。
   A new version will come out this autumn. 今年秋天將會出新的版本。

精選句子與延伸

1. She gets an employee's discount on top of the sale price! 她可以拿到減價後的價錢再加上員工折扣。＝She gets the sale price plus employee discount.

2. I saw a before-and-after video someone posted, I can see why that mask is so expensive, seems like it does wonders! 我有看到有人上傳使用前後對照的影片，難怪那面膜這麼貴，看起來就像是在創造奇蹟。
   本句中有兩個 see，第一個 saw，see 的過去式，是看到的意思，第二個see則是理解的意思。在一般網路用語中常見的 OIC，即為 oh, I see. 為 "喔，我明白了" 的意思。
   do wonder 創造或是施行奇蹟。與 work miracle 意思相同。
   這個句子可改寫成 I saw a before-and-after video, and I can understand why that mask is so costly, seems like it works wonders.

公司內部社團

Employee 1	Hey there, welcome to our company, it's really big but it'll be easier for you to find your own group of friends if you find a good group for yourself.	嗨，歡迎加入我們公司，這公司很大，但如果你能加入你喜歡的社團的話，將會比較容易找到屬於你的一群朋友。
New Worker	What do you mean group? Like a department?	你所指的社團是？像是部門嗎？
Employee 1	No, there are people who are in different groups in each department. There is group for sports, reading, fitness, and even a veteran's group. I am in the soccer group.	不是，在每一個部門會有許多人分屬於不同的社團。有體育、讀書、健身甚至有退伍軍人社。我是足球社的。
New Worker	That sounds cool, I love soccer. I play with my friends every Sunday morning.	聽起來很酷，我喜歡足球。我每星期天早上會和朋友一起踢球。
Employee 1	Then you would be perfect to join my group! We go out with other members in the group from time to time to play soccer as well.	那你來加入我的社團就再好也不過了！我們和其他社員也常會一起出去踢球。
New Worker	Well sign me up.	那我要報名。

Employee 2　Well if you like soccer, you have to join the general sports group then as well. I am also in the fitness group; we go and work out every Friday after work.

如果你喜歡足球的話，那你也要加入綜合運動社。我還有參加健身社，我們每個星期五下班後會去做訓練。

New Worker　Yeah, that sounds good; it would help me stay in shape.

耶，聽起來不錯；這有助於我保持良好的健康狀況。

Employee 2　These groups that the company has is a way to help keep the employees together, there are so many of us working here, if we don't have these groups, many of us would never know the other exists.

公司裡的這些社團是為了凝聚員工，我們這麼多人在這裡工作，如果沒有這些社團的話，我們許多人都不會知道對方的存在。

New Worker　I feel like it is a good way to help people cooperate even through different departments. I feel comfortable here already.

我覺得這是一個促進人們合群的好方法，甚至是來自於不同的部門。我已經在這感到舒適自在了。

Employee 1　It could be a lot of stress working in a big company such as this, but joining these groups and finding people who share your common interests takes a lot of stress away.

在像這樣的大公司上班壓力可能會很大，但是參加社團找到和你有相同興趣的人有助於減輕壓力。

New Worker　Yeah, I can see how that works. How do I become a member of each group?

對，看得出那效果。我要怎樣成為各個社團的團員呢？

Employee 2　You can talk to the group leader saying that you are interested to join their group.

你可以去找社長，告訴他你有興趣參加他們的社團。

Employee 1	Don't forget to leave your number and e-mail with them so they can contact you when they are having an event. Some groups even have forms you have to fill out but the sports ones are really simple and only need your name, number, and e-mail.	別忘記留下你的電話號碼及email給他們，他們才能在有活動時聯絡你。有些社團甚至需要填一些表格，但是運動性質的社團比較簡單，只要留下你的名字，電話及email。
New Worker	Wow, that sounds really exciting, where can I find the group leader for the soccer group?	哇，聽起來真讓人激動，我在那裡可以找到足球社的社長啊？
Employee 1	He is in a meeting right now but you can find him on the second floor and the second room on your right at noon.	他現在正在開會，但你可以在中午時在二樓第二間右手邊的房間找到他。
New Worker	Oh, thanks, is there a list of all the groups we have?	喔，謝啦，有公司所有社團的清單嗎？
Employee 2	There is one but it's from last year, groups get created all the time so I guess you have to ask around to find out. I'll give you the old list right now.	有一張是去年編列的，但社團一直在增加，所以我建議你四處打聽看看。我先給你之前的社團列表。
New Worker	Thanks guys.	謝啦。
E1 and E2	No problem.	不客氣。

Dialog 2

Employee1	Hey, you know next week is the 9/11 memorial?	你知道下星期是911紀念日嗎？

New employee	Yeah, I know that, everyone always makes it into a big deal around this time of the year.	是的，我知道，每年的這段期間大家總是將它當作件大事。
Employee 1	Well, that's because it is a big deal. You know we have a group in our company that dedicates to those who lost their lives during the terrorist attack right?	那是因為它的確是件大事。你知道我們公司有一個社團是為了那些在恐怖攻擊中犧牲的人而設的，對吧？
New Worker	I have heard about it.	我聽說過。
Employee 1	Basically, everyone in this company is a part of the group. You should join us too.	基本上，公司裡的每個人都是這社團的一份子。你也應該加入我們。
New Worker	What do you do in the group?	這社團主要在做些什麼？
Employee 1	Every year when it gets close to 9/11, we would decorate all the offices with pictures or names of those who have lost their lives on that day.	每年快到9月11日時，我們會在所有的辦公室裡佈置上那些在那天失去生命的人的照片或是名字。
New Worker	So the group only has one event for the entire year?	所以這個社團一整年只有一個活動？
Employee 1	Well, we are sort of like a veterans group as well. So we do special things for those who lost their lives in Iraq or still in Iraq fighting for this country.	嗯，我們的性質類似於退伍軍人社。所以我們會為了那些在伊拉克失去生命的，或是仍在伊拉克為國家作戰的人做些特別的事。
New Worker	So all the members of the company are a member?	所以，公司所有的成員都是一員？

Employee 1 Yeah. On 9/11 last year we lit 2,996 candles in front of the front entrance of our company for the number of people that died on that day. It shows our support to those families who had lost a loved one.	對。在去年9月11日時，我們在公司正門前點燃了相當於當時死亡人數的2，996隻蠟燭。用以表示我們對在那一天失去心愛的人的家庭的支持。
New Worker Wow, that is a very thoughtful thing to do for those families.	哇，對那些家庭而言這非常的貼心。

💬 精選單字及片語

1. sign up   報名，申請；跟…簽訂合同
   He heard her beautiful singing, and persuaded the company to sign her up.
   他聽見她美妙的歌聲，便說服公司簽下她。

2. work out   進行鍛鍊，訓練；筋疲力盡；解決。
   I work out regularly to keep fit.
   我定期地鍛鍊身體以維持健康狀況。

   In fact, I was worked out.
   事實上我已精疲力盡。

   It doesn't work out.
   這無法解決事情。這是行不通的。

3. stay in shape   維持良好的健康狀態，維持身材。
   Swimming can help you to stay in shape by targeting all areas of your body.
   游泳可以讓你活動到身體的每一個部位，有助於維持健美的身材。

   She takes diet pills to keep her figure.
   她服用減肥藥來維持身材。

4. veteran(s) *n.*   退伍軍人；老兵；經驗豐富的人，元老。
   The new CEO was not able to dominate those veterans in the board of shareholders.
   新上任的執行長未能控制住股東會議上的那些元老。

💬 精選句子與延伸

1. It could be a lot of stress working in a big company such as this, but joining these groups and finding people who share your common interests takes a lot of stress away. 在像這樣的大公司上班壓力可能會很大，但是參加社團找到和你有相同興趣的人有助於減輕壓力。＝It could be very stressful to work in this big company, and it may be helpful to release a lot of stress by joining these groups and finding people to share common interests.

2. Some groups even have forms you have to fill out but the sports ones are really simple and only need your name, number, and e-mail. 有些社團甚至需要填一些表格，但是運動性質的社團比較簡單，只要留下你的名字，電話及e-mail。
句中的sports ones，ones指的是groups社團；number指的是contact number / phone number聯絡電話號碼。
fill out （表格）填寫

3. You know we have a group in our company that dedicates to those who lost their lives during the terrorist attack right? 你知道我們公司有一個社團是為了那些在恐怖攻擊中犧牲的人而設的，對吧？
dedicate to 把（時間、精力）用於…；致力於…
We dedicate ourselves to creating a truly outstanding service.
我們致力於創造極為優越的服務品質。

4. On 9/11 last year we lit 2,996 candles in front of the front entrance of our company for the number of people that died on that day. It shows our support to those families who had lost a loved one. 在去年9月11日時，我們在公司正門前點燃了相當於當時死亡人數的2,996隻蠟燭。用以表示我們對在那一天失去心愛的人的家庭的支持。
在本文中的9/11指的是2001年9月11日，一般稱為911恐怖攻擊事件 9/11 terrorist attack。在英文的讀法中為了有別於911求救電話 (nine-one-one)，應讀做nine-eleven。
lit (v.) 動詞light的過去式及過去分詞。在這做「點燃」，「點亮」解釋。可在後面接up使用，有點亮、點燃，容光煥發的意思。但有一個特殊的用法，在美國俚語中All lit up. 指的是人在吸毒時因被毒品麻醉而呈現的狀態。

員工旅遊

Dialog 1

Ralph	Alright everyone, in today's meeting we will be talking about our company's annual weekend field trip. Does anyone have any ideas regarding where it should take place?	好了，各位，在今天的會議上我們要討論的是一年一次在週末舉辦的公司旅遊。有沒有人有任何構想要在哪裡舉行呢？
Jordan	What is our budget this year?	今年的預算是多少呢？
Ralph	Our company did very well this year so they added an extra $2000 to our budget totaling to $8000 dollars.	我們公司今年的業績不錯，所以他們多加了2000元在這次的預算中，一共是8000元。
Nancy	How about a local hot springs?	在本地的溫泉如何？

Rachel	We went there last year, and since we have an extra $2000 to spend I say we go further out, and let's have something fresh this time.Have you ever seen the movie "The Hangover?"It makes me always want to see those various wedding chapels, luxury hotels, and the Mojave Desert in Vegas. There are so many shows in Las Vegas, such as Cirque du Soleil Shows, musical shows, magic shows, comedy shows, and of course the adult shows that you guys love the most. Besides casinos and shopping malls, there are also so many world-class spas in those magnificent hotels, I already feel relaxing when I mention Las Vegas.	我們去年就去過了，既然我們多了2000元可以花，我想我們可以去遠一點的地方，我們這次來一點新的花樣。你們有沒有看過 "醉後大丈夫" 這部電影？這部電影讓我一直都想去看看在拉斯維加斯的那一些各式各樣的結婚小教堂，豪華飯店，及莫哈韋沙漠。在拉斯維加斯有好多的秀，例如有太陽馬戲團秀、音樂秀、魔術秀、喜劇秀，以及當然有你們男生最喜歡的成人秀。除了賭場及購物中心之外，在那些華麗宏偉的飯店裡還有許多世界級的水療休閒中心，當我談到拉斯維加斯時就已經覺得放鬆了。
Jordan	Let's go to Las Vegas! They have spas in the hotel for the girls and guys can go out and relax a little bit as well.	那就去拉斯維加斯吧！女的可以在飯店裡享受SPA，男的可以出去並放鬆。
Nancy	That seems like a good idea.	似乎是個不錯的主意。
Ralph	Do we all agree on Las Vegas?	那大家都同意去拉斯維加斯嗎？
Everyone	Yes.	對。

Ralph	This year we're going by bus since it's in another state, it's cheaper. Nancy, find a few transportation companies and compare price and services. We have a higher budget but we still need to conserve because during this time of the year the hotel room prices go up.	今年我們將搭巴士去，因為是要到另一州，這樣比較便宜。Nancy，請找幾家運輸公司，比較價錢及服務。我們有較高的預算，但還是要省一點，因為在這個時候的飯店房價比較高。
Rachel	My cousin said Bally's hotel is very nice, and in the middle of the strip. It's a good price as well, shall we book that hotel?	我表弟說巴利酒店不錯，而且位於拉斯維加斯大道的中段。價錢也不錯，我們要不要就訂那間飯店？
Ralph	Rachel, would you look into that and come back to me with the prices? Find out if they have a group discount.	Rachel，你可不可以去查一下價錢再告訴我？看看他們有沒有團體折扣。
Jordan	Should we plan any additional events during the trip such as helicopter ride to the Grand Canyon or hiking trip?	那我們要不要計畫一些旅途中的活動像是搭直昇機到大峽谷或是郊遊？
Ralph	Yes, the helicopter trip to Grand Canyon can be put down for the first day we arrive. Now since it's almost Christmas and New Year I think this year we can do something a little more special and go to the New Year's count down. The lights will still be up from Christmas and we can all gather for the countdown, what do you guys think?	好，到大峽谷的直昇機之旅可以放在我們抵達的第一天。現在既然已經快到聖誕節及新年了，我想今年我們做點特別的，來個新年倒數好了。從聖誕節時掛的燈會持續到那時候，我們可以聚在一起倒數，你們覺得如何？

Jordan	That is a perfect idea! Since Bally's is in the middle of the strip, we'll get a good view to all the fireworks.	真是個好主意！既然巴利酒店就在大道的中段，我們能清楚的看到所有的煙火。
Nancy	Should I send all the employees an e-mail of the dates and times plus events tomorrow?	那我要不要在明天發e-mail給所有的員工，告知日期，時間加上活動？
Ralph	Yes, make sure to include to be here at 7 am as the bus leaves at 8 and we will not wait for anyone. Rachel, if you can book the rooms as soon as possible, I know people from all over the world gather there during the New Year and rooms sell out fast. Also try to book all the rooms on the same floor.	要，還要確認加上早上7點在這集合，8點巴士準時出發，逾時不候。Rachel，麻煩儘早訂房，我知道在新年時會有從世界各地的人聚集在那，房間很快就會被訂光。還有要盡量將訂房集中在同一個樓層。
Rachel	Yes sir.	是的，長官。
Ralph	Well that concludes our meeting today, everyone report their information to me tomorrow morning.	我們今天會議到這結束，大家明天早上要將所有相關資訊向我報告。
Everyone	OK.	OK。

💬 精選單字及片語

1. field trip　校外旅行，實地考察旅行。用以指員工旅遊時還可用 staff travel, incentive tour 等。

2. hot spring　溫泉
   Is that resort celebrated for its hot spring?
   那個觀光勝地是以溫泉而著稱的嗎？

3. transportation company　運輸公司；在本文中是指遊覽車公司，但也可指運輸貨物的公司。
   They are running a transportation company.
   他們經營一家運輸公司。

4. conserve *vt.*　節省；保存。
   It is very important to conserve energy.
   節省能源是非常重要的。

5. look into　調查；查問；看進…裡面
   The manager promised to look into the matter.
   經理承諾要調查這件事。

6. helicopter(s) *n.*　直昇機。　*vt.*　用直昇機運送；　*vi.*　搭直昇機。
   The wounded soldier was helicoptered to the hospital.
   受傷的士兵被用直昇機送到醫院。
   Mr. President helicoptered to the capital.
   總統先生搭乘直昇機到首都。

7. as soon as possible　儘快，及早，趁早。在文件上常會以縮寫標註成 ASAP。
   We have to improve our efficiency as soon as possible.
   我們必須儘快提高工作效率。

8. book a room　預定房間
   book *v.*　預定，登記。
   I booked a concert ticket, a flight and a room for him.
   我幫他訂了一張演唱會的票，一班飛機及一個房間。

💬 精選句子與延伸

1. Our company did very well this year so they added an extra $2000 to our budget totaling to $8000 dollars. 我們公司今年的業績不錯,所以他們多加了 2000 元在這次的預算中,一共是 8000 元。＝The company makes good profits this year, so we have $6000 in the budget, plus extra $2000.
   totaling(v.) 總共。total 的現在分詞。此為美式拼法,也可拼成 totalling(英式拼法)
   budget(n.) 預算
   The lion's share of budget is rental.
   預算中絕大部分是房租。
   The lion's share 最大份額

2. My cousin said Bally's hotel is very nice, and in the middle of the strip. It's a good price as well, shall we book that hotel? 我表弟說巴利酒店不錯,而且位於拉斯維加斯大道的中段。價錢也不錯,我們要不要就訂那間飯店?
   strip(n.) 帶狀地帶;長條。strip 在本文中指的是拉斯維加斯大道 Las Vegas Boulevard,一般俗稱為 The Strip。拉斯維加斯大道全長約 7 公里,是拉斯維加斯最繁華的地區,匯集了許多豪華飯店,購物中心及餐廳,由於沿著這條大道的所有飯店都是可以免費進入參觀,所以 in the middle of the strip 也成了遊客在飯店選擇上的首選。

3. Well that concludes our meeting today, everyone report their information to me tomorrow morning. 那我們今天會議到這結束,大家明天早上要將所有相關資訊向我報告。
   conclude(v.) 結束,終止; 推斷;決定。
   What did you conclude from that matter?
   你從那件事得到什麼結論?

Unit 10 老闆不是人!（抱怨老闆或主管）

Dialog 1

Employee 1 Can you believe it? Our boss just deducted $100 from my pay for being late!

你相信嗎？我們老闆因為我遲到而從我薪水裡扣了100元。

Employee 2 Wow, that's almost a day's worth of pay.

哇，那幾乎是一整天的薪資。

Employee 1 I know. How unfair is that? It's not like he was never late before!

我知道。這多不公平啊？又不是他從來都沒遲到過。

Employee 2 Well, he is the boss after all; he can come in whenever he wants.

他畢竟是老闆；他想什麼時候來都可以。

Employee 1 OK, but as a boss I think he should set some good examples for his employees don't you think?

OK，但是身為一個老闆，我認為他應該以身作則，你不這樣認為嗎？

Employee 2 What do you mean?

你的意思是？

Employee 1 If he comes in on time every morning, wouldn't it motivate everyone else to want to be here on time as well? It would also show a good boss image.

如果他每天早上都準時到，這樣不是也會激勵其他人也要準時嗎？這樣也能表現出好老闆的形象。

Employee 2	The boss has a lot of things to do every day besides sitting in here with us though. Do you think you would be on time every day if he was on time? You were late every single day this week.	老闆除了跟我們坐在這之外，每天還有許多的事要做。你認為如果他準時的話，你也能每天都準時嗎？你這一個禮拜每天都遲到。
Employee 1	I have a child that wakes me up in the middle of the night; it's hard to get a good night's sleep.	我的孩子總在半夜吵醒我，很難一覺睡到天亮。
Employee 2	A lot of us have kids, we all get here on time most of the time. You just have to find a way to schedule things out. Maybe you should try going to bed early.	我們很多人都有孩子，我們大多能準時到。你要想個辦法解決這件事。也許你可以試試早點睡。
Employee 1	Fine, I'll try that, and also what is it with the boss's weird requests, I know I am his personal assistant and I run all his errands but telling me to scrub the toilet and hand write all his invitation addresses is a little too much, isn't it?	好，我會試試看，還有老闆那些奇怪的要求是怎樣，我知道我是他的私人助理，我是任他差遣的，但是要求我刷馬桶還有手寫他所有邀請函的地址有點太過份了，不是嗎？
Employee 2	Well as his personal assistant, you tend to his personal needs as well.	嗯，身為他的私人助理，你要遵照他的個人需求。
Employee 1	We have professional cleaners to clean our floors and bathrooms though! I feel like I am being treated unfairly.	我們可是有專業的清潔人員在清潔打掃樓面及廁所！我覺得我受到不公平對待。
Employee 2	Then are you going to quit?	那你要辭職嗎？

Employee 1 This is my only job, I need the income.

這是我唯一的工作，我需要這份收入。

Employee 2 Find a new job.

找份新的工作。

Employee 1 I have been trying to look for a new job lately but nothing yet.

我最近試著在找新的工作，沒有進展。

Employee 2 Maybe you should ask the boss why he is treating you badly first, maybe he has his reasons.

也許你該先問問老闆為什麼這樣對你，也許他有他的理由。

Employee 1 Yeah… you're right, I will confront him today.

嗯，你是對的，我今天來問問他。

Employee 2 Good luck!

祝好運！

Dialog 2

Employee 1 Hey, I just got the article I wrote about the car accident back and the boss threw it back in my face and told me it was basically crap.

嘿，我剛拿回我寫的那篇有關車禍的文章，老闆將它丟在我的臉上，還告訴我這基本上是篇廢話。

Employee 2 Was it crap?

是胡扯的嗎？

Employee 1 No, I worked really hard on this; I even went and interviewed the family!

不，我很用心的。我甚至還去採訪那家人！

Employee 2 What problems did he say with your article?

那他說你的文章有什麼問題嗎？

Employee 1	He says that there is no sense of urgency or excitement, that it was a boring piece that no one wants to read.	他說文章裡沒有任何迫切或是激動的感覺，是很無聊的一篇，沒有人會想看。
Employee 2	Wow, that is pretty harsh.	哇，這樣有些太過苛刻了。
Employee 1	He yelled at me a lot. He said that my recent work hasn't been as good and said that if this keeps going on, he will fire me.	他對我大吼大叫。他說我最近的工作不如往常的好，還說如果一直這樣的話，他要開除我。
Employee 2	Maybe you should seek help from others?	也許你應該尋求其他人的幫忙？
Employee 1	Yeah, I talked to Lisa before I came to talk to you and she said she will take a look at my article and see where I can improve.	對，在我跟你說這事之前，我跟Lisa談過了，她說她會看我的文章看是否有需要改進的地方。
Employee 2	That's good, don't worry, I have gotten yelled at by the boss plenty of times. It's all for a good cause, it helps us write better.	這樣很好，別擔心，我被老闆吼過好多次了。都是為了我們好，可以讓我們寫得更好。
Employee 1	Honestly, I just think that the boss is putting a lot of workload on me recently that is causing my articles to be so bad.	老實說，我認為最近老闆給我的大量工作造成我文章寫不好。
Employee 2	A lot of things have been going on, everyone's workload has increased double this week.	很多事都在持續進行，每個人這星期的工作量都增加了一倍。

Employee 1	No, not just this week, it's been like this for over a month now, I am so overloaded with work, I can barely breathe!	不，不只是這個禮拜，大概有超過一個月了，我的工作量超過我所能負荷，我都快不能呼吸了。
Employee 2	Did you ever try telling the boss that he's giving you too much work to cover?	你有沒有告訴過老闆他分派給你太多工作呢？
Employee 1	Yes, but every time I bring it up, he would always be on his phone or on the computer not listening to me.	有，但每當我提起時，他就在講電話或是用電腦就是沒聽我說。
Employee 2	Did you do something to upset him?	你有做什麼惹惱他的事嗎？
Employee 1	Not that I know of...	據我所知沒有…
Employee 2	Then maybe you should find a time to sit down with him and talk about it soon.	那也許你該儘快找個時間跟他坐下來談一談。

💬 精選單字及片語

1. deduct *vt.* 扣除，減除。
   That means tax is deducted for you before you get paid.
   那表示在你得到收入前就已經先扣稅了。

2. it's not like… 又不是。在 it's not like 後接完整的句子用法，是表示「又不是…」，常用於在解釋的情況，或是為自己辯解。句子的前面加上 It's not like，則會變成完全相反的意思。
   What's the big deal? It's not like I didn't tell you I have a girlfriend.
   這有什麼了不起的？又不是我沒告訴你我有女朋友。（i.e. 我告訴過你我有女朋友。）

3. run errands for 供差遣，為人辦事、跑腿。在使用這個片語時，需注意 errands 需為複數型態，不可用單數型態

He's always running errands for his mother.

他常替他媽媽跑腿辦事。

4. yell at 對…大叫。包含有正面及負面的情緒，正面的是為了讓對方聽清楚而大聲喊；負面的是對某人大吼，需以語氣及情境來判斷。

I heard someone yelled at me "Go, Jessie, go!"

我聽到有人大聲對我説「加油，Jessie，加油！」（這句也可解釋為我聽到有人對我大吼著「走啊，Jessie，走！」）

5. bring up 提出，談到。

I would like to bring up a question.

我想提出一個問題。

6. not that I know of 據我所知沒有，據我所知不是這樣。

🗩 精選句子與延伸

1. I think he should set some good examples for his employees. 我想他應該為員工樹立個好榜樣。

set a good example 做好榜樣，做模範。

2. The boss has a lot of things to do every day besides sitting in here with us though.

老闆除了跟我們坐在這之外，每天還有許多的事要做。

besides 除此之外。在英文中的「除此之外」有兩種，一種是包含在內，另一種則是排除在外，besides為包含在內。

though 雖然；然而；儘管；可是；不過。在句中though可做「雖然」解釋，在口語中though置於句尾，發音需上揚，為一種語氣的表現，類似中文的「啊」或是「呢」。

Unit 11 禮貌地拒絕同事要求

Employee 1 Hey Sarah, can you write up these reports for me?

嘿，Sarah，妳可以幫我完成這一些報告嗎？

Sarah No, sorry. I have enough reports of my own.

不，對不起。我自己有很多報告。

Employee 1 But we are in this project together, so you have to at least write half of it.

但我們這個專案項目是一起的，所以妳必須至少要完成一半。

Sarah I have done every report this year; I think you should do this one because I really am swamped.

今年的每一份報告都是我做的；我認為妳應該要做這一份因為我真的忙得不可開交。

Employee 1 You write better reports than I do though.

妳的報告寫的比我好。

Sarah I really am sorry but I cannot help you with this one. Plus I have to leave tomorrow for a convention in another state.

我真的很抱歉但這個我不能幫妳。再加上我明天必須離開到別州出席一個會議。

Employee 1 You can take it on the road or the plane and you can do the report on the road?

妳可以將這報告帶上路或是飛機，妳可以在途中完成這份報告？

Sarah I have other reports for other projects that I am still typing up. If I help you write this report, I wouldn't have time for my other projects.

我另一個項目還有一份我正在繕打中的報告。如果我幫妳寫這一份報告，那我可能就不夠時間作我的專案了。

Employee 1	The deadline is tomorrow though, so can't you just write it really quick?	明天就是最後的期限了，所以妳就不能很快的寫一下嗎？
Sarah	I have two reports due tomorrow. I only have half of one done right now. These things can't be rushed; you should have done it sooner.	我有兩份報告明天要交。我目前只有完成其中一份的一半而已。這些事是不能草草了事的；妳早就應該要寫了。
Employee 1	We should at least talk about the data for the report.	我們至少要討論一下有關這份報告的資料吧。
Sarah	If you have any questions regarding data, you can always ask me.	如果妳有任何有關資料的問題，妳可以問我。
Employee 1	Yeah that would be helpful thanks. Can you help me do the part for calculations?	好，這會有些幫助，謝啦。妳能幫我完成計算的這一部分嗎？
Sarah	No, I am not doing any part of your report for you.	不行，我不能幫妳做報告的任何一個部分。
Employee 1	Why not?	為什麼不行？
Sarah	Because if I spend time on your report, it is taking away time from my own reports. My job depends on these reports.	因為如果我花時間在妳的報告上，將會佔去我自己的報告的時間。我的工作是要靠這些報告的。
Employee 1	I see. I'll just try to do it myself then. Hopefully I will get it done on time.	我懂了，我會試著自己完成的。希望我能準時完成。
Sarah	Yeah good luck.	嗯，祝好運。
Employee 1	Thanks. Have a safe trip by the way.	謝啦。順便說一下祝旅途平安。
Sarah	Thanks	謝謝。

Dialog 2

Kate	Excuse me, Mr. Ferguson, do you have a minute?
Mr. Ferguson	Oh, hi, Kate. Yes, I do have a minute. But I have to meet a client 15 minutes later, so if you can finish your talk within 10 minutes…
Kate	It won't be long, I just need maybe 5 minutes.
Mr. Ferguson	Ok, please come on in, and have a seat.
Kate	Thank you, Mr. Ferguson.
Mr. Ferguson	All right, we don't have much time, so let's cut to the chase.
Kate	Sure, I need to talk to you about your new secretary.
Mr. Ferguson	Zack? Ok, please tell me what's going on.
Kate	I think I have some problems working with him.
Mr. Ferguson	But in my point of view, he's quite qualified for this position. Does his behavior or attitude make you feel that he's not qualified to be my secretary?

對不起，Ferguson先生，你有空嗎？

喔，嗨，Kate。有，我空。但我在15分鐘之後必須要見客戶，所以如果你能在10分鐘之內說完的話…

不會很久，我只需要大約5分鐘。

Ok，請進，請坐。

謝謝你，Ferguson先生。

好吧，我們沒有很多時間，所以直接切入主題吧。

好的，我要和你談一談有關你的新秘書。

Zack？好，請告訴我發生什麼事了？

我認為我和他共事有些問題。

但是我的意見是，他還蠻稱職的。是他的行為或是態度讓妳覺得他不夠資格做我的秘書？

Kate	No, but he sometimes makes me feel annoying, and he's kind of bossy.	沒有，但他有時讓我感到很煩躁，而且他有些跋扈。
Mr. Ferguson	If it's just a personal problem, and I would prefer it if you two could work it between yourselves.	如果這只是個人問題的話，我傾向於你們兩個人能夠自己解決。
Kate	I think you at least should talk to him.	我認為你至少要和他談一談。
Mr. Ferguson	No, I won't. Kate, you should know that Zack is my secretary. And he's done pretty well so far. He's well-organized, and very considerate. I don't see any point that makes him disqualified as my secretary. And you, Kate, I think you should put more efforts on your work, not on my secretary. No hard feelings. I also think you've done very well recently, but you just don't have to aim at Zack.	不，我不會和他談的。Kate，妳應該知道Zack是我的秘書。還有到目前為止，他做得很不錯。他很有組織性，還非常細心。我不覺得有什麼讓他不夠資格當我的秘書。還有妳，Kate妳應該將更多的精力放在工作上，而不是我的秘書。不要介意。我也認為妳最近做得不錯，但妳不必要針對Zack。
Kate	All right, I understand.	好吧，我懂。
Mr. Ferguson	Kate, I think you have to talk to Zack in a placid mood, and I'm sure as long as you get to know him, maybe you'll like him.	Kate，我覺得妳應該心平氣和的和Zack談一談，我確定只要妳了解他，也許妳會喜歡他的。

💬 精選單字及片語

1. write up　全部寫出，詳細描寫。
   I must write up a note of the lecture.
   我必須完成這一份講稿的綱要。

2. swamp *v.*　忙得不可開交，使陷入困難，淹沒。
   We are swamped with work.
   我們被工作壓得喘不過氣。

3. type up　繕打，打成定稿。
   Please type up a copy and publish on the notice board for everyone to read.
   請將副本打印出來並公布在公告欄上給大家看。

4. come on in　進來。on 在這有加重，強調語氣的作用，與 come in 意思相同。
   Please come on in, we are just about to have dinner.
   請進來，我們才正要開始吃晚餐。

5. cut to the chase　切入主題。俚語，直接說重點，不要猶豫，或是說一些無關緊要的，也可說是 "打開天窗說亮話"。

6. placid *adj.*　平靜的，寧靜的，溫和的。
   She was a placid child and nearly cried.
   她是個溫和的孩子很少哭鬧。

精選句子與延伸

1. If I help you write this report, I wouldn't have time for my other projects.

   如果我幫妳寫這一份報告，那我可能不夠時間作我的專案了。

   在這一個 if 的假設句中，if 條件句是現在式，而結果句為語氣助動詞 (would)+原形動詞 (have)，是一種未來假設可能會成為事實的用法，在這裡代表 Sara 有可能無法完成報告，也有可能完成。

2. These things can't be rushed; you should have done it sooner.

   這些事是不能草草了事的；妳早就應該要寫了。

   these things 在這裡指的是 reports（報告），這句話是改寫自 "Some things can't be rushed."（有些事是急不得的。），這一句話在 Lohas（樂活）這一種生活形態興起之後開始流行起來，常可在討論旅遊，生活及健康的文章中看到。

3. No hard feelings.

   不要介意。

   在這裡是指 Ferguson 先生叫 Kate 不要介意他所說的話，因為他是提出意見給 Kate，而不是指責。

   hard 在英文中的用途很廣泛，除了指 "硬，難" 之外，還可以用在說態度很差，對人很兇，很嚴厲，或是一種令人難以調適，平和的狀態，在安慰人時，或是為自己說的話消毒時，也能說 "No hard feelings." 請對方不要難過，不要見怪等。

Unit 12 新客戶開發

Dialog 1

Sales　Hi, Jenny, my name is Cathy and I'm calling from ABC International, we are a computer repair business located in Taipei. The reason for my call today is that a friend of yours, Maria, recently had us repair her desktop and she kindly passed on your details.

嗨 Jenny，我的名字是Cathy，我代表ABC International。我們是一間在台北當地的電腦維修公司。我今天打電話給妳的原因是因為你的朋友，Maria，最近使用了我們的服務。她把你的聯絡方式給了我們因為她認為你也會需要我們的服務。

Jenny　Hello, Cathy, thank you for your call, but I am not sure if I need your service.

哈囉 Cathy，謝謝你打電話來，但是我不確定我需要你們的服務。

Sales　Can I ask you, how many PCs do you have at home? And how are they working out for you in terms of performance? How have you found your current PC repairer to be?

Jenny，我想請問一下你家裡有幾台電腦？它們目前性能表現如何？你有需要維修嗎？

Jenny　I have 3 computers, and they have worked OK for the last few years. Two of them are running a bit slow, but I plan to buy new ones soon.

我有三台電腦，過去幾年都沒有甚麼大問題。有兩台最近跑得比較慢，但是我想直接買新的。

Sales	Before you buy new computers, I highly recommend considering our repair services. A well maintained computer can run for many years and save you money on buying a new computer. We specialize in repairs to home PCs and we're known widely in the area for the quality and efficiency of our work – in fact you may have seen us in the local paper only last month when we won the small business award in our category.	在你決定買新的之前，我建議你考慮我們的維修服務。一台完善保養的電腦可以持續使用好幾年，省下你買電腦的錢。我們修電腦的品質和效能在台北是非常有名的——你應該有在上個月的報紙裡看到我們的到中小企業在電腦服務業的獎項。
Jenny	Really, I thought PC repairs are very expensive, and I would save more money by buying a new one.	真的阿，我一直以為修電腦很貴，不如直接買新的省錢。
Sales	We offer a low cost alternative for PC repairs. We are able to do that because we are a word of mouth company who keeps our advertising costs down.	Jenny，我們能夠給客戶優惠待遇因為我們都是靠口耳相傳的好服務來拓展業務。不需要多花廣告費用。
Jenny	If that's the case, please tell me more.	既然如此，那請多告訴我一點。

Sales	We understand how frustrating sometimes slow computers can be. We currently have a special offer for the next 10 days to help improve the performance of your computer for 50% off! We can send someone to your house as early as this Friday. If that sounds like something you want to do, I can transfer you to our scheduling department right now.	我們瞭解性能不佳的電腦很讓人頭痛。我們現在有一個優惠服務。在未來的十天內，我們所有的維修項目都是半價！我們能夠到府維修，最快在星期五就派人過去。如果這是你想要的，我可以馬上把你轉給我們的預約部門。
Jenny	Sounds great, I am ready to take that deal.	聽起來很棒，我要買這個服務。
Sales	Thank you very much Jenny, you will definitely enjoy the savings and enjoy working with us. I will transfer you now, goodbye.	謝謝你Jenny，你絕對會對省下來的費用以及我們的服務感到非常滿意。我現在就幫你轉接，再見。
Jenny	Thank you for the offer, bye!	謝謝你介紹給我這樣的方案，再見！

Dialog 2

Sales	Hello, welcome to XYZ mobile, how may I help you today?	你好，歡迎光臨XYZ 電信，今天我能怎麼為您服務？
Jenny	Hi, I want to buy a new phone for my son.	你好，我想要買一台新的手機給我兒子。

| Sales | Great, I can certainly help you with that. Do you know what kind of phone and service plan you want? | 沒問題，我可以幫您服務。請問你有特別想要的電話跟月費方案嗎？ |

Jenny I do, I want to use plan A and the new smart phone from Orange.

我想要方案 A 跟新的橘子牌智慧型手機。

Sales Great choice! Let me get that phone for you. Can you provide me with your account information?

非常好的選擇！讓我拿那支電話給妳。你能夠給我你的帳號嗎？

Jenny Yes, my account number is _____, and my access ID is _____.

我的帳號是 _____，我的登入ID是 _____。

Sales I notice here that you make a lot of international phone calls. May I suggest that you and your son both purchase our international discount calling program? This should save you some money each month.

我發現你打很多國際電話。我想要建議你跟妳兒子買我們的國際通話專案。這應該能夠幫你每個月省下一點錢。

Jenny If that's the case, please tell me more!

如果是這樣，請你多告訴我一點！

Sales For an additional 10 dollars every month, you can participate in a program that discounts all of your international calls by 30%. If you make more than 2 hours of international calls, you should break even with the additional cost!

每個月多繳10塊錢，你能夠參與這個方案讓你所有的國際電話都打七折。如果你每個月講超過兩小時的國際電話，這樣就很划算能省到錢。

Jenny Sounds great, please sign me up!

聽起來太好了，請幫我sign up加入！

Sales   OK, no problem! We are always looking for ways to provide high quality services to our clients at reduced cost!

OK，沒問題！我們的目標一直都是為客戶省錢但是保有高品質的服務！

Jenny   I appreciate that, and I will definitely be back for more of my wireless needs in the future!

非常感謝，我未來如果還有需要一定會繼續回來跟妳們買的！

💬 精選單字及片語

1. pass on　傳遞；前進
   If there's no further discussion, maybe we can pass on.
   如果沒有更多要討論的話，或許我們可以進入下一個議題。

2. PC (abbr.) personal computer　個人電腦。
   The PC business is a conservative industry.
   個人電腦產業是個保守的產業。

3. in terms of　根據，就…而言，從…方面來說。
   He thought of everything in terms of money.
   他看待每一件事都是從金錢的角度為出發點。

4. word of mouth　口碑，口述，口傳。
   The news was passed on by word of mouth.
   這消息被口頭傳開了。

5. if that's the case　如果是這樣的話
   If that's the case, we will change our target.
   如果是這樣的話，那我們將改變我們的目標。

6. appreciate v.　感激，欣賞，領會
   I would appreciate some feedback on my site.
   如能對我的網站提出一些建議的話，我將感激不盡。

精選句子與延伸

1. We are a computer repair business located in Taipei. 我們是一間在位在台北當地的電腦維修公司。

   computer repair business＝computer repair company

   located in 位於

   The new building will be located in the CBD (central business district).

   新的大樓將會建在商業中心區。

2. We understand how frustrating sometimes slow computers can be. 我們瞭解性能不佳的電腦有多讓人頭痛。＝We do understand that most people get frustrated with the slow computers.

   frustrating *adj.* 使人沮喪的，產生挫折的。

   I found the unexpected delays extremely frustrating.

   我發覺這些意料外的耽擱非常地令人感到沮喪。

3. We are always looking for ways to provide high quality services to our clients at reduced cost! 我們的目標一直都是為客戶省錢但是保有高品質的服務！＝Our goal is to provide quality service to our customer with a lower price.

   look for 尋求，尋找

   He'll be looking for a new special assistant.

   他將要找個新的特助。

   way(s) (n.) 方法

   Reading is a good way to unwind.

   閱讀是個放鬆的好方法。

4. I will definitely be back for more of my wireless needs in the future! 我未來如果還有需要一定會繼續回來跟妳們買的！

   在本句中的wireless needs 指的是行動電話服務方面的需求，包括費率的更改，門號變動，行動上網等服務。

   wireless (adj.) 無線的。

   Our office needs to install the wireless network.

   我們辦公室需要安裝無線網路。

Part Three

英文簡報

Have an English Agenda

Unit 13 事項確認

Dialog 1

Sales	Hi Jenny, this is Caitlyn calling from ABC International. I want to confirm with you about the computer maintenance package that you have purchased from us on last Friday	嗨，Jenny，我是ABC國際公司的Caitlyn。我想要和您確認一下您在上個星期五時向本公司所購買電腦維修方案。
Jenny	Hi Caitlyn, thanks for calling to confirm.	嗨，Caitlyn，謝謝妳來電確認。
Sales	No problem, I want to first verify that you have purchased package A and you have set up an appointment with us on Friday morning at 10am, is that correct?	不客氣，我首先要跟您確認的是您購買的是A方案，並約在星期五早上10點，這樣是否正確？
Jenny	Oh, no. Caitlyn, in fact,I told the representative of your company's scheduling department that I want to purchase plan B at that time instead of plan A! And now that I think about it, Friday is not good for me. I was thinking about calling you to reschedule the appointment for me before this call.	喔，不。Caitlyn，事實上，我那時候和妳們公司預約部門的代表說我要購買的是B方案而不是A方案！而且我想了一下，星期五那天對我來說不太方便。在這一通電話之前我還正在想著要打給妳幫我重新安排預約的時間。

Sales	Oh I apologize for the dreadful mistake we made, let me get that changed for you. As for the appointment rescheduling, what day would work better for you?	喔，我為我們所犯的嚴重錯誤感到抱歉，讓我幫您做修改。至於重新安排時間的部份，請問您約在那一天比較恰當呢？
Jenny	I will be available on Monday morning.	我星期一早上有空。
Sales	We can send one of our engineers out at 9am.Jenny, is that a good time for you?	我們可以安排我們一位工程師在早上9點的時候到。Jenny，這時間對妳來說方便嗎？
Jenny	Yes, that should be fine.	是，應該可以。
Sales	OK, let me reconfirm with you, Jenny. The plan you purchased is service plan B and you have made an appointment with us on Monday morning at 9am. Is that correct?	好的，讓我再跟您確認一次，Jenny。您所要購買的是B服務方案，及妳和我們約在星期一早上9點鐘。這樣正確嗎？
Jenny	Sounds great, thank you for reconfirming.	聽起來不錯，謝謝妳的再次確認。
Sales	My pleasure, thank you very much again for your business. And if you have any other questions, please do not hesitate to contact us.	我的榮幸，再次非常感謝您的購買。如果您有其他任何的問題的話，請不要猶豫，直接聯絡我們。

Dialog 2

Sales	Hi, this is Bob calling from XYZ Mobile. May I speak to Jenny please?	嗨，我是XYZ電信的Bob。請問一下Jenny在嗎？
Jenny	Oh, hi, Bob. This is she.	喔，嗨，Bob。我就是。
Sales	Hi, Jenny, I want to confirm with you about the international calling discount plan that you have signed up for. Our records indicate that you call Taiwan a lot, is that correct?	嗨，Jenny，我想要和您確認一下有關您所選擇的國際電話折扣方案。我們的紀錄顯示您經常打到台灣，對嗎？
Jenny	Yes, that is correct.	對，沒錯。
Sales	In that case, I want to make you aware that this international calling plan is not the best one available for you. I apologize if our store associate did not give you more information, but there is a specific plan for discount calling to Taiwan that will save you even more money.	如果是那樣的話，我想要跟您說一下這一個國際電話的方案並不是最適合您的。我很抱歉如果我們的門市服務人員沒有提供給您更多的相關資訊，但這裡有一個打到台灣的折扣方案可以讓您省更多錢。
Jenny	Oh, what is the difference?	喔，有什麼不同嗎？
Sales	If you use the original plan that you purchased, you will get the best discount if you call a lot of different countries. But if you only call Taiwan, this new plan will save you more than 10%.	如果您選擇原來的方案的話，那需要打到許多不同的國家才能最優惠的費率計算。但如果您只有打到台灣的話，這個新方案將能為您節省超過百分之十。

Jenny	Oh, I did not know that, thank you for telling me this. I only have to pay additional 10 dollars every month for the originalplan, how much should I pay for the alternative that you suggest?	喔，我不知道耶，謝謝你告訴我這個。我每月只需多付10元在原先的方案上，你所建議的這一個替代方案要付多少錢呢？
Sales	Same as the original plan, $10 per month. So do I have your permission to change you to this new plan?	和之前的方案一樣，每月10元。那您是否答應讓我為您更改成這個新方案？
Jenny	Yes, that should be fine.	是的，應該沒問題。
Sales	OK, let me reconfirm with you, you are now on our new Taiwan discount calling program.	好的，讓我和您再確認一次，您現在選擇的是我們新的台灣折扣話費方案。
Jenny	Sounds great, thank you for following up with me on this.	聽起來不錯，謝謝你讓我知道這方案。
Sales	My pleasure, thank you very much again for your business.	我的榮幸，再次非常感謝您選擇本公司。

💬 精選單字及片語

1. confirm with...　與…確認
   According to the company policy, we have to confirm with you on this phone.
   根據公司規定，我們必須透過這通電話和您做確認。

2. maintenance *n.*　維護，保持
   Who is responsible for the facility maintenance?
   誰負責設備的維修呢？

3. verify *vt.*　確認，證明，判定
   Please carefully verify each item that I've marked.
   請將我已經標出的每一個項目仔細的核對一下。

4. indicate *vt.*　指示，指出　*vi.*　以手或是燈號指示人或是車輛的轉向（常用於英式英文中）
   The witness indicated the suspect.
   證人指認出嫌犯。

   Do not forget to indicate before you pull out.
   將車輛開出時別忘了要打方向燈。

5. permission *n.*　允許，許可，同意
   Do you get permission to take photographs here?
   你有得到可以在這裡拍攝相片的許可嗎？

6. reconfirm *v.*　重新確認；重新批准
   You must reconfirm your flight reservation 72 hours before your flight.
   您必須在班機起飛之前最少 72 小時再次確認您的航班。

精選句子與延伸

1. And now that I think about it, Friday is not good for me. 而且我想了一下，星期五那天對我來說不太方便。＝And now I recall that I'll be busy on Friday.（現在我想起來，我星期五那天會很忙。）
   think about 考慮
   I have been thinking about that all the time.
   我一直都在考慮那件事。

2. Oh, I apologize, let me get that changed for you. 喔，我很抱歉，讓我幫您做修改。＝Oh, I'm so sorry about that, I will correct the mistake.
   apologize(vi.) 道歉，認錯，賠不是。
   I have to apologize for the delay.
   我必須為了這次的耽擱道歉。

3. In that case, I want to make you aware that this international calling plan is not the best one available for you. 如果是那樣的話，我想要跟您說一下這一個國際電話的方案並不是最適合您的。
   in that case 那樣的話；如果是那樣的話。
   If you don't like your job, in that case why don't you quit?
   如果你不喜歡你的工作，那你為什麼不辭職呢？

4. Oh, I did not know that, thank you for telling me this. 喔，我不知道耶，謝謝你告訴我這個。＝Oh, I didn't know that, thank you for the information.＝Oh, I didn't know that, thank you for informing me.

Unit 14 約定會議時間

Dialog 1

Jenny	Hi, Bob, can we setup a meeting to talk about the new product launch?	嗨，Bob，我們可以安排討論新產品上市的會議嗎？
Bob	Yes, sure John, when do you suggest we have this meeting?	當然可以，John，你建議在什麼時候呢？
Jenny	I was thinking maybe have this meeting on Friday afternoon, after lunch.	我想也許在星期五下午，午餐後。
Bob	That'll work for me and our team, but John, please remember that this launch is for Asia, so we have to have this meeting with our other colleagues in the Taiwan office and their difference are in the different time zones. So I don't think Friday afternoon is going to work.	對我來說沒有問題，但是John，請記住這次上市是針對亞洲地區，所以我們必須和我們其他在台灣辦公室的同事們一起開會，而他們是在不同的時區。所以我不認為星期五下午可以。
Jenny	You are right, Bob, I totally forgot about it. Let me check everyone's calendar. With the time difference, when do you think it is appropriate to schedule this meeting for our colleagues in the Taiwan office?	你是對的，Bob，我完全忘了這回事。讓我和大家確認一下行程。有時差的問題，你覺得安排什麼時間和台灣辦公室的同事開會比較恰當呢？

Bob	I think it's reasonable to have a conference call on Thursday evening in US time, Friday morning in Taiwan time. This way we are not taking up too much of everyone's off-work hours.	我覺得在美國時間的星期四傍晚，台灣時間的星期五早上來召開電話會議比較合理，這樣的話我們才不會佔用大家太多的下班時間。
Jenny	Great idea, ok, let's setup the product lunching meeting on Thursday evening and I will send out a confirmation e-mail to the Taiwan office and our teammates.	好主意，ok，那我們就將產品發表的會議定在星期四傍晚，我會將確認的e-mail發給台灣辦公室及我們的隊友。
Bob	Sounds good! Also remember to invite our manager and let our colleagues to adjust their schedules and leave time for this meeting. Oh, before you begin this, maybe you should contact Taiwan office's Brian first, to make sure if they can have this meeting with us on Thursday evening in US time.	很好！要記得請經理參加這次的會議，還有讓我們的同事調整他們的行程，空出時間給這一個會議。喔，你開始做這之前，或許你應該先和台灣辦公室的Brian聯絡，確認他們是否能夠在美國時間的星期四傍晚和我們一起開會。
Jenny	Ok, I will, thank you for your suggestion, Bob!	好的，我會的，謝謝你的建議，Bob！
Bob	You're welcome.	不客氣。

Dialog 2

Jenny	Hi, Brian, this is John from the Los Angeles Office. We want to set up a meeting to prepare for the new product launch. What time will you and your team be available on Friday morning?	嗨，Brian，我是洛杉磯辦公室的John。我們要為了準備新產品的上市來召開會議。你和你的團隊在星期五早上什麼時間比較方便呢？
Brian	Hi, John, Please give me a second, let me check my schedule first. Oh, John, I am sorry, but this Friday morning we have a meeting with a local client.	嗨，John，請等一下，讓我先查一下我的行程。喔，John，我很抱歉，但是這個星期五早上我們和本地的一個客戶要開會。
Jenny	Oh, that will not work then, but I really think we need a meeting to prepare ourselves for the launch next week. Do you have any good suggestion?	喔，那就不行了，但我真的認為我們需要開個會為下星期的發表會做準備。你有沒有什麼好的建議呢？
Brian	Can we possibly do it on Thursday night our time in Taiwan, your Thursday morning?	那有沒有可能在台灣時間的星期四晚上，你們那的星期四早上開呢？
Jenny	No, I don't think so. our team manager will be out of office on Thursday morning for a private appointment.	不行，我想沒辦法。我們團隊的經理在星期四早上有一個私人行程，不會在辦公室裡。
Brian	Then we really need to find another time.	那我們就需要再找其他時間。
Jenny	Will you be opposed to the idea of having this meeting at Friday night?	你們會反對在星期五晚上開會的這個主意嗎？

Brian   I am sure it is not preferable, but if it is necessary, my team and I can accommodate Friday night.

我確定一定是不太願意，但如果是必要的話，我的團隊和我可以遷就在星期五晚上。

Jenny   OK, then let's set the time to be Friday night, 9 pm Taipei time, is that agreeable?

好，那我們就約個時間在星期五晚上，台北時間9點，同意嗎？

Brian   I think that will work.

我想可以。

Jenny   Thank you, Brian, I am sure this will be a productive meeting and allow us to have a successful launch.

謝謝你，Brian，我確定這將是一個富有成效的會議，能讓我們有個成功的產品發表會。

💬 精選單字及片語

1. launch *v.* （新產品）推出，發表；（活動，企劃）發動，展開
   If we want to launch our product on time, then we'll have to work against the clock.
   如果我們要準時推出我們的產品，那我們必須和時間賽跑。

2. time difference 時差
   What is the time difference between Taipei and Tokyo?
   在台北及東京的時間相差多少呢？
   除了 time difference 之外，英文中還有一個另外時差的講法，那就是 "Jet lag"，兩者的不同是在於 jet lag 指的是乘坐飛機後，因兩地的時間差異所導致不適應的時差感。
   I got jet lag for a week after coming back from Canada.
   我從加拿大回來之後有一個禮拜的時間有時差。

3. conference(s) *n.* 會議，正式的討論，大會。
   The conference will be held in Chicago.
   會議將在芝加哥舉行。

4. local client(s) 本地客戶＝local customer
   The restaurant's business basically relies on local clients.
   這間餐廳的生意基本上都是靠本地的顧客。

5. opposed *v.* 反對；使相對，使對照
   Many parents oppose bilingual education in schools.
   許多父母反對學校進行雙語教育。

6. accommodate *v.* 遷就，迎合；容納
   We have made every effort to accommodate your opinions.
   我們已經盡力遷就你的意見。

7. productive *adj.* 有成效，收穫的；具生產力的
   a productive meeting 富有成效的會議
   The volcano soils are generally the most productive.
   火山土壤通常是最為肥沃的。

精選句子與延伸

1. I totally forgot about it. Let me check everyone's calendar.　我完全忘了這回事。讓我和大家確認一下行程。

   句中的it指的是time difference 時差。

   check everyone's calendar 查一下每個人的日程表，也可以説 check everyone's schedule。

2. I think it's reasonable for a conference call on Thursday evening US time, Friday morning Taiwan time.　我覺得在美國時間的星期四傍晚，台灣時間的星期五早上來開電話會議比較合理。

   conference call 通常會被簡稱為 con call，指的是電話會議。而視訊會議在英文中則稱為 video conference。

3. This way we are not taking up too much of everyone's off-work hours.　這樣的話我們才不會佔用大家太多的下班後的時間。

   take up 佔用（時間或是空間）

   I won't take up any more your time.

   我將不再佔用你任何的時間。

   off-work hours 工作外的時間，下班後的時間。

4. We want to set up a meeting to prepare for the new product launch.　我們要為了準備新產品的上市來召開會議。＝We want to call a meeting for the product launch.

   set up 設置，在這做召開（會議）解釋。

   prepare for 為…做準備

Unit 15 新客戶開發/寒暄與聯繫/推廣新廣告

Dialog 1

Caitlyn	Hi, Jenny, this is Caitlyn from ABC International; I am calling as a follow up to the service you received from us last week. Do you have a few minutes to tell us about your experience?
Jenny	Hi, Caitlyn, good to hear from you. Yes, I do have a few minutes.
Caitlyn	Great, I want to first check if the service provider showed up on time for the appointment?
Jenny	Yes, he did.
Caitlyn	Was he able to quickly resolve your issues and did so in a courteous manner?
Jenny	Yes, he was very efficient and polite.

嗨，Jenny，這裡是ABC國際的Caitlyn，您上星期有接受我們公司的服務，我打來做個追蹤調查。請問您現在有時間告訴我們您的經驗嗎？

嗨，Caitlyn，真高興聽到妳的聲音。有的，我現在有空。

好極了，我想要首先了解我們的服務人員是否有在約定的時間準時出現？

有，他有。

那他是否能很快的解決您的問題並且保持有禮貌的態度呢？

是的，他非常的有效率及有禮。

Caitlyn	Terrific. Now that you have had some experience with us, I want to see if you are interested in our long term contracts. It is a one year contract, and you can call us anytime for consultation. We will also provide on-site service 4 times, all for the price of 3 separate regular visits.	太好了。現在您有過接受我們公司服務的經驗，我想要瞭解一下您對我們公司的長期契約是否有興趣呢？契約期間是一年，您可以隨時找我們做諮詢。我們還會提供4次免費的到府服務，全部只要3次個別定期檢視的錢。
Jenny	Wow, that sounds like a great deal, sign me up!	哇，聽起來蠻優惠的，那我要加入！
Caitlyn	Excellent,so how would you like to pay for this long term contract? We receive cash, checks and major credit card.	太好了，那您要用什麼方式來支付這一個長期契約的款項呢？我們接受現金，支票及主要的信用卡付款。
Jenny	I want to pay by master card.	我要用萬事達卡。
Caitlyn	Great, I will send you the credit card authorization form with the contract, just simply fill in the blanks. And then please send them back with the business reply envelope that I enclosed. Thank you again for your support and I am confident that we can continue to satisfy all of your computing needs!	好極了，我會將信用卡授權書籍合約一併寄給您，只要在空白處填上您的資料即可。然後請將它們放進我隨信所附上商業回覆信封寄回。再次感謝您的支持，我有信心我們能滿足您所有在電腦方面的需求。
Jenny	No problem, thank you for doing an excellent job.	沒問題，謝謝妳為我做的這些。

Dialog 2

Caitlyn	Hi, Jenny, this is Chris calling from Toyota Motor CorporationMotor Corporation, how are you today?	嗨，Jenny，我是豐田汽車的 Chris，您今天好嗎？
Jenny	Hi, Chris, I am doing well.	嗨，Chris，我很好。
Caitlyn	Great, I am calling to check how your car is doing. According to our records, your car is due for a routine service next month.	好極了，我打來想知道您車子的車況。根據我們的紀錄顯示，下個月您的車子該做定期保養。
Jenny	Oh, thank you for the reminder, I totally forgot about it. My car has been running fine, but I am sure it needs the proper maintenance.	喔，謝謝你的提醒，我差一點忘了。我的車運作狀況還不錯，但我確定它需要一些適當的維修。
Caitlyn	Yes, periodic service has always been the key to keep the car running smoothly. I would like to recommend you to set up an appointment now.	沒錯，定期保養一直都是維持車輛順利運作的關鍵。我想要建議您現在安排一個預約。
Jenny	I would like to, but I am not sure when I will be free actually. How about that? I will put this on my calendar and call you back after I have figured out my schedule.	我有這個意願，但事實上我不確定我什麼時候有空。這樣如何？我會將這寫在我的行事曆上，在我確認行程之後再回電給你。
Caitlyn	That would be great. You could call me to set up the appointment, and you also could visit our website to schedule an appointment then. Our website provides great coupons every month for services.	那太好了。您可以來電讓我為您安排預約事宜，您也可以在我們的網站上做預約。我們的網站上每個月都會有不同的服務折價券。

Jenny	That's wonderful, I love coupons. I think I'll schedule the appointment on the website.	太好了，我愛折價券。我想我會在網站上做預約。
Caitlyn	That would be wonderful. We,Toyota Motor always try to provide the best values to our customers. If you have any other questions, please do not hesitate to contact us. Thank you again for choosing Toyota Motor, we hope you have a great day!	那非常的好。我們豐田汽車總是試著提供給我們的顧客最優惠的價格。如果您有其他任何問題的話，請隨時和我們聯絡。再次感謝您選擇豐田汽車，我們祝您有美好的一天！
Jenny	Thanks for your information, and hope you have a great day, too!	謝謝你提供的資訊，也祝你有個美好的一天。

💬 精選單字及片語

1. a follow up *n.* 追蹤訪查，定期複查，後續動作。作為名詞或是形容詞使用時也可以寫成 follow-up, followup。但作為動詞使用時，則只寫作 follow up。
   Is there anyone willing to do the follow-up?
   有人願意做後續的追蹤調查嗎？

2. show up 出現，露面。
   He didn't show up for our wedding because he forgot.
   他在我們的婚禮上沒有出現因為他忘記了。

3. courteous *adj.* 謙恭有禮的。
   She made courteous remarks in reply to journalists.
   她以有禮貌的談吐回答了記者。

4. on-site *adj.* 現場的
   I think the on-site training is very important.
   我認為現場訓練是非常重要的。

5. due for 輪到，到…時候了，應該…了。
   She's due for promotion soon.
   很快就要輪到她升官了。

6. coupon(s) *n.* 優惠券；參賽表，訂貨單（多為附在報刊雜誌）。
   Please fill in and return the attached coupon.
   請填寫所附上的訂貨單並寄回。

精選句子與延伸

1. Was he able to quickly resolve your issues and did so in a courteous manner?
   那他是否能很快的解決您的問題並且保持有禮貌的態度呢？
   in a manner 用一種方式；有些，有點兒。in a courteous manner 用有禮貌的方式。
   resolve issue 解決問題
   Effective and proficient agents always can resolve issues on the first call.
   有效率及熟練的代理人總是能在第一通電話就解決問題，

2. I want to see if you are interested in our long term contracts. 我想要瞭解一下您對我們公司的長期契約是否有興趣呢？＝I would like to know that if you're interested in our long term contracts.
   see(v.) 在本句中做「知道」，「瞭解」解釋。

3. No problem, thank you for doing an excellent job! 沒問題，謝謝妳為我做的這些。
   thank you for doing an excellent job. 通常被解釋成 "感謝你在工作上的優異表現"。在本句中，excellent job 指的是 Caitlyn 致電告知長期契約的優惠及協助 Jenny 加入方案。

4. My car has been running fine, but I am sure it needs the proper maintenance. 我的車運作狀況還不錯，但我確定它需要一些適當的維修。
   proper maintenance 適當維修，維護。
   The vehicle requires proper maintenance to ensure its proper functioning.
   車輛本身需要適當的保養來確保其正常功能。

5. Yes, periodic service is always key to keep the car running smoothly. 沒錯，定期保養總是維持車輛順利運作的關鍵。
   periodic service 定期保養
   key to 關鍵，要訣
   The key to success is to be ready from the start.
   成功的關鍵在於一開始時就要做好準備。

Part Four

電話溝通
English Phone Calls

Unit 16 代為接聽客戶電話

Dialog 1

Michael	Hi, this is Michael from AIC Global. How can I help you?	嗨，AIC 全球的，我是Michael。請問有什麼需要我為您服務的？
David	Hi, Michael, my name is David. I need some help with my internet service.	嗨，Michael，我叫David。我需要網路服務上的協助。
Michael	Sure. Can you describe to me what the problem is?	沒問題，David。您可以為我描述一下您的問題是？
David	The internet service just stopped working and I'm not sure why.	網路服務突然就停止了，我不確定是什麼原因。
Michael	OK, are you sure that all the cables are plugged in and all the lights are working on your modem?	好的，那您確認過所有的線路都連接在插座上，還有您數據機的信號燈是否有亮？
David	Yes, all the cables are plugged in, and let me check the lights. (Pause) Yes, the lights are all blinking.	是的，所有線路都是接上的，讓我看一下燈號。（暫停）有，所有的燈都有在閃爍。
Michael	OK, great. Did you try to power cycle your modem?	好的，很好。那您有試過重新啟動您的數據機嗎？
David	Power cycle?	重新啟動？

Michael	Yes, unplugging your modem and letting it rest for about 30 seconds before you turn it back on.	是的，將數據機的電源拔除，並停留大約30秒，再將它的電源接上。
David	Oh no, I didn't try that. Let me see if that works.	喔，沒有，我沒試過。讓我試試看。
Michael	Any progress?	有任何進展嗎？
David	Actually yes, that seemed to do the trick.	實際上有，看起來好像成功了。
Michael	Great. David, is there anything else I can help you with?	好極了。David，那還有其他我能為您效勞的嗎？
David	No, Michael, thanks for your help.	沒有了，Michael，謝謝你的幫忙。
Michael	You're welcome. Thank you for calling, and have a great day.	不客氣，謝謝您的來電，祝您有美好的一天。
David	Thanks, you too.	謝謝，你也是。

Dialog 2

| Leila | Hi, this is Leila from TGA Services. We hope to provide you with excellent customer service. How may I be of service to you today? | 嗨，這裡是TGA服務，我是Leila，我們希望能提供給您卓越的客戶服務。請問今天有什麼我能為您服務的呢？ |
| Kelly | Hi. Leila, I want to return a product that I ordered online. | 嗨，Leila，我想要退掉一個我在網路上訂購的產品。 |

Leila	OK sure, can I have your name and online tracking number?	OK，沒問題，可以給我您的姓名及網路追蹤號碼嗎？
Kelly	Sure, my name is Kelly, and my online tracking number is 53978.	當然，我的名字是Kelly，我的網路追蹤號碼是53978。
Leila	Great, thanks Kelly, let me look that number up. It says here you purchased a chef's knife. Is that correct?	好極了，謝謝您Kelly，讓我查一下這個號碼。這裡顯示您訂購的是一把廚師刀。對嗎？
Kelly	Yes, that is correct.	是的，沒錯。
Leila	Is there a reason that you wanted to return your purchase?	請問一下您要退貨的理由是？
Kelly	I decided that I didn't want the knife any more.	我認為我不再需要這把刀。
Leila	OK, that is fine. Can I have the credit card number, expiration date, and CVV number that you used to purchase the knife?	好的，沒問題。可以給我您購入這把刀時所使用的的信用卡號碼，有效期限及驗證碼嗎？
Kelly	Yes, it is a VISA 4185 3288 4958 3273, expiration 07/14, CVV 244.	可以，我用的是VISA 4185 3288 4958 3273，有效期限07/14及驗證碼244。
Leila	OK, great thank you for that information. I just made the return, you should see credit back on your bank statement tomorrow.	OK，很好，謝謝您提供的相關資訊。我剛為您做了退款，您應該明天就能在您的銀行對帳單上看到退的款項。
Kelly	Great, thank you.	好極了，謝謝你。

Leila	You're welcome. Is there anything else I can help you with?	不客氣，請問還有什麼能為您服務的呢？
Kelly	Nope, that's it.	沒有，就這樣了。
Leila	OK, have a nice day and thank you for calling TGA Services.	OK，Kelly 祝您有美好的一天及感謝您來電TGA服務。
Kelly	Thanks.	謝謝。

💬 精選單字及片語

1. plug *v.* 插上（插頭，線路）plug in 插上插座以接通。
   Where can I plug in my hair straightener?
   我在哪裡可以插上直髮器的電源呢？

2. blink *v.* 閃爍；眨眼。
   According to a research, liars blink less frequently than normal during the lie, and then speed up about 8 times faster than usual afterward.
   根據一項調查指出，說謊的人在說謊時眨眼的頻率會比平常少，之後會加快到比平時多八倍左右。

3. power cycle 重新啟動；動力循環。
   We have been power cycling devices to sign back on.
   我們一直在重新啟動裝置來重新登錄。

4. return 退貨，返還
   We have a 30-day return policy on all items purchased.
   我們對所有購買的品項提供30天的退貨政策。

5. track 追蹤；監測。tracking number 追蹤號碼
   The hunter tracked the deer and managed to catch it.
   獵人追蹤一頭鹿，並設法要捕到它。

6. expiration *n.* 截止，終止，屆滿。
   You'll get refund at the expiration of the lease.
   你在租約到期時，就能拿到退款。

精選句子與延伸

1. I need some help with my internet service.　我需要網路服務上的協助。
   internet service　網際網路服務。我們一般常見的 ISP (internet service provider) 網路服務業者，就是專門提供使用者在網路上活動的各種服務之業者。

2. Actually yes, that seemed to do the trick.　實際上有，看起來好像成功了。＝As a matter of fact, it works.（事實上，它成功了。）
   do the trick　獲得成功，達到效果。
   The medicine should do the trick.
   這個藥應該會有效。

3. How may I be of service to you today?　請問今天有什麼我能為您服務的呢？

4. Can I have the credit card number, expiration date, and CVV number that you used to purchase the knife?　可以給我您購入這把刀時所使用的的信用卡號碼，有效期限及驗證碼嗎？＝Can I have your credit card number follow by the expiration date and CVV number that you used to buy the knife?
   CVV number＝card validation value number 驗證碼

Unit 17 新客戶開發／回覆客戶問題

Dialog 1

Sam	Hi, my name is Sam, how are you doing this morning?	嗨，我是Sam，您今天早上好嗎？
Nelson	Hi, Sam, I'm doing well.	嗨，Sam，我很好。
Sam	That's Great, what can I do for you, sir? Or are you looking for some certain rate plans or phone services?	好極了，我可以為您做些什麼呢，先生？或是您是不是想知道一些費率方案或是電話服務相關內容呢？
Nelson	Yes, actually I was wondering if you could introduce some different rate plans to me.	對，事實上我剛在想你是否能為我介紹一下一些費率方案。
Sam	Sure, no problem. Excuse me, sir. May I have your phone number and your name please? I would like to check your contract status for you.	當然，沒問題。不好意思，先生，我是否能告訴我您的電話號碼及您的大名呢？我想要幫您確認一下您的合約狀態。
Nelson	My phone number is xxxx-xxxxxx, and my name is Nelson Wang. I believe that my contract expired three months ago.	我的電話號碼是xxxx-xxxxxx，我的名字是Nelson王。我相信我的合約在3個月前已經期滿了。

Sam	Yes, that's right, Mr. Wang. It shows that your contract matured in our records. And I notice that there's an excellent offer for you just today. If you upgrade your phone service, and we'll offer a free mobile phone for you.	是的,沒錯,王先生。在我們的紀錄中顯示您的合約已滿。另外我還注意到今天有一個超值的優惠能提供給您。如果您今天升級您的電話服務,我們將會贈送一隻免費的新手機給您。
Nelson	Oh, really? What kind of phone?	喔,真的嗎?什麼樣的手機?
Sam	We're offering an iPhone 4s—from your record I see that you currently have an iPhone 4?	我們送的是iPhone 4s – 從您的紀錄來看,您現在使用的是iPhone 4嗎?
Nelson	Yes, I do. What kind of upgrade do I need to do?	是的,沒錯。那是要升級成怎樣的方案?
Sam	If you upgrade to "unlimited data", we will give you the free iPhone 4s.	如果您升級成「上網吃到飽」方案,我們將贈送一隻免費的iPhone 4s。
Nelson	Actually, I've been needing more data, that sounds like a great idea.	事實上,我一直都需要更多的資料傳輸量,聽起來是個不錯的主意。
Sam	Great, let me put you through to our customer representatives who can help you with that procedure.	很好,讓我將您轉到我們客服代表,他可以幫您完成這個手續。
Nelson	Great Sam, thanks for your help.	好的Sam,謝謝您的協助。
Sam	It's my pleasure.	這是我的榮幸。

Dialog 2

| Tonya | Hi, my name is Tonya, and we have a great deal on beauty products today. | 嗨，我是Tonya，今天我們的美容產品有優惠喔。 |

Ryan Hi, Tonya, I'm sorry, I don't have the time for buying any products today.

嗨，Tonya，不好意思，我今天沒有時間購買任何產品。

Tonya This won't take up too much of your time. We have a promotion for a cleanser, toner, and makeup remover for the price of just the cleanser. This is a great deal.

這不會花費您許多的時間。我們今天的優惠是一罐洗面乳，化妝水及卸妝乳只要一罐洗面乳的價錢。這真的非常優惠。

Ryan How do I know if these products work well?

那我怎麼知道這些產品好不好用？

Tonya These products are safe, all natural and organic, and make your skin look fresh after every use. We have scientific proof of anti aging effects as well.

這些產品很安全，全部都是純天然及有機，每次用完後，可以讓您的肌膚看起來明亮乾淨。

Ryan Anti aging effects? Do you have any brochures with this information?

有抗老的效果嗎？你有相關資訊的宣傳手冊嗎？

Tonya	Yes, we do, and the cleanser, toner, and make up remover come with a free DVD of our company that also includes the scientific information. It's a great buy.	有，我們有，還有洗面乳，化妝水及卸妝乳都附有一片免費的我們公司的DVD其中包括有相關的科學資訊。這真的很值得買。
Ryan	I'm not sure, I need some time to think about it.	我不太確定，我需要一些時間考慮。
Tonya	Are you sure? It's a great buy, and if you buy now, we'll throw in an extra cleanser for free, so it will be four products for the price of one.	您確定嗎？這真的很值得，還有如果您現在購買，我們將會多送一瓶洗面乳，所以是四樣產品只要一樣產品的價錢。
Ryan	Hmm, if you say it like that, then sure I'll buy it.	嗯，既然妳都說成這樣了，那我當然會買。
Tonya	Great! I can take your payment information at this time.	太好了，現在跟您確認一下您的付款方式。
Ryan	OK, let me find my wallet.	OK，讓我找一下我的皮夾。

🗨 精選單字及片語

1. currently *adv.* 現在，通常，一般。
   Our new project is currently under review.
   我們新的項目正在審核當中。

2. put through 實行；完成；使經歷；（電話）接通
   We expect to put through the challenge.
   我們希望能順利完成這項挑戰。

   Please put me through to Mr. Kim.
   請幫我接Kim先生。

3. deal(s) *n.* 交易；許多，大量；待遇。
   I got a good deal on the apartment.
   我便宜的買到這間公寓。

   They spent a great deal of money as well as time.
   他們耗費了大量的金錢及時間。

   The manager has promised her a new deal.
   經理答應要給她更好的待遇。

4. organic *adj.* 有機的。
   The organic fertilizer keeps the soil in good cultivation.
   有機肥料能讓土壤適於耕種。

5. fresh *adj.* 明亮乾淨。fresh 一般做新鮮解釋，但用於形容皮膚，則有明亮、乾淨的含意。
   Her skin was fresh and golden as though she had been dipped in honey.
   她的膚色明亮閃耀著金色的光彩就好像浸泡過蜂蜜一般。

6. brochure(s) *n.* 小冊子，資料手冊。
   The product's features are all detailed in our brochure.
   產品的特點在我們的手冊中有詳盡的介紹。

精選句子與延伸

1. If you upgrade to "unlimited data", we will give you the free iPhone 4s. 如果您升級成「上網吃到飽」方案，我們將贈送一隻免費的 iPhone 4s。

   unlimited data＝unlimited data usage 上網吃到飽，無限的資料傳輸。這裡指的是手機的上網費率方案，data 在這指的是網路的檔案傳輸量，unlimited data 就是我們一般所稱的手機上網的「吃到飽方案」。

   Optus offers unlimited data roaming for Aussie travelers.
   Optus 為在澳洲的旅客推出了上網漫遊吃到飽方案。

2. Actually, I've been needing more data, that sounds like a great idea. 事實上，我一直都需要更多的資料傳輸量，聽起來是個不錯的主意。

   本句中的 I've been needing 為 have been + Ving 是現在完成進行式，用以表示從過去的某一刻開始的動作持續到現在，並仍在持續進行當中，在 Nelson 說這一句話時，他傳輸量不足的問題尚未解決。

3. It's a great buy, and if you buy now, we'll throw in an extra cleanser for free, so it will be four products for the price of one. 這真的很值得，還有如果您現在購買，我們將會多送一瓶洗面乳，所以是四樣產品只要一樣產品的價錢。

   throw in 加送，附帶奉送
   You can have the table for $100, and I'll throw in 2 chairs as well.
   這張桌子賣妳 100 元，我還奉送兩張椅子。

4. Hmm, if you say it like that, then sure I'll buy it. 嗯，既然妳都說成這樣了，那我當然會買。

   if you say so 既然你這麼說，如果你說。包含有就這樣做，不再與對方提出相反意見或是質疑的感覺。
   If you say so, and we can't argue with that.
   既然你這麼說，那我們也就不再爭論。

Unit 18 電話中推廣新產品

Dialog 1

Mary	Summer Time, this is Mary speaking, how may I help you?	Summer Time，我是Mary，有什麼能為您效勞的？
Victor	Hello, may I speak with Mr. Grey, please?	哈囉，請問Grey先生在嗎？
Manager	I will put you through immediately, please hold.	我將立刻為您轉接，請稍後。
Victor	Thanks.	謝謝。
Grey	Hello.	哈囉。
Victor	Hi, Mr. Grey. This is Victor Green with HarbourT. I am sure you are busy, and I want to respect your time, so I will be brief, and before I introduce our product, I would like to know that, Mr. Grey, have you ever heard of Harbourt?	嗨，Grey先生。我是HarbourT的Victor Green。我想您應該很忙，為了尊重您寶貴的時間，所以我將盡量簡短，在我介紹我們的產品之前，我想知道Grey先生是否有聽說過HarbourT？
Grey	Nope.	沒有。
Victor	OK, we are the leading provider of merchant services and transaction processing equipment, including the Harbourt point of sale systems.	好的，我們是提供商務服務及交易處理設備的領導品牌，其中也包括了HarbourT銷售點管理系統。

Grey	So, you are selling POS system, right?	所以，你是在賣POS系統的？
Victor	Not exactly, we are also a direct processor for all major credit cards including American Express,Checkand Debit Card.	不完全是，我們同時也是負責所有主要信用卡包括美國運通卡，記帳卡及支票卡的交易處理服務商。
Grey	Hmmm… as a matter of fact, we are just a mom-and-pop business and still in start-up mode. I don't think we have upfront cash to invest on a new POS system.	嗯…事實上，我們只是小生意，也剛開始起步。我不認為我們有可預先支出的現金來投資在新的POS系統上。
Victor	We totally understand what you are worried about. The precise reason I'm calling you today is that we will provide our POS hardware and software to your business for free in exchange for a 5-year agreement to our credit card transaction processing services. It's a limited-time offer.	我們完全可以瞭解您所擔心的。我今天打來最主要的原因是我們將免費提供POS硬體及軟體設備供您的生意使用，只要您加入我們為期5年的信用卡交易處理服務。這是一項限時優惠。
Grey	That sounds great. But we don't accept credit cards in our business.	這聽起來很棒。但我們店裡並不收信用卡。
Victor	Mr. Grey, I would like to know that have you ever had the embarrassing situations of turning the sales away because your business is not credit card unfriendly?	Grey先生，我想知道您是否曾遇過因為不收信用卡而將生意推出門的尷尬情況？
Grey	Yes, sometimes.	是的，有時候。

Victor	OK, according to our research, it indicates that card transactions actually consist of more than 50% of all sales transactions. Besides, accepting credit cards can ensure a more than 20% increase in sales and even foot traffic in your store.	OK，根據我們的調查指出信用卡交易大概佔了所有銷售交易的百分之50以上。除此之外，接受信用卡交易可以達到增加百分之20以上的銷售量，甚至還能帶動店內的人潮。
Grey	Oh, I didn't know that there are so many advantages to accept credit cards. But as I know, most businesses pay up to 5% on credit card transaction fees. The rate is a little bit too high for a small business owner like me.	我不知道收信用卡有這麼多好處。但是據我所知，大部分的店家支付高達百分之5的信用卡交易費用。這個費率對於像我這樣小店的老闆來說有一些太高了。
Victor	That's a good point. Harbourt does understand what a small business owner wants, we charge less than 2% for each credit card transaction.	您的意見非常好。Harbourt瞭解小型企業主的需求，我們只收取低於百分之2的信用卡交易費。
Grey	Wow, that sounds great.	哇，那聽起來不錯。
Victor	If that interests you, we will send one of our representatives, his name is Gary, to your area this week, which day works best for you?	如果您有興趣的話，我們將派一位代表叫做Gary，這個星期到您那區一趟，那一天最適合呢？
Grey	I will be available on Thursday.	我星期四時有空。
Victor	Morning or afternoon?	早上或是下午？
Grey	Afternoon.	下午。
Victor	How about 2 pm at your store?	那下午2點在您的店裡？

Grey	OK.	好的。
Victor	Great, let me reconfirm with you, Gary will call on you in your store at 2 pm on Thursday.	好極了，讓我跟您再確認一次，Gary將會在星期四下午2點鐘到您的店裡做拜訪。
Grey	OK. Oh, one more thing, you mentioned about the free Harbourt POS system, do I have to pay for the shipment, installation, and training?	好的。喔，還有一件事，你提到的免費的Harbourt POS 系統，我需要支付運費，安裝費及訓練費用嗎？
Victor	No, you don't have to, it's completely free. As long as you sign up a 5-year commitment to our processing services. Once the 5 years are up, you own the POS system outright.	不，不需要，它完全是免費的。只要您加入我們為期5年的處理服務合約。一旦期滿5年，您就完全的擁有那台POS系統。
Grey	OK, thanks for informing me this program.	OK，謝謝您告訴我這一個優惠。
Victor	It's my pleasure, Mr. Grey, and thank you very much for your precious time.	是我的榮幸，Grey先生，並感謝您寶貴的時間。

💬 精選單字及片語

1. point of sale systems　銷售點管理系統，一般稱為 POS 系統。結合了收銀機，銷售，庫存，及進貨等的管理功能。POS 是 point of sales 的縮寫，而隨著 POS 系統的應用不斷的擴大，現在也有廠商將它改稱為 point of service system 服務點管理系統。

2. debit card　記帳卡，是種結合存款帳戶，兼具信用卡及提款卡的功能。一般所見到的 VISA 金融卡即是記帳卡的一種。

3. mom-and-pop　小型的家庭式經營的生意。mom 是媽媽，pop 是爸爸的意思。
   If we want to become the leading brand in the industry, then we have to move beyond the mom-and-pop operation and play hard ball.
   如果我們要成為業界的領導品牌，那我們必須突破小型企業的經營方式，並採取強勢的手段。

4. start-up　（公司或工程）剛在開辦的階段
   It grew from a tiny start-up to an international coporation.
   它從一個一個小小的新公司發展成為一個跨國集團。

5. upfront *adv.*　提前支付的；在最前面的。　*adj.*　率真，坦率
   We don't take any upfront payment.
   我們不收任何預付的款項。
   I like Molly, because she's an upfront lady.
   我喜歡Molly，因為她是個坦率的女士。

6. installation *n.*　安置，裝置
   The new system installation will take several days.
   新系統的裝置會花上幾天的時間。

🗨 精選句子與延伸

1. Have you ever had the embarrassing situations of turning the sales away because your business is credit card unfriendly? 您是否曾遇過因為不收信用卡而將生意推出門的尷尬情況？

   turn away 拒絕

   A doctor cannot turn away a dying person.

   醫生是不能見死不救的。

   credit card unfriendly 不收信用卡；credit card friendly 收信用卡。在英文中常會以在後面接 friendly 來表示對其是有助益，不會拒絕的。例如 eco friendly，environmentally friendly（環保的）。

2. Accepting credit cards can ensure a more than 20% increase in sales and even foot traffic in your store. 接受信用卡交易可以達到增加百分之 20 以上的銷售量，甚至還能帶動店內的人潮。

   foot traffic 人潮。traffic 除了指交通工具的流動之外，也可用來指人的流動。

   The shop is in the corner hardly with any foot traffic.

   這間店在那幾乎沒有人潮經過的角落。

3. Gary will call on you in your store at 2 pm on Thursday. Gary 將會在星期四下午 2 點鐘到您的店裡做拜訪。

   在英文中，習慣先寫地點，再寫時間，並以由小到大的順序排列。例如在本句中先寫 in your store 店裡（地點）→2 pm 下午（時間 - 小）→Thursday 星期四（時間-大）

4. Once the 5 years are up, you own the POS system outright. 一旦期滿 5 年，您就完全的擁有那台 POS 系統。

   本句也可解釋成：一旦期滿 5 年，您就能立即擁有那台 POS 系統。

   outright(adv.) 徹底的，完全的；立即的。

   We won outright in the election.

   我們在選戰中大獲全勝。

績效評估

Dialog 1

| Dave | Hi, Pete. Please have a seat. How are you today? | 嗨，Pete。請坐。你今天好嗎？ |

| Pete | Honestly, I'm quite nervous. | 老實說，我很緊張。 |

| Dave | That's normal. I also get tensed up before my performance reviews. Just take a deep breath, I believe that will make you feel better. | 那是正常的。我在面對我的績效評估前也都非常緊張。深呼吸，我想你會感到好一點的。 |

| Dave | Thanks. | 謝謝。 |

| Dave | Okay, let's have a look at your performance appraisal. In general, your performance through this year has been satisfactory. Some aspects of your performance are pretty strong, and others aspects need to be improved. | Okay，我們來看一下你的績效評估。整體而言，你今年的績效表現還算令公司滿意。你的工作表現有些方面相當不錯，但有些方面則需要加強。 |

| Dave | I don't get it. Why I get only satisfactory? I got the employee of the month for 3 times this year. The customer surveys show that they are very happy with our customer service. | 我不懂。為什麼我只拿到滿意的評比？我今年得到三次的本月最佳員工。顧客調查中顯示顧客都非常滿意我們的客戶服務。 |

Dave	Indeed, our customers are all happy with our service, and you deserve lots of credit for that. However, as a senior representative, you should realize that when the quality of customer service is very high, and usually the efficiency has fallen. It caused that your department is over budget.	的確，我們的顧客都非常滿意我們的服務，而你的功勞最大。然而，身為一個資深的客服人員，你應該了解當客戶服務品質非常高時，通常效率就會降低。這造成你的部門超出預算。
Dave	I know that our department is slightly over budget, but I think the most important part of my job is to keep our customers happy and help them to solve their problems.	我知道我們的部門有些超出預算，但我認為我的工作中最重要的是讓顧客滿意及幫助他們解決問題。
Dave	Like I said before, some aspects of your performance do need improvement. You have to get a good balance between the quality of customer service and work efficiency.	正如我之前所說的，你的工作表現中有些方面是需要改進的。你必須在顧客服務品質及工作效率之間得到一個好的平衡點。
Dave	So I have to work at improving the quantity of calls handled.	所以我必須致力於增加通話的數量。
Dave	That's correct, and maybe you could make a standard chart for the customer service to speed up the procedure.	沒錯，或許你可以製作顧客服務的標準流程來加快服務速度。
Dave	Thank you, Dave. It is a brilliant idea.	謝謝你，Dave。這是個好主意。
Dave	You are welcome. Let me know if you need help.	不客氣，如果需要幫忙時告訴我一聲。

Dave　　Yes, I will.

好的，我會的。

Dialog 2

Manager　Let's go over the weekly performance reviews. I have got good news and bad news. I will give you guys bad news first.

我們來看一下每週的業績評估。我有好消息及壞消息。我想先告訴你們壞消息。

Staff A　Hold on, sir. Let me take a deep breath.

經理，等一下。先讓我吸口氣。

Manager　Our team was low in ranking last week. All of the numbers were at the lower level for performance reviews.

我們隊上星期的名次落後。所有績效評估中的指數都低於標準。

Staff B　What's wrong?

怎麼會這樣？

Manager　That's what I want to know. As a whole, our personal reviews were okay. There were no negative reviews for any of us in this team, but the problem was our sales numbers have been too low on last week.

這正是我想知道的。整體而言，我們的個人評估都還好。我們隊中並沒有任何人有負面的評估，但問題在於上星期我們的銷售業績太差了。

Staff C　I think that's not completely our fault, all my clients know that our company's going to launch a new product line, but we don't have any information of the new line so far…

我認為這並不完全是我們的錯，我所有的客戶都知道我們公司正準備推出一系列新的產品，但目前我們並沒有與新產品相關的任何資訊……

Manager	You mean our clients are interested in our new product line?	你的意思是我們的客戶對我們的新產品線有興趣？
Staff C	Yes. As the market has recently shrunk, our clients want to adopt our new product to attract more potential customers. Most of my clients stop ordering our existing products, because they've got words that the new product will be launched next week.	是的。隨著市場逐漸的萎縮，我們的客戶要採用我們的新產品用以吸引更多的潛在顧客。我有很多客戶已經不再訂購現有的產品，因為他們收到消息，新產品將在下星期推出。
Manager	Is there anyone at the same situation?	有沒有人遇到相同情形？
Everyone	I am!	我
Manager	It was just as I had conjectured. Luckily, the new product will be launched tomorrow, and Sally will email you related information. About good news, congrats, everyone, our team has won the first prize at the annual sales competition. We will get extra bonus for this month.	正如我所猜測的一樣。還好，新產品將在明天推出，Sally會將相關資訊email給你們。關於好消息，恭喜大家，我們在年度的銷售競賽中得到第一名。這個月會有額外的獎金。

💬 精選單字及片語

1. appraisal(s) *n.* 評價，評估，鑑定
   A performance appraisal is a review of an employee's assigned duties and responsibilities.
   績效評鑑是針對員工所被交付的工作及其職責所做的評估。

2. some… others 有些…有些…用於特定的範圍可數名詞中使用，使用 some… others… 則會有部分不包含在 some… others… 中。
   The students in the classroom are busy, some are reading and others are crafting.
   教室裡的學生都在忙，有些在讀書，有的在做工藝品。

3. deserve credit for 因…值得受到讚賞
   He deserves credit for the work he did on that project.
   他是那個項目的最大功臣。

4. to launch a new product line 推出新的產品系列（包含多種產品為同一主題的延伸）
   to launch a new product 推出一樣新產品
   We decided to launch a new product to increase the revenue.
   我們決定推出一項新產品來增加獲利率。

5. adopt *vt.* 採用；收養；批准
   They adopt new techniques in raising cows.
   他們採用新的養牛技術。

6. conjecture *v.* 推測；臆測
   I can't conjecture what his motives are.
   我無法猜測他的動機是什麼。

💬 精選句子與延伸

1. I also get tensed up before my performance reviews. 我在面對我的績效評估前也都非常緊張。＝I get nervous before my performance reviews, too.
tense up 緊張
Work swiftly, but don't tense up; relax your body and mind and never tighten up.
工作要趕不要急；身心要鬆不要緊。（聖嚴法師自在語）

2. You have to get a good balance between the quality of customer service and work efficiency. 你必須在顧客服務品質及工作效率之間得到一個好的平衡點。
work efficiency 工作效率，也可成為workforce productivity
balance(s)(n.) 平衡，穩定，天平

3. I have got good news and bad news. 我有好消息及壞消息。
news(n.) 消息，新聞。news 為不可數名詞，接單數動詞。
e.g. The news comes from a reliable source. 這消息來自於可靠的來源。
a news 為常見的錯誤用法，如果要強調是一則消息或新聞時，可寫做 a piece of news。

4. They've got words that the new product will be launched next week. 他們已經收到消息，新產品將在下星期推出。＝They have received the news that we will launch a new product next week.
get words 獲得消息，聽說，得知。

Unit 20 銷售計畫

Dialog 1

Manager	Alright, everyone, we are here today to hold this meeting, because we have to make a sales plan for the final quarter. As we discussed last week, we did not do very well for the third quarter, so we have to make some plans to stimulate the sales. Hopefully, we could reach the annual sales target. I need some concrete solutions, anyone?	好了，各位，我們今天的會議是要為最後一個季度制訂銷售計畫。如我們上星期所討論的，我們在第三季的表現並不太好，所以我們必須提出一些方案來刺激銷售量。希望我們能達到年度銷售目標。我需要一些具體的解決方法，有誰要提出意見嗎？
Staff A	How about lower the prices of our products? It may give a boost to our sales.	降低我們的產品的價格可以嗎？可能會增加我們的銷量。
Manager	It's not very creative. I prefer something more creative, not just reducing the price.	不太有創意。我希望是較具有創造性的，而不只是降低價格。
Staff A	I know it's not very creative, but according to the research, we are the most expensive supplier in the market.	我知道沒什麼創意，但是根據調查中顯示，我們是市場中最貴的供應商。
Manager	That is because we supply the products of the best quality, and we have a good reputation for high standards of the product quality.	那是因為我們供應最佳品質的產品，及我們以高標準的產品品質而聞名。

Staff A	Indeed, our company is famous, because our products of the best quality. However, I found that it's necessary to discuss our pricing strategy. In my regular client visits, I found that many clients are very interested in our product B, but they changed their minds after they know the price of product B, they always choose product C instead of product B.	的確，我們公司是因最佳品質的產品而出名。然而我發現有必要來討論一下我們的價格策略。在我例行的客戶拜訪中，我發現許多客戶對我們的B產品有興趣，但在知道B產品的價錢之後改變心意，他們總是選擇C產品，而不是B產品。
Manager	uh-huh! That's very interesting. Tell me more about it.	嗯哼！這情況很有趣。跟我再多說一些。
Staff A	Okay. We all know that our product B and C are quite similar in their functions. I was very curious about why the prices of these two products are so different, so I checked the actual cost of both products, I found out that product B is a high profit margin product, and there is some room for reduction. On the contrary, the product C is a low margin product, it doesn't generate significant profit in our sales. So I suggest that maybe we should pick up some products for reduction, and that should make us more competitive in the market.	Ok，我們都知道我們的產品B和C在功能上極為相近。我對這兩樣產品的價格相差這麼多感到非常好奇，所以我查了這兩樣產品的實際成本，我發現B產品是個高獲利產品，而且還有降價的空間。相反的，C產品獲利空間較少，並不會對我們的銷售帶來明顯的利益。所以我建議也許我們應該挑選出幾項商品來調降價格，這樣應該會讓我們在市場上更具競爭力。

Manager	Hmm…about picking up some products for reduction and revising our pricing strategy. I think we can put that to the annual sales plan, and we only slightly reduce the price of product B for this quarter to test the market. Do you agree?	嗯…有關挑選一些商品來調降價格以及修正我們的價格策略的部份，我認為我們可以將那個放在年度的銷售計畫中，我們這一季先針對B產品的價格做稍微地調降來測試市場反應。你贊成嗎？
Staff B	No problem. And I think we will all have to go all out to promote the product B in the coming quarter.	沒問題。還有我認為我們在下一個季度必須盡全力的推銷B產品。
Manager	That's for sure. Does anyone else have opinions? How about our new product? How's the market reaction toward our new product?	這是當然的。還有誰要提出意見？我們的新產品如何？市場對我們新產品的反應怎麼樣？
Staff B	The new product has been launched so far which is very well received by the market, and I suggest a new product promotion to motive sales.	新產品推出至今，市場的接受度很高，我建議促銷新產品來刺激銷售量。
Manager	OK, please be sure to inform the marketing department, and let them make a good strategy for the promotion. About the sales quota for this season, is that possible to revise up?	好，請確記要通知行銷部門，讓他們為新產品的促銷制定一個好的策略。有關於這一季的業績標準，有沒有可能調高呢？
Everyone	Oh, no…	喔，不…

Manager	OK, I know our performance target was decided at the beginning of this year, and the local market slowed down a little bit, but I'm not going to revise down this season's sales quota, 'cause I have confidence in you guys and our new product.	OK，我知道我們的業績目標是在今年年初就設定好的，還有本地市場有一點點的衰退，但我並不打算下修本季的銷售配額，因為我對大家及我們的新產品有信心。
Staff C	Hey, guys, we will try our best, right?	嘿，各位，我們會竭盡所能，對吧？
Everyone	Yes!	對！
Manager	I am very glad to have all of you in my team. OK, Steve, can you responsible for the market analysis?	我非常高興你們大家能在我的團隊中。OK，Steve，你能負責市場分析嗎？
Staff C	Yes, sure.	好的，沒問題。
Manager	And Joan, you and Nelson, take in charge of the sales action plan, will ya?	還有Joan，你和Nelson負責銷售行動計畫，可以嗎？
Staff A&B	Yes, sir.	是，長官。
Manager	OK, everybody, please e-mail me the report by Wednesday, and we will have discussion on Friday's meeting.	OK，各位，請在星期三之前將報告e-mail給我，我們會在星期五的會議中討論。

🗨 精選單字及片語

1. quarter(s) *n.* 四分之一；一季，季度。在財務報表上或是銷售計畫中常會以 Q 加上數字代表第幾季，如 Q4 則是第四季（最後一季）。
   The US economy saw a 3.3% increased in the 3rd quarter of this year.
   美國第三季的經濟成長增加了 3.3%。

2. stimulate *v.* 刺激；激勵，鼓勵。
   I found her conversation very stimulating.
   我發現她的話非常能激勵人心。

3. concrete solution 具體的解決方法。concrete 在這為形容詞，為 "具體的"，"實在的"。
   The concrete solution depends, of course, on the circumstances.
   具體的解決方案理當依不同情況來決定。

4. instead of 而不是，而非。接在這個片語後的詞是沒有發生的。
   I gave him advice instead of money.
   我給了他忠告而非金錢。

5. actual cost 實際成本
   The actual cost of this project was more than we expected.
   這個項目的實際成本超出我們所預期的。

精選句子與延伸

1. We are here today to hold this meeting, because we have to make a sales plan for the final quarter. 我們今天的會議是要為最後一個季度制訂銷售計畫。＝We are holding this meeting today because we have to make a Q4 sales plan.

   sales plan 銷售計畫

2. On the contrary, the product C is a low margin product, it doesn't generate significant profits in our sales. 相反的，C 產品獲利空間較少，並不會對我們的銷售帶來明顯的利益。＝In contrast with product B, C product generates less profit in our sales.

   on the contrary 相反的，正好相反的，反之。

   You think you are smart, on the contrary, we all assure that you are foolish.
   你自認聰明，相反的，我們卻覺得你很傻。

3. I'm not going to revise down this season's sales quota, 'cause I have confidence in you guys and our new product. 我並不打算下修本季的銷售配額，因為我對大家及我們的新產品有信心。

   revise *vt.* 修改，修訂，校訂；複習。

   I am revising for my exam. 我正在複習功課準備我的考試。

   用於數據的修改時：revise up 上修

   　　　　　　　　　revise down 下修

   have confidence in 對…有信心

   Do you have confidence in yourself?
   你對你自己有信心嗎？

Unit 21 專案進度討論

Dialog 1

Manager Hey, everyone, let's have a project status meeting in the meeting room.

嘿,各位,我們到會議室開一下專案進度會議。

Manager I got the news that the boss will be here to check up the Sydney branch store project status in the afternoon. He wants to know what's holding us back on that project.

我剛得到消息,老闆今天下午要過來檢查雪梨分店的專案進度。他想要知道專案進度停滯的原因。

A The Sydney branch store project has been stopped for just a few days, there was a snag in the filing process to get the necessary construction permits.

雪梨分店專案只是先暫停了幾天,在申請必要的建設許可證過程當中遇到了一點阻礙。

Manager And the reason is?

那理由是?

A The location we choose is in the heritage conservation area, so we need to get a construction certificate to refurbish the building.

我們所選擇的地點是在文化遺產保存區域中,所以我們必須要拿到建設許可證才能翻新整棟建築。

Manager Will it take long?

會需要很長的時間嗎?

B We've already consulted with our duty planner, and she replied that it will take about 2 weeks to examine our specs.

我們已經和我們的責任設計師諮詢過了,她回答的是將會需要2個星期左右的時間來審核我們的工程設計書。

Manager	Is this project going to be behind schedule?	那這一個專案的進度會被耽誤嗎？
B	No. It's still on schedule. We already knew the development application and thought about some other possible challenges when we were planning the project.	不。進度仍在預計的當中。我們在策劃這一個專案時已經知道這個開發申請的事也考慮過其他有可能發生的挑戰。
Manager	Is that possible to finish this project in advance?	那有可能提前完成這一個專案嗎？
C	No, I don't think so. We do have ample time to work out this project, but we only can guarantee that the project can be finished on time to ensure the quality.	不，我不這樣認為。我們確實有足夠的時間來進行這一個專案，但我們只能保證能如期完成這一個專案，來確保其品質。
Manager	I appreciate all your efforts on this project, and I hope you guys can keep track of the progress of this project.	我感謝你們大家在這專案上所付出的努力，我希望你們能持續追蹤這個專案的進度。

Dialog 2

Crisity	Jenny told me that you have a word for me?	Jenny告訴你有話對我說？
Darren	Yes, please come on in.	沒錯，請進。
Crisity	What's the matter? You look so serious.	怎麼回事？你看起來很嚴肅。
Darren	We have heard that our competitor's going to launch a product which is quite akin to our new product next month.	我們聽說我們的競爭對手在下個月要推出的產品和我們新產品相當類似。
Crisity	Is it true?	是真的嗎？
Darren	Yes, it is. We've also heard they're almost ready, so I wanna know how's that new product project going? We have to finish first, or they'll take over the market before we get started.	是的，是真的。我們還得到消息他們已經幾乎準備好了，所以我要知道新產品專案進行的怎樣？我們必須先完成，要不他們將在我們開始之前就佔據了整個市場。
Crisity	The project's nearly done. Basically, we have almost done the final version, and I could have it all finished by Friday afternoon.	這個專案已經快完成了。基本上，我們已經幾乎要完成最後的版本，我可以在星期五下午之前完成專案。
Darren	That's good, but remember do take your time to look over this project, we can't afford to make any mistake on it.	這樣很好，但是記得要花些時間好好的將整個專案檢查一遍，我們無法承擔在這個專案上犯錯的代價。

Crisity	Ok, I can check up every detail on this weekend, and have it finished by Monday.	Ok，我可以利用這個週末來仔細做檢查，在星期一之前完成。
Darren	Great, and we will finish it just in time. The B project can be suspended for the time being, so we can concentrate on the new product project within the next few days.	很好，那我們將能及時完成。B專案可以先暫時擱置一段時間，所以我們可以在接下來的這幾天專心在新產品專案上。
Crisity	From the next week on, and we'll be in less of a hurry. We will have plenty of time to do the B project.	下星期開始，我們就不用這麼趕了。我們將有大把的時間來做B專案。
Darren	That's right, we still have one month to finish project B before the deadline. Let's put our effort into the new product project now, and make sure everyone knows that we have to finish it before Friday.	沒錯，在最後期限之前我們還有一個月的時間來完成B專案。讓我們現在全力投入在新產品專案上吧，務必讓大家都知道我們一定要在星期五前完成它。
Crisity	Yes, I will.	好的，我會的。

💬 精選單字及片語

1. project status meeting　專案進度會議
    The manager re-emphasized the importance of this project at the project status meeting.
    經理在專案進度會議中再次強調這個專案的重要性。

2. snag(s) *n.*　阻礙，小困難或障礙。
    The only sang is that I can't afford it.
    唯一的障礙是我付不起這些錢。

3. refurbish *v.*　整修，翻新（房子）。
    We have spent a lot of money on refurbishing our office.
    我們花了很大一筆錢來翻新我們的辦公室。

4. hold back　阻擋，阻礙；隱瞞。
    The dam was not strong enough to hold back the flood water.
    水壩不夠堅固，無法阻擋洪水。

5. akin *adj.*　相似的；同源的；關係密切的。
    Her life story is akin to an idol drama.
    她的人生故事就好像是一部偶像劇。

6. in less of a hurry　不這麼匆忙 (in a hurry + less of)
    I tried to leave in less of a hurry to pretend as nothing happened.
    我試著離開時不要這麼匆忙來裝作什麼事都沒發生過。

7. suspend *v.*　暫停，延緩。
    Without any support, he was compelled to suspend his experiment.
    沒有任何的支援，他被迫中斷他的實驗。

🗨 精選句子與延伸

1. I got the news that the boss will be here to check up the Sydney branch store project status in the afternoon.
   我剛得到消息，老闆今天下午要過來檢查雪梨分店的專案進度。
   project status 專案進度
   I report on the project status and issues to my client regularly.
   我定期的向客戶報告專案的進度及相關事宜。

2. Jenny told me that you have a word for me?
   Jenny 告訴你有話對我說？
   = Jenny said you want to talk to me.

3. But remember do take your time to look over this project, we can't afford to make any mistake on it.
   但是要記得要花些時間好好的將整個專案檢查一遍，我們無法承擔在這個專案上犯錯的代價。
   在這個句子當中容易犯的錯誤是將重點放在 "你的時間" 上，但如果將 take your time 這個常用的片語抽出，便能發現重點是在 "不用急，慢慢來" 必須謹慎，多花些時間在檢查上面。
   take your time 不用急，慢慢來
   look over 仔細檢查，審視。

4. We can concentrate on the new product project within the next few days.
   我們可以在接下來的這幾天專心在新產品專案上。
   concentrate on 專心於，集中注意力在。
   You should concentrate on the road while driving.
   開車時你應該要集中注意力在路上。
   within the next few days 在最近幾天內
   The cinema will be shown within the next few days.
   這部電影將在這幾天內會上映。

Unit 22 產品定位

Dialog 1

Manager	In today's meeting, we'll discuss the marketing plan for the next fiscal year. Before that, I want to know regarding to the company's losses last season, Josh, in your point of view, where do the problems lie?	在今天的會議中，我們要討論下一個會計年度的行銷企劃。在那之前，我想要知道對於我們公司上一季的虧損，Josh，依你的看法，問題出在哪裡？
Josh	I think the major cause was the visibility of our new product was rather low, and this should be ascribed to ineffective promotions.	我認為主要的原因是出在我們新產品的曝光度不夠，這應該歸咎於宣傳效果不佳。
Kenny	I disagree. I think the product positioning was not clear enough, so we were unable to reach the target audience of the new product.	我不同意。我認為產品定位不夠清楚，所以才沒辦法找到新產品的目標客群。
Manager	All right, gentlemen. Let's get down to the nitty-gritty. No children quarrels allowed. It sounds to me that you two both are passing the buck. What we have to do now is to find a solution.	好了，兩位。讓我們認真的討論些實質的問題。不要像小孩一樣的拌嘴。我聽起來像是你們兩個人在推卸責任。我們該做的是要找到解決方法。
Josh	Shall we reposition the product?	我們要重新定位產品嗎？

Manager	No, I don't think so. I prefer to enhance the product positioning. So Josh, please tell me what's the benefit of this product?	不，我不這樣認為。我希望能強化產品定位。所以，Josh，請告訴我這個產品的優點是什麼？
Josh	It's stylish, multifunctional, and inexpensive.	它造型漂亮，功能很多，而且價錢也不貴。
Manager	Ok, Kenny, what kind of position did you choose when making the promotion plan?	Ok，Kenny，你在制定促銷計畫時選擇的產品定位是什麼？
Kenny	Style and price positions.	造型及價格定位。
Manager	Ok, so we focus on the style position and price position for the next campaign, any problem?	Ok，那我們就在下一次的宣傳活動中專注於造型及價格的定位上。有任何問題嗎？
Josh&Kenny	No.	沒有
Manager	Ok, you two should have a serious talk. I have faith in both of you, and let's even the odds!	Ok，你們兩個應該要好好的談一談。我對你們兩人有信心，讓我們來扳回一城。

Dialog 2

A	The advance technology is the selling point of this product.	先進的技術是這一個產品的賣點。
B	Unfortunately, the price of this new product vis-à-vis the average price on the market is extremely high.	很可惜，這一個新產品相對於市場上的平均價格來說非常的高。
C	Maybe we should adjust the price according to the market.	也許我們應該依照市場來適度調整價格。
B	I'm afraid we can't do anything about the pricing. This model of computer has extradinary capabilities, and most existing computer systems can not handle it, so we have to update the entire computer system to be compatible, which makes it costly to launch.	我恐怕我們在定價上無法更動。這一款的電腦有優越的性能，大多數現有的電腦系統無法匹配，所以我們必須更新整個電腦系統使其能相容，因此上市的成本十分昂貴。
A	Anyway, price position has never been our style. In the cost-wise aspect, we may be not that competitive. How about the quality? The reliable quality of our product is the reason why our products are in customers' good graces.	反正，價格定位從來都不是我們的風格。在以成本作為考量的方面，我們也許並不這麼具有競爭。那品質方面呢？我們產品的可靠品質是我們產品受到顧客青睞的原因。
B	The quality of this model is stable and reliable. It has passed the test and the result is up to standard.	這一款的品質相當的穩定及可靠。它已經通過測試，而且結果高出於標準。

C So how about the product positioning for this model? As usual, quality and style?

所以那這一款產品要做怎樣的定位呢？跟往常一樣，品質及造型定位嗎？

A Yes, I think so. And I want to conduct a research of the price-performance ratio before planning.

對，我也這麼想。還有我想在制定計畫之前做一個性價比的調查。

C Ok, no problem, anything else?Oh, maybe we can consider the placement marketing, I think this model will be in high favor with the young people.

Ok，沒問題，還有其他的嗎？喔，也許我們可以考慮置入性行銷，我覺得這一款應該會受到年輕族群的歡迎。

B I am with you, we can embed this product in the music videos, and some trendy dramas to increase its visibility.

我贊成，我們可以將這一個產品置入到音樂錄影帶，及一些偶像劇中，增加它的能見度。

💬 精選單字及片語

1. fiscal *adj.* 會計的，財政上的。
The decrease of taxation is an important fiscal policy.
減稅是一項重要的財政政策。

2. get down to 開始認真的對待，處理。
I am going to get down to studying English this year.
我今年要開始認真的學英文。

3. nitty-gritty (nitty-grittiies) *n.* 事情真相，本質。
I like to do business with those who get right into the nitty-gritty.
我喜歡和那種直截了當的人做生意。

4. vis-à-vis *prep.* 與…相比，相對於；面對面。
His salary vis-à-vis the national average is rather high.
他的薪資與全國平均薪資比起來相當的高。

5. cost-wise *adj.* 從成本角度來看，考慮成本的。名詞+wise 從…角度來看，關於。
It makes the most sense cost-wise and safty-wise.
從成本及安全的角度來考慮是最為合理的。

6. price-performance ratio 性價比，性能與價格的比較。
The price-performance ration of this laptop is pretty good.
這台筆記型電腦的性價比很不錯。

精選句子與延伸

1. It sounds to me that you two both are passing the buck.
   我聽起來像是你們兩個人在推卸責任。
   pass the buck 推卸責任，互踢皮球；將責任交付給他人。
   這個片語的起源來自於牌桌上，在以前的美國西部，玩撲克牌時，會輪流發牌，而輪到某人發牌時，會將用鹿角做把手的小刀 "buck" 傳到他手上，久而久之，buck 被沿用為有 "責任" 的意思，而 pass the buck 則有 "推卸責任" 的含意。
   I don't know enough about it to decide, so I'll pass the buck to you.
   我對這件事的瞭解不夠不足以做決定，所以我將請你全權負責。

2. I have faith in you, and let's even the odds!
   我對你們兩人有信心，讓我們來扳回一城。
   faith in 對…的信心。
   She began to lose faith in herself.
   她開始對她自己失去信心。
   even the odds 扳回一城，扳回劣勢。odds 是 "勝算" "逆境" 的意思，even 則是 "打平" "使相等"，所以 even the odds 則可解釋成 "扳回劣勢"。

3. The reliable quality of our product is the reason why our products are in customers' good graces.
   我們產品的可靠品質是我們產品受到顧客青睞的原因。
   in somebody's good graces 受到…的喜愛，得到…的好感。
   I shouldn't be the one to ask her, because I'm not in her good graces.
   我不應該負責去問她，因為她對我沒有好感。

4. I am with you.
   我贊成。
   照字面上的解釋應為 "我與你同在"，但在對方提出意見，回答 "I'm with you"，則表有贊同之意。也常聽到 I am with somebody on something 的說法，則是表與某人在某件事上有同樣的看法。
   I am with Peter on his advice.
   我贊成 Peter 提的意見。

Part Five

上班族生活大小事

All about the Office Work

Unit 23 小組進度討論

A	How's the Emory's case going?	那個Emory的生意進展如何？
Hank	Well, I'm just going to tell you that their representative rang me before this meeting, and he wants to know if we can make the delivery before next Wednesday, and they need confirmation on those orders today.	嗯，我才正準備要告訴你，他們的代表在開會前打電話給我，他想要知道我們能不能在下星期三前出貨，還有他們今天要確認訂單。
A	Gina, how long does it take to complete the purchase order confirmation?	Gina，完成採購訂單的確認需要多久的時間？
C	It depends on the circumstances. The earliest we can get back to him is tomorrow morning. Hank, maybe you should ask him if it would be possible to extend the confirmation deadline to tomorrow morning.	需依情況而定。我們最早能在明天早上回報他。Hank，也許你應該要問他是不是有可能將確認的期限延到明天早上？
Hank	I have already informed him, but he insisted that he must know the result today, 'cause they have to go to press for the advertisement.	我已經告知他了，但他堅持他必須在今天知道結果，因為他們必須要印製廣告。

A   Is there any way we can speed up the process of checking inventory? Is that possible to make our factory staffs stay over for it?

有沒有辦法盡快的核對庫存呢？是不是有可能讓我們的工廠員工加班完成呢？

D   That will be costly. It will probably take 3 staffs approximately 4 hours to finish the inventory check and the order confirmation. That will be an increase on the labor fee by about 10%.

那將會是一筆不小的支出。這大概需要3個員工約莫4小時的時間來完成核對庫存及訂單確認。大約會增加10%的勞務費用。

A   Ok, Hank, please contact the Emory's representative, and tell him that we can get back to him with the order confirmation before 9 p.m., however it will be an increased cost of 10% in their order. Or we can get back to him tomorrow morning to confirm those orders. Let him make the call!

Ok, Hank，請聯繫Emory的代表，告訴他我們能在晚上9點之前回報他訂單確認事項，然而他們的訂單則會增加10％的費用。或是我們會在明天早上跟他確認訂單。讓他來做決定！

Hank   Ok, chief, I'll call him immediately.

好的，老大，我即刻去聯絡他。

Dialog 2

A　What's the latest progress of the hotel renovation?

飯店整修的最新進度是什麼？

B　It could be finished by the end of this month, two weeks ahead of our schedule.

整修工程大概在月底時能夠完工，比我們所預期的早兩個星期。

A　So how about the pipeline replacement?

那管線更換的部分呢？

C　The laying of pipelines has been nearly completed, except for a few joints in some suits.

管線的鋪設工程已經接近完工，除了幾間套房中的一些接頭處尚未完成。

A　Including the presidential deluxe suite?

那包括總統套房嗎？

C　Yes. We have to wait till the new hot tub arrives before we install the pipeline in the presidential suite's bathroom.

對。總統套房內的管線配置必須要等到新的按摩浴缸到了才開始鋪設。

D　Excuse me, I had just returned from my annual leave, did I miss anything? I remember that the new hot tub had been installed in the presidential suite before my vacation. Are we going to install the second one?

不好意思，我才剛放完年假回來上班，我是不是錯過什麼了？我記得在我放假前總統套房內新的按摩浴缸已經裝好了。我們是要再裝上第二個嗎？

C No, it's a long story so I will boil it down. President was not satisfied with the layout especially that installed hot tub. He didn't see that tub fit in with the atmosphere of our presidential suite. So he asked the contractor to remove the hot tub and ordered a new model.

不。說來話長，所以我就長話短說了。總裁對整個格局不太滿意，特別是那一個按摩浴缸。他覺得那個浴缸跟我們總統套房的氛圍不太合適。所以他要求承包商將那一個按摩浴缸拆掉，並訂購一個新款式。

D Oh, I see.

喔，我懂了。

A When will the new hot tub arrive?

新的按摩浴缸什麼時候會到？

B Probably one more week. The supplier had informed us that tub is the latest model and they have to import it from US.

大概再一個星期左右。供應商已經告知過我們那個浴缸是最新款的，他們必須從美國進口。

A All right, please contact the supplier and confirm the delivery schedule.

好。請聯絡供應商並確認交貨日期。

B Yes, I will.

好的，我會的。

💬 精選單字及片語

1. purchase order confirmation　採購訂單確認。purchase order 採購單）一般會稱為 PO，在交給供應商之後，供應商會在訂單產生或是訂單變更時作一個確認的動作，告知貨源是否充足，可訂購量，價格相關費用等，稱為採購訂單確認。

2. labor(s) *n.*　勞力；勞工。
You look tired, you need to rest from your labor.
你看起來很累，你需要放下工作休息一下。

3. make the call　做決定。這一個片語很容易會被誤會是要打電話的意思，"打電話" 我們通常會說 "make a (phone) call"。而在一群人在討論要做怎樣的決定，或是選擇時，如果有人對你說 "Your call"，則是要求你來決定的意思。
It's really not your call.
這不是你能作主的。

4. pipeline(s) *n.*　管線，管路，管道。
The main water pipeline was sabotaged by rebels.
這條主要的供水管線被反叛者給破壞了。

5. contractor(s)　承包商，承包者；立契約者。
My boss has given me a free hand in deciding which contractor to use.
我的老闆讓我全權負責承包商的選擇。

6. hot tub(s) *n.*　按摩浴缸。一般的浴缸稱為 "bath tub"，雖然一般也是放熱水，但 hot tub 則是具有調節水溫的功能，且有水療的功能。一般也稱為 jacuzzi，取自於第一個製造出按摩浴缸的知名品牌。
We have a hot tub in the garden, which children love playing in.
我們在花園裡有一個按摩浴缸，孩子們喜歡在裡面玩。

精選句子與延伸

1. It depends on circumstances.
   需依情況而定。
   circumstance(s) (n.) 狀況，情形，境遇。
   在這個句子中 circumstance 需加 s，因為是廣泛的指各種情況，所以要使用複數型態。

2. I have already informed him, but he insisted that he must know the result today, 'cause they have to go to press for the advertisement.
   我已經告知他了，但他堅持他必須在今天知道結果，因為他們必須要印製廣告。
   = I already told him, but he insisted to get the result today, because they must let the ad printed.
   go to press 付印，付梓。
   The book you want to order hasn't even gone to press yet.
   你要訂的那一本書甚至還沒開始印呢。

3. I had just returned from my annual leave, did I miss anything?
   我才剛放完年假回來上班，我是不是錯過什麼了？
   放完⋯假回來上班 可以寫做 "return from⋯"，例如 "She had returned from her vacation." （她收假回來上班）。
   miss 在這裡做 "錯過，漏掉" 解釋。

4. It's a long story so I will boil it down.
   說來話長，所以我就長話短說了。
   It's a long story. 說來話長。當對方詢問事由，而因為要解釋或是述說的部分有些繁瑣，就可以用這一個片語，而有時可被認為是有不想多說或是解釋的含意在。
   boil down 熬煮，煮濃；濃縮某事，歸納某事。可以用在煎藥，煲湯上，也被引申為將事情去蕪存菁，歸納整理的意思。而和 It's a long story 放在一起，則解釋成 "長話短說"。

Unit 24 討論難纏的客戶要求

 Dialog 1

A Have you discussed our most recent proposal with your client?

你有沒有和你的客戶討論過我們最新的提案呢？

B Yes, but they are as yet unwilling to agree to each term of the contract. I think they only want discount without the long-term cooperative commitment. They have booked a conference room for next Friday, and the secretary asked me to give them 20% discount, what am I supposed to reply?

有，討論過了，但他們到目前為止都還不同意合約上的任一條款。我認為他們只想要折扣但並不打算給予長期合作的承諾。他們在下星期五訂了一間會議室，他們的秘書要求我給他們8折的優惠，我現在應該怎麼回覆？

A As usual, quote them with 5% discount. Tell the secretary that it's really not your call, and you can't give her more than 5% discount without that contract, otherwise…

照舊，報給他們95折的優惠。告訴那位秘書這不是你能做決定的，沒有合約那你就沒辦法給他們高於5%的折扣，要不然…

B My boss will fire me.

我的老闆會炒了我。

A That's a good answer.

這是個不錯的回答。

C Chief, one of my clients wants to know if she can use the conference room A on Wednesday afternoon from 2 p.m. to 5 p.m. for "free".

老大，我有一位客戶想要知道她是否能在星期三下午3點到5點之間 "免費" 的使用A會議室。

A It sounds interesting, tell me about the story.

聽起來很有趣，告訴我整件事。

C That lady called yesterday, and booked the conference room A on Wednesday. She was very polite and said she'll have afternoon tea with her friends in the conference room A. And then I quoted her the price of that conference room, and she suggested me to check with my honcho, because she thought she can use that room for free.

那位女士昨天打電話過來預約了A會議室星期三的時段。她非常的有禮，並說她要和她的朋友在A會議室中用下午茶。隨後我報給她會議室的費用，她建議我向我的上司確認，因為她認為她應該能夠免費使用。

A Did she tell you the reason?

那她有告訴你原因嗎？

C She said she's a big fish's wife.

她說她是某位重要人士的太太。

A Do you know the name of that big fish?

你知道那位重要人士的名字嗎？

C Yes, he's xxxx.

知道，他是XXXX。

A OK, I'm sure that lady's not boss' wife, and not my wife, either. Send her the quotation as polite as you can, if she insists not paying for the room, cancel her booking.

OK，我確定那位女士不是老闆的太太，也不是我的太太。盡可能有禮貌的將報價單傳給她，如果她堅持不付費的話，取消她的預定。

C Yes, sir.

是的，長官。

Dialog 2

A Bob, I thought you have already got some ideas for the product's name.

Bob，我以為你對那產品的名字已經有好幾個點子了。

B I did, and I have discussed with their head of the creative department. I have given her ten different names for the product so far, but she didn't like any of them.

我是有啊，而且我已經和他們創意部門的老大討論過了。我至今已經給了她10個產品的名字了，但她一個都不喜歡。

C Oh, do you have any clue about what's going wrong?

喔，那你知不知道哪裡出了問題呢？

B I gave her five names this time, and she said they were too negative.

我這次給了她5個名字，她說它們太過於負面了。

D That I can understand, most clients want their products have positive images instead of the negative ones.

這我可以了解，大部分的客戶希望他們的產品有正面的形象，而不是負面的。

B Hmm… no, you don't understand. She said she wants something decadent when I first gave her five positive product names.

嗯，不，你不了解。當我第一次給她5個正面的產品名稱時，她說她要有些帶點頹廢感的。

D Oh, well, what can I say? I'd better bite my tongue.

喔，嗯，我能說什麼呢？我最好不要說話好了。

B Please don't. I need your advices, all of you.

請不要這樣。我需要你們的意見，你們大家的。

A Yep, let help Bob brainstorm a bit.

對，讓我們來幫Bob一起想一些辦法。

C Two heads are better than one, more-over here are four heads.

兩個腦袋總比一個強，更何況這裡有四個腦袋。

B Thank you, guys!

謝謝你們大家。

D I have an idea, how about we produce three kinds of names, positive, neutral and decadent. And Bob, you give these names to their head of the creative department at the same time, let her choose one.

我有個主意，我們來想三種不同型態的名字如何，正面的，中性的及頹廢的。還有Bob，你要同時將這三種名字交給他們創意部的老大，讓她來做選擇。

B It's a good idea. Thank you so much, Derek.

這是個好主意，非常謝謝你，Derek。

D No problem, we are a team.

小意思，我們是一個團隊嘛。

A Ok, so I'll responsible for the positive names.

Ok，所以我負責正面的名字。

C Oh, I love decadent ideas, leave it up to me.

喔，我愛頹廢的思想，將它交給我。

D It seems we two have to take the neutral names.

看起來我們兩個必須要選中性的名字了。

💬 精選單字及片語

1. commitment(s) *n.* 承諾，答應。
   This restaurant has a commitment to provide the best service.
   這家餐廳承諾要提供最好的服務。

2. book *v.* 預定，登記。
   Could you please book me a room?
   你可以幫我預定個房間嗎？

3. honcho(s) *n.* 上司，頭兒。美國俚語，源自於日文中軍隊的班長 han'chô，可用來稱呼主事者，經理，老闆等，也常見到 "head-honcho" 的說法。
   We are getting a new head-honcho.
   我們要有個新的工頭了。

4. decadent *adj.* 頹廢的，墮落的。
   I don't agree with the decadent opinions in the book.
   我不贊同這本書中消極的意見。

5. neutral *adj.* 中性的，中立的。
   Journalists should be politically neutral.
   新聞從業者應該保持政治立場上的中立。

6. leave it up to me 把它交給我，由我負責。也可說成 leave it to me。
   Don't worry, just leave it up to me, and I can handle it well.
   別擔心，把這事交給我，我會好好處理的。

精選句子與延伸

1. Do you know the name of that big fish?
   你知道那位重要人士的名字嗎？
   在這裡的 big fish 指的不是大魚，也不是我們中文中能帶來利益的大魚，這個詞在英文中指的是「重要人士，有影響力的人」。也可以說是「big cheese」，或是「big gun」。

2. Ok, I'm sure that lady's not boss' wife, and not my wife, either.
   Ok，我確定那位女士不是老闆的太太，也不是我的太太。
   在用英文說 "也" 的時候，大家第一個想到的應該是「too」，「too」適用於肯定句中，而否定句中則要用「either」，「too」及「either」的用法相同，都是置於句尾，前面要記得加上逗號。話說每當我聽到有母語不是英語的人在談話間正確說出either，我都會在心中大大的稱讚一番，因為這個錯誤很小，小到有時連母語是英語的人也會不小心在談話間說錯。

3. Oh, well, what can I say? I'd better bite my tongue.
   喔，嗯，我能說什麼呢？我最好不要說話好了。
   oh, well 這兩個狀聲詞連接在一起說，有表示無可奈何的感覺。
   bite one's tongue 不小心咬到舌頭；保持沈默，想說但卻不能或是不願意說。
   I have to bite my tongue to keep from telling her what I think.
   我必須不發一言免得告訴她我所想的。

4. Two heads are better than one.
   兩個腦袋總比一個強。
   這個諺語意思與我們常說的「三個臭皮匠勝過一個諸葛亮」一樣，只是在人數上有些差異。用以描述在解決問題上，兩個人一起想，成功的機會會大過只有一個人。

Unit 25 討論難以處理的客戶

 Dialog 1

A Sorry, I am late. Jerry and I just finished a meeting with a client. Jerry's showing our client out now, and he'll be here in a minute if he has a chance to get away.

對不起，我遲到了。Jerry和我剛結束與客戶的會議。Jerry正在送客戶出去，他很快會到，如果他有機會脫身的話。

B Ok, please have a seat. Jenny had told us before this meeting. So what's going on? It sounds like Jerry's in trouble?

Ok，請坐。Jenny已經在開會前告訴過我。所以發生了什麼？聽起來像是Jerry有麻煩了。

A The thing is… Oh, Jerry's here. Let him tell you.

事情是這樣的…喔，Jerry到了。讓他自己說吧。

C Sorry, I'm late.

對不起，我遲到了。

B That's ok. Please have a seat. Tommy said that you have something to tell me.

沒關係，請坐。Tommy說你有話跟我說。

C Yes. I have. Chief, I want to know is that possible for me to pass this project to other colleagues?

是的，我有話要說。老大，我想知道是否能將這個項目轉交給其他同事負責？

D I think chief will agree to that, but before that you have to tell us what happened. Do you have any complaint to make? We are all your ears.

我想老大會同意的，但在這之前你必須告訴我們發生了什麼事。你有沒有要抱怨的？我們都很願意傾聽的。

162

C I think you should know that Tommy and I had sat through a nearly 4-hour meeting with that client. He wants to meet again on Friday to discuss the progress.

我想你們應該知道我和Tommy撐了快4個小時和客戶開會。他要在星期五時再和我們碰面一次討論進度。

B It all sounds very reasonable to me, anything went wrong?

整件事在我聽起來十分合理，哪裡出錯了嗎？

C The problem is that client seemed only interested at me, and asked nothing about the project but my personal profile. He made me feel uncomfortable.

問題是客戶看起來只對我有興趣，只問我的個人資料而不是和這個項目有關的。他讓我感到很不舒服。

D So how about the project? Got any useful information?

所以這個項目談的怎樣呢？有沒有得到任何有用的資訊？

A Nope, we got only one sentence about that project. He wants a new brand image, something creative, and strong.

沒有，我們只得到一句話與這個項目有關。他要一個全新的品牌形象，要有創意，有力量的。

D That's all you got? In the 4-hour meeting?

這是你們知道的全部？在4個小時的會議中？

A That was bought with Jerry's email address.

那可是用Jerry的電子郵件地址換來的。

B Jerry, I'll let Jenny to take over this project. Jenny, please find some excuses to explain to that client. One more thing, if this client harasses any of you, please report to me forthwith.

Jerry，我會讓Jenny接替這個項目。Jenny，請找一些藉口向這個客戶解釋。還有一件事，如果這個客戶騷擾你們任何一位的話，請立即向我報告。

Dialog 2

A I can't stand Mrs. Dolores any more.

我再也無法忍受Dolores太太了。

B What did she do this time?

她這次又做了什麼？

A She asked me to prostrate myself for the delay.

她要我為了遲到下跪。

C Oh my gosh. I can't believe that you dared to be late for her appointment.

喔我的天啊。我不敢相信妳居然敢在她的預約時遲到。

A I didn't mean to it. I did inform her that I was fully booked on that day, but she insisted that I must put her in. I told her that there's a scheduling conflict, and I might be 30 minutes late for her appointment, and she said okay.

我不是有意的。我告訴她我那一天的預約全滿，但她堅持我必須將她排進去。我告訴她這跟我其它的行程有衝突，所以她的預約我會晚到30分鐘，她說可以的。

B Why didn't you ask her to change the time? I mean to make an appointment at a later spot.

那妳為什麼沒有要求她改時間呢？我的意思是約晚一點的時間。

A I did, but she didn't listen to my advice and went her own way.

我有，但她不聽我的意見，一意孤行。

C So how late you were?

所以妳晚到多久。

A I was only 10 minutes late and 20 minutes earlier than I expected.

我只晚到10分鐘，比我預計的早到20分鐘。

B Oh, poor you.

喔，妳真可憐。

C How did you response to her request?

那妳對她的要求如何回應呢？

D	Did you really go down on your knees and ask for forgiveness?	妳真的有下跪乞求原諒嗎？
A	I was going to. Fortunately, Shirley came out to pour oil on troubled waters.	我正準備要跪。幸好，Shirley 出面調解。
D	You were lucky. Last time during the treatment, Mrs. Dolores asked me to sing a song for her, I declined politely. And she became furious instantly and swore at me roundly. I was scared to cry.	妳真幸運。上次在療程當中，Dolores太太要求我為她唱首歌，我禮貌的回絕。她立刻變得暴怒起來還狠狠的咒罵我一頓。我被嚇哭了。
A	Alas, maybe we should ask Shirley to teach us how to deal with awkward customers.	唉，也許我們應該請Shirley教我們怎麼處理奧客。
E	That is good proposal,I will record it in the minutes.	這是一項好的提議，我會將它記錄在會議記錄中。

💬 精選單字及片語

1. sit through　一直坐到…結束。
   I can't stand to sit through that class again.
   我無法忍受再一次坐在那聽完那門課了。

2. harass *v.*　騷擾，擾亂。
   He uses his power to sexual harass his employees.
   他利用他的職權性騷擾他的員工。

3. forthwith *adv.* 即刻，立刻。

The agreement between us is terminated forthwith.

我們之間的協議即刻終止。

4. prostrate oneself 俯臥，拜倒，屈服。

They prostrated themselves before the emperor.

他們向皇帝跪拜行禮。

5. roundly *adv.* 嚴厲地。

I was roundly condemned for my mistake.

我因為犯錯而受到嚴厲的指責。

6. minutes *n.* 會議記錄。

The secretary took down the minutes in shorthand.

秘書將會議記錄以速記的方式寫下來

精選句子與延伸

1. Jerry's showing our client out now, and he'll be here in a minute if he has a chance to get away.

Jerry 正在送客戶出去，他很快會到，如果他有機會脫身的話。

在以 if 做引導的假設句中，可分為以 if 為首的條件子句和結果子句，因發生的時間點不同，是否為事實等，這兩個子句所使用的時態也不同。本句中，條件子句 if he has a chance to get away 為現在式，而結果子句 he'll be here in a minute 為未來式，是未來假設的一種，如能達成條件子句，一定會成為事實；當結果子句是現在式或是語態助動詞加原形動詞時，則代表結果有可能發生也有可能不發生。

show someone out 送客，陪同或是護送某人出去。

Please show our guests out of the factory.

請將我們的客人送到工廠外。

2. That was bought with Jerry's email address.

那可是用 Jerry 的電子郵件地址換來的。

在這裡的 that 指的是客戶說出的一句與專案項目相關的話，bought 在這裡可以解釋成 "做出犧牲而換取"，所以是以 Jerry 的電子郵件地址換來與專案有關的訊息。

3. Did you really go down on your knees and ask for forgiveness?

妳真的有下跪乞求原諒嗎？

= Did you kneel down to apologize?

在句子中的 knees 是複數，用以表明是雙膝下跪，在 go down on one's knees 這一個片語中，必須使用複數的 knees。而下跪求婚時，是單膝跪下，我們則用 get down on one's knee。

4. Fortunately, Shirley came out to pour oil on troubled waters.

幸好，Shirley 出面調解。

pour oil on troubled waters 試著平息爭端，調解。這一個片語猛一看容易被誤解為是火上加油的意思，但仔細推敲後則能看出為第三者出面調解紛爭的意思。troubled waters 指的是混亂的狀況，而在渾水中灑油，意圖讓水面趨於平緩，有大事化小，小事化無的寓意。

5. Alas, maybe we should ask Shirley to teach us how to deal with awkward customers.

唉，也許我們應該請 Shirley 教我們怎麼處理奧客。

alas 是一個狀聲詞，表嘆息，跟中文中的唉差不多。

awkward customer 難搞的客人，我們一般俗稱的奧客。awkward 在這裡做「難對付的」，「棘手的」解釋，另外還常會聽到也有人稱難搞的客人為「difficult customer」。

Unit 26 討論新的行銷計畫

Dialog 1

Manager All right, everyone. Let's begin. The reason we are here today is for our new marketing strategy. Before that, I have to emphasize again that the mission of our company is to serve our customer the highest quality coffee and provide outstanding and personalized service in a warm welcome coffeehouse atmosphere.

好了，各位，讓我們開始。我們今天在這裡的原因是為了新的行銷策略。在這之前，我必須重新強調我們公司的宗旨是要供應顧客最高品質的咖啡，及提供絕佳及個人化的服務在具熱忱歡迎的咖啡館氛圍中。

A I want to know if that is possible to reduce the prices for our coffees.

我想要知道是否有可能調降我們咖啡的價錢？

Manager I don't think the price oriented marketing strategy is suitable for our company. In its simplest term, it's just not our style.

我不認為價格取向的行銷策略適合我們公司。以最簡單的話來說，這不是我們的風格。

B But some of our competitors have reduced prices for their coffees, and in fact, they do draw in more customers.

但我們有些競爭對手已經調降他們的咖啡價格，而且事實上，他們的確吸引了更多的顧客。

C I second that. In my opinion, to compare with the coffee quality, I think customers are more care about the price.

我也同意這一點。我的意見是，與咖啡品質相比，我覺得顧客更關心價格。

Manager	I disagree. Most of our customers are highly discerned, and they know our coffee is far better than the coffee you buy in the other places.	我不同意。我們大多顧客是非常敏銳的，而且他們知道我們的咖啡要比在其他家買的來得好。
A	Yeah, chief, you are right. There is no doubt that we have achieved the top of mind awareness when it comes to the best taste brewing. It's the main differentiation between our competitors and us.	好吧，老大，你是對的。無庸置疑的，在提到咖啡最佳口感上，我們是顧客心目中的第一品牌。而這也是競爭者和我們最主要的區隔。
Manager	So, we can use this differentiation strategy to show our appreciation to the customers?	所以我們可以利用區隔策略來向顧客展現我們的價值？
B	Oh, I have an idea. As what we discussed before, money is tight for everyone these days, and some of our loyal customers may don't want to spend money for the morning coffee. Why don't we use the superiority of our coffee beans as our core competency? It's a perfect timing for us to sell coffee beans for people who prefer to brew coffee at home.	喔，我想到一個主意了。像我們之前所討論的，現在大家的手頭都有點緊，所以我們有些忠實顧客可能不會想要花錢在早晨咖啡上。我們為什麼不利用我們咖啡豆上的優勢來做為我們的核心主力？對我們而言這是一個絕佳的時機開始販售咖啡豆給那些喜歡在家煮咖啡的人。
Manager	That sounds great, but we'd better brainstorm some more ideas, and do some research.	這聽起來不錯，但我們最好還是多腦力激盪幾個點子，並做一些調查研究。

Dialog 2

A　Here, everyone, I apologize for calling this emergency meeting.I just finished a marketing meeting with the executive management this morning. Unfortunately, none of our ideas were accepted.

各位，請注意一下，我很抱歉召開這一個緊急會議。我今天早上才和高層主管開完行銷會議。很遺憾的是，我們所有的想法都沒有被接受。

B　It's awful, I thought we have put forward some great ideas.

這太奇怪了，我覺得我們所提出的想法都很不錯。

C　That's right. I talked about our ideas with Paul last week, and he seemed to be very supportive to our plan. So what happened in the meeting?

沒錯，我上個星期才和Paul討論過我們這些想法，他看起來很支持我們的企畫。會議上到底發生了什麼？

Manager　Some people did not take to our ideas very well, and that was in my expectation. But the worst thing was that Paul did not support me during the meeting.

有些人並不非常喜歡我們的想法，這是在我預料之中的事。但最糟糕的就是Paul在會議上並不支持我。

D　Do you know the reason? So we can revise the plan, and take those objections into account.

那你知道原因嗎？那我們就能重新審視這個企畫，並將那些遭到反對的因素也考慮進去。

A Regrettably, I don't think that even revised proposal will be accepted. It seems like the executive management wants to suspend all relevant marketing activities, due to the anti-extravagance campaign announced by the Chinese President two days ago. And we all know that China is our largest market in Asia. Maybe "hands-off" is the best new marketing strategy for our company for the moment.

D So we don't have to do anything currently?

A Not exactly, remember we talked about the charity event? It can be considered as a kind of marketing strategy. Now I think we have plenty time to prepare that, but we'll have to draw in our horns and keep the whole event in low key.

很遺憾的是，即便是重做的企畫我也不認為會被接受。這情形看起來像是高層主管們打算要暫停所有相關的行銷活動，原因出在兩天前中國總理所頒佈的禁奢運動。而且我們都知道中國是我們在亞洲最大的市場。也許 "順其自然" 是目前對我們公司而言最好的新行銷策略。

所以我們現在不需要做任何事？

並不盡然，記得我們討論過的慈善活動嗎？它可以被認為是行銷策略的一種。現在我們有大把的時間可以準備，但是我們必須比以前謹慎節制，並要保持低調。

🗨 精選單字及片語

1. draw in 吸引；使捲入，參與；深呼吸。
   This cinema is drawing in large crowds every night.
   這部電影每晚都吸引了大批的人潮。
   It won't be easy for you to draw her in.
   對你而言要將她捲入這事並不是那麼簡單。

2. I second that. 我同意，我附議。
   這一個用語是其源於在國會或是議會中的用語，對於提出的議題，必須有第二人的附議，才能更進一步的討論，甚至是表決。後來被使用在日常用語中，代表我同意他說的，也可說 "I second it." 或是 "Second"。

3. brainstorm v. 腦力激盪，集思廣益，集體研討。
   Let's have a meeting and brainstorm some good ideas.
   讓我們來開個會及一起構想一些好點子。

4. take to 喜歡
   The first season was terrible, but for some reasons the viewers took to it.
   第一季糟透了，但不知為何觀眾卻開始喜愛上這齣戲。

5. anti-extravagance 禁奢，反對鋪張浪費。extravagance 是 "奢侈，揮霍，奢侈品" 的意思。anti-extravagance 也可指是對於宣告破產的人的禁奢條款。

6. hands-off 順其自然，不插手，不干預。
   He takes a hands-off approach when it comes to the children quarrel.
   遇到孩子們吵架時，他採取不插手的方式。

精選句子與延伸

1. There is no doubt that we have achieved the top of mind awareness when it comes to the best taste brewing.
   無庸置疑的，在提到咖啡最佳口感上，我們是顧客心目中的第一品牌。
   top of mind awareness 又簡稱為 TOMA，是指在提到某個行業時，在顧客心中所想到的第一個品牌或是產品。有可以寫做 top-of-mind awareness。

2. It's the main differentiation between us and our competitors.
   而這也是競爭者和我們最主要的區隔。
   當在句子中有出現多個人稱時，排列的順序請記住以下幾個原則
   1. 單數人稱為 2 (you), 3 (he) and 1 (I)
   2. 複數人稱為 1 (we), 2 (you) and 3 (they)
   3. 當第 3 人稱單數的 he 和 she 擺在同一個句子中，一般是男先女後。
   differentiation(s) (n.) 差異，區分。在行銷上，我們稱之為區隔。

3. Now I think we have plenty time to prepare that, but we'll have to draw in our horns and keep the whole event in low key.
   現在我們有大把的時間可以準備，但是我們必須比以前謹慎節制，並要保持低調。
   draw in one's horns 這個片語的寓意是要比以前更小心，謹慎，而也可當作是要節制，特別用錢方面要節省開銷，緊衣縮食。這裡的 horns 是複數，因為這個片語據說是來自於蝸牛的動作，當感受到危險時，會將頭及兩隻觸角縮回殼中。
   low-key 低調。同義詞還有 low profile。

Unit 27 討論參展人員工作配置

Dialog 1

A I hereby call this meeting to order. First, I want to thank you all in attendance today. I know it's a busy day for all of you. We have a lot of material to cover today. Did everyone get an agenda? Ok, in today's meeting, we are going to discuss the related matters of the trade show in Chicago.

我在這裡宣布會議開始。首先，我要感謝大家今天出席這個會議。我知道大家今天都很忙。我們今天有許多的資料要處理。大家是不是都拿到一份議程表了呢？好的，在今天的會議中，我們將要討論在芝加哥貿易展中的相關事項。

B Great, so we are going to Chicago.

太棒了，所以我們要去芝加哥了。

A Yes, it has been evaluated by the executive management, and they all agree that our company will be able to get its name out there by attending this trade show. Calm down, everyone, I can understand how excited you are, but we have to talk about the work assignments. Ok, who's going to contact the travel agent?

是的，經過管理高層的評估之後，他們都一致認為我們公司將能藉由參加這一次的貿易展來提高知名度。冷靜一下，各位，我能了解你們有多興奮，但我們必須討論一下工作分配的事。Ok，誰要負責聯絡旅行社？

C Can't we do the booking by ourselves?

我們不能自己訂嗎？

A I prefer not, it's much easier to let the travel agent arrange everything for us, besides we'll need the invoice to reimburse the expenses.

我希望不要，由旅行社為我們安排所有的事簡單多了，除此之外，我們也需要代收轉付收據來報銷費用。

C Oh, I see. I can do that.

喔，我懂了，我來負責。

A Ok, thank you Sara, and you better check with the financial department first, ask them about the maximum per diem.

Ok，謝謝妳Sara，還有妳最好先和財務部確認一下，詢問他們每日津貼最多為多少。

C Okay.

好的。

B I'll contact the express company.

我會聯絡快遞公司。

D I will be in charge of the sales literature.

我會負責銷售的文宣資料。

A Darren, don't forget about everyone's business cards, make sure all of us have enough cards.

Darren不要忘記大家的名片，確保我們大家都有足夠的名片。

D Ok, I got it.

Ok，我了解。

Dialog 2

A We have two more days to prepare for the trade show. I know some of you felt disoriented with the jet lag when we first arrived. Karen, Sara, have you both got over the jet lag?

我們還有兩天的時間可以準備貿易展。我知道你們有些人剛來的時候有因為時差的造成生理節奏失調所產生的昏沈感。Karen，Sara妳們倆現在時差調過來了嗎？

B I feel much better after a good night's kip.

我在好好的睡了一整晚後，感覺好很多了。

C So do I.

我也是。

A Great. We will be very busy for the next week, so all of you should take good care of yourselves. Ken, did you check with the express company? When will our goods arrive?

很好，我們皆下來的一整個星期都會非常的忙碌，所以你們大家要好好的照顧你們自己。Ken，你有聯絡過快遞公司了嗎？我們的貨品什麼時候能到？

D Our goods will arrive tomorrow afternoon.

我們的貨品明天下午能到。

A When can we finish our exhibit booth decoration?

我們什麼時候能完成我們的展覽攤位的裝潢呢？

B The exhibit booth decoration has been substantially completed. We will make a few minor adjustments tomorrow, and then embark on the booth display. We will debug the equipment the day after tomorrow.

展覽攤位裝潢的部份已經大致完成了。我們明天會再做幾個小小的調整，然後開始著手進行攤位展示的部份。我們會在後天調整設備。

A Who's responsible for setting up the web-enable kiosks?

誰負責設定可上網的多媒體自動化服務機呢？

C　That's my task. All three kiosks have been set up this afternoon, they run smoothly, and enable our visitors to order our products online.

那是我的工作。全部3部多媒體自動化服務機已經在今天下午設定完畢,他們運行的還蠻順暢的,可以讓參觀者上網訂購我們的產品。

A　Great! All of you are hardworking these days. You all did a good job. I think I should take you out for a drink, what do you think?

好極了!你們大家這幾天都十分努力的在工作。大家都做得很好。我想我應該要帶你們去喝一杯,你們覺得如何呢?

All　Hoorays!

萬歲!

💬 精選單字及片語

1. in attendance　出席，當值。
The manager is very busy and can't be in attendance at today's conference.
經理非常忙碌無法出席今日的會議。

2. trade show　貿易展，商展。
Many of our rivals will be attending the Sydney trade show.
許多我們的競爭對手將會參加雪梨貿易展。

3. reimburse *v.*　償還，付還。
We will reimburse you for your traveling expanses.
我們會報銷你的旅費。

4. kip *n.*　【英，非正式】睡覺，一段睡眠時間。
I'm going to lie down and try to get some kip.
我要躺下來小睡一會兒。

5. kiosk(s) *n.*　多媒體自動化服務機。kiosk 在英文中原來是指小亭子或是販賣書報的小亭子等，後來沿用到指可提供服務或是販賣商品的機器，例如是商品導覽系統，自動販賣機或是 ATM 等都可以算是 kiosk。

6. dispose *v.*　使有意於，使傾向於。
His bad records do not dispose me to trust him.
他的不良記錄讓我無法信任他。

💬 精選句子與延伸

1. You better check with the financial department first, ask them about the maximum per diem.

   妳最好先和財務部確認一下，詢問他們每日津貼最多為多少。

   per diem 每日津貼，每日定額。per diem 是拉丁文，意思是每天。每日津貼是逐日計算的津貼，這其中包含飯店住宿費用及餐飲費用。

2. I will be in charge of the sales literature.

   我會負責銷售的文宣資料。

   = I'll be responsible for the sales literature.

   sales literature 銷售文宣，這其中包括有廣告傳單，商品目錄，說明書，商品簡介等與銷售相關的印刷品，書面資料，可以提供給潛在客戶，以達到增加銷量的目的。

   in charge of 負責。

   Who's in charge of the administration in your company?

   在你的公司理事誰負責行政的部份？

3. So do I.

   我也是。

   我們曾在 Unit 24 中介紹過 too/either 的用法，在英語中「也」的說法還有另外 3 種，那就是 so、neither 及 also。so/neither 的用法相同，均為置於句首，其後的子句為倒裝句，先寫動詞再寫主詞，唯一的不同是 so 是用於肯定句，neither 則是用於否定句。

   A: I don't like her. 我不喜歡她。

   B: Neither do I. 我也是。/ 我也不喜歡。

Unit 28 介紹公司

Dialog 1

Fion Ladies and gentlemen, thank you for attending our coffee lecture. My name is Fion Radford, I am the regional manager of G J's Coffees. Today I would like to give a 20-minute talk on our company and products. Then I will give you all some demonstrations of our famous coffee drinks. After my demonstrations, I will give all of you a chance to make your own coffee with our professional coffee machine.

各位女士各位先生,謝謝你們大家來參加我們的咖啡講座。我的名字是Fion Radford,我是G J's Coffees的區域經理。今天,我將會花約20分鐘的時間來介紹一下我們的公司及產品。然後我將會為你們示範製作一些我們公司有名的咖啡飲品。在我的示範之後,我會讓各位都有機會能使用我們專業的咖啡機來做出屬於你們自己的咖啡。

Fion　We founded G J's Coffees in Australia more than 20 years ago with the ambition to serve the best coffee. We currently have more than 400 stores throughout the country, and we think there's room for more. Our CEO and General Manager are both coffee lovers and experts. They set their sights on bringing specialty gourmet coffee to Australia. So in 1992, the first G J's Coffees store was opened in Sydney. Can anyone see this screen clearly? Great, this is the picture of our first store. Can anyone of you tell me what do you feel from this photo?

A　Clean and warm.

Fion　That's right. Clean environment and warm atmosphere are just two major elements of Gloria J's Coffees Stores. You can find them both in our every store. Even today, we have more than 500 coffee houses in 38 markets around the world, they are all in different styles but definitely with clean environment and warm atmosphere.

我們在20多年前帶著要供應最好的咖啡的抱負於澳洲創立G J'S Coffees。我們現今在全國有超過400家的分店，而且我們認為還有增加的空間。我們的執行長及總經理都是咖啡愛好者及專家。他們將引進精品極品咖啡到澳洲視為目標。所以在1992年，第一家的G J's Coffees店面在雪梨開幕。請問一下大家看得清楚螢幕嗎？好極了，這是我們第一家店的照片。有誰可以告訴我你們從照片中感覺到什麼？

乾淨及溫暖。

沒錯。乾淨的環境和溫暖的氛圍是G J's Coffees店面最主要的兩個元素。你能在我們任何一家店裡感受到這兩樣。甚至到了今天，我們在全世界各地的38個國家有超過500間的分店，他們全都有著不同的風格但絕對會有乾淨的環境及溫暖的氛圍。

Dialog 2

Paul: Good afternoon, ladies and gentlemen. Welcome to our monthly business meeting. Today we are going to hear a short presentation from one of our members before lunch. And now without any further ado, we would like to welcome Mr. James Smith.

James: Thank you, Paul. Ladies and gentlemen, I am James from Smith & Co. Today I would like to give you a brief introduction to our consulting firm. I will talk about what we do and how we do it inside the firm. Firstly, I'm going to tell you a little bit about our firm, then more about our service in the second part. Please don't hesitate to let me know, if you have any questions while I'm presenting. I have also prepared a handout for everyone. Here you are, please take one and pass it along. Thank you.

各位女士各位先生，午安。歡迎來到我們每個月的商務會議。今天我們將會在午餐前由我們的一位會員做段簡短的報告。現在我們言歸正傳，讓我們一起歡迎James Smith先生。

謝謝你，Paul。各位女士各位先生，我是Smith & Co.的James。今天我要為你們簡短的介紹我們的諮詢公司。告訴你們我們的公司在做些什麼，及如何去做。首先，我要簡短的跟你們介紹我們公司，詳細的介紹我們的服務在第二個部分。如果在我報告時，各位有任何問題的話，請不要遲疑，立刻告訴我。我也準備了綱要給各位。來，這裡麻煩你，請拿一份並傳下去。謝謝。

James　Now you can see this slide on the first page of the handout. Smith & Co. is a global management consulting firm. We are the trusted advisor to the world's leading businesses, governments and institutions. Our firm was founded in 1935 by Kevin Smith. My dear grandfather, and I think he couldn't have imagined to reach his small firm would eventually have. Seventy-eight years later, the firm has grown into a global partnership serving more than half of the Fortune 1000.

現在你們可以在綱要的第一頁中看到這一張投影片。Smith & Co.是一個全球性的管理諮詢公司。我們是受全世界有名的企業，政府及機構所信賴的顧問公司。我們的公司是在1935年時由Kevin Smith一手創辦。我親愛的祖父，我想他應該無法想像他的小公司之後的規模。78年之後，這家公司成長成為一家為超過一半以上的全球前1000強企業服務的全球夥伴關係。

💬 精選單字及片語

1. ambition(s) *n.* 雄心，抱負。
   You will achieve your ambition if you work hard.
   如果你努力的話，你的抱負是有可能成功的。

2. specialty *adj.* 特色的，專門的。specialty coffee 精品咖啡，咖啡豆的評比標準，在 1996 年由 Eran Knutsen 女士提出，2004 年美國精品咖啡協會技術標準委員會發佈相關的評比標準。

3. gourmet *adj.* 美味的（高品質但通常價格也昂貴）。gourmet 在做為形容詞使用時，需注意後面一定要加一個名詞，無法單獨使用，是定語形容詞。例如，我們可以說 gourmet food，但不能說 the food is gourmet。

4. without further ado 言歸正傳，立即，不多說。
   Okay, without further ado, let me turn over to Isabella.
   Ok，不多說，讓我們轉回給Isabella。

5. the Fortune 1000 由 Fortune （財富）雜誌評選出的世界前1000強企業。
   Hiring Demand by the Fortune 1000 companies grew by 2.9% from last month.
   從上個月起，世界前1000強企業的聘僱需求增加了2.9%。

💬 精選句子與延伸

1. Today I would like to give a 20-minute talk on our company and products.

今天，我將會花約 20 分鐘的時間來介紹一下我們的公司及產品。

在做簡報時，通常會先簡單介紹一下主講者，內容，也會和聽眾說一下大約會花多長的時間。20-minute 是形容詞，意思是「20 分鐘的」，talk 在這一句中則為名詞。

2. Can anyone see this screen clearly?

請問一下大家看得清楚螢幕嗎？

在簡報當中難免會出現會有觀眾「靈魂出竅」或是「不務正業」的時後，這個時候可以運用一些小技巧來將觀眾的「魂魄」召回。例如本句，除了詢問觀眾之外，也請他們將注意力放到螢幕上，有利於接下來要說的話題。

3. Please don't hesitate to let me know, if you have any questions while I'm presenting.

= During my presentation, if you have question, please let me know.

如果在我報告時，各位有任何問題的話，請不要遲疑，立刻告訴我。

這一個句子是一種迂迴的說法，常見於書信往來，電子郵件，及電話當中。可以被認為是非常客氣的講法。

hesitate (v.) 猶豫，躊躇。

They hesitated at nothing to gain their ends.

他們不惜一切以達目的。

4. I have also prepared a handout for everyone. Here you are, please take one and pass it along.

我也準備了綱要給各位。來，這裡麻煩你，請拿一份並傳下去。

在簡報中，主講者常會準備講義或是綱要給觀眾，有助於觀眾對報告內容能更清楚的了解，也方便觀眾能做筆記，對於內容的專心度上有相當的幫助。

handout(s) (n.) 綱要，講義。這個詞來自於 hand out（發，傳）這一個動作，用於指稱免費發放的東西，如樣品、講義等。

here you are 是指 "給" 的這一個動作，用於在遞給對方，但尚未完成這一個動作時，給的這一方來說。

Unit 29 介紹產品

Fion Now, I believe that all of you might have the basic concept of G J's Coffees. And I would like to move to introduce our products, the most favorite G J's coffee drinks in Australia. In the first part, I have mention about G J's Coffees' ambition. And does anyone remember what kind of ambition we have?

A To serve the best coffee.

現在，我想你們大家應該對G J's Coffees有基本的認識了。我想要接下來介紹我們的產品，在澳洲最受到喜愛的G J's 咖啡飲品。在第一個部分，我有提到G J's Coffees的期望。有沒有任何人記得我們有什麼樣的期望？

提供最好的咖啡。

Fion　Bingo, and here is a $10 gift card for you, thanks for your answer. You can reload the card in our official website or in any of our coffee houses. With this card, you'll get 5% off in each transaction, and get a special offer for the online registration and your birthday. That's our latest product, and I truly think it's worth it, so I can't help myself to talk a lot about the card. Ok, back to our point. To serve the best coffee in a clean environment with warm atmosphere is our mission, besides we're also dedicated to provide outstanding and personalized service to our customer. So now we serve 18 types of hot drinks, and 12 types of cold drinks with alternatives, for example you can choose from dairy to soy, or you like it sweet or not sweet. We try our best to meet our customers' needs. Have any questions so far?

賓果，這裡有一張含有$10的禮物卡送你，謝謝你的答案。你可以在我們的官網上或是任何一家我們的咖啡館內儲值。有了這一張卡，你每一次的交易都會有95折的優惠，而且上網註冊及你的生日都能得到特別的優惠。這是我們最新的產品，而且我覺得真的很值得，所以我情不自禁地談論這一卡。Ok，回到我們的主題。提供最好的咖啡在一個有溫暖氣氛的乾淨環境中是我們的使命，除此之外，我們還致力於提供頂尖卓越及個人化的服務給我們的顧客。所以我們現在提供18種熱飲，及12種冷飲可以做不同的選擇變化，舉例來說，你可以選擇牛奶或是豆漿，或是你喜歡甜的或是不甜的。我們都會盡力滿足顧客的需要。到目前為止有任何問題嗎？

Dialog 2

James	As you can see on this slide, we mainly provide consulting service to our clients in 3 aspects…	正如你們在這一張投影片所看到的，我們主要提供給客戶的咨詢服務可分成3個方面…
A	Excuse me, James. Can you speak louder? We can't hear you from the back of this room.	對不起，James。你可以說大聲一點嗎？我們在後面聽不到你的聲音。
James	Sure, no problem. Is this volume fine with everyone?	當然，沒問題。這樣的音量，大家覺得可以嗎？
A	Yes, it's much better now. Sorry for the interruption.	是的，這樣好多了。不好意思我打斷你的簡報。
James	No worry, mate. And here, I would like everyone to look at this chart carefully. It shows our divisional ratios in these three aspects. Oops! The picture on the screen is very blurry, isn't it? Could someone dim the light please? Thank you, Paul.	別擔心，朋友。還有這裡，我想要大家仔細的看一下這一個圖表。在這圖表中可以看出我們這三個方面所佔的比例。糟糕，在螢幕上的圖片非常模糊，不是嗎？有沒有誰可以幫忙調暗燈光？謝謝你，Paul。
Paul	You are welcome.	不客氣。
B	James, we still can't see the chart clearly.	James，我們還是看不清楚那一張圖表。

James　I apologize for this, and I think this projector's broken down. Just my luck! Maybe today is not a perfect day for my presentation. All right, please forget about the microphone and the projector. As this situation, strange things happened, no matter how well-prepared you are. So does it in the real life, no matter how big the company is, or how well-development the firm is, crisis always happened. Under these circumstances, what my consulting firm can do is to find out the problem and provide radical solutions. Furthermore, we help to transform companies into sharper, smarter, better versions of themselves with our expertise and experience in various industries. My presentation ends here, thank you.

我為這個感到抱歉，我想這一個投影機壞了。真倒楣！或許我今天不宜做簡報。好吧，請忘掉麥克風或是投影機。如同這一個情形，奇怪的事發生，不論你準備的有多充分。在真實生活中也是一樣，不論這一家公司規模有多大，或是這一家公司的發展有多好，危機總是會發生。在這種情況下，我的顧問公司能做的就是找出問題並提供有效的解決方法。更進一步，我們利用我們在各行各業的專門知識及經驗來協助這些公司改造成為更靈敏，更有智慧，更具願景。我的簡報在這結束，謝謝。

精選單字及片語

1. concept(s) *n.* 概念，觀點，想法。
An infant has no concept of right and wrong.
嬰兒沒有是非的概念。

2. gift card 禮物卡，禮券卡。類似於我們的儲值卡，但裡面已經有固定的金額在，在國外非常流行做為禮物送人，因為這類型的禮物卡通常會有相當的折扣或是回饋金，跟我們的儲值卡相同，有分為記名及不記名的，卡內的金額用完的話，有的是可以儲值，有些則不行。

3. dairy(ies) *n.* 乳製品
I am allergic to dairy.
我對乳製品過敏。

4. chart(s) *n.* 圖表。
Here is the sales chart of last quarter.
這裡是上一季的銷售圖表。

5. interruption(s) *n.* 中斷，打斷。
Constant interruption of her work annoyed her.
對她的工作不停地干擾，惹惱了她。

精選句子與延伸

1. You can reload the card in our official website or in any of our coffee houses.
   你可以在我們的官網上或是任何一家我們的咖啡館內儲值。
   reload (v.) 再裝，重新裝。reload a card （將卡片）加值，儲值。而這裡的 card 是指儲值卡，禮物卡等，reload 是一個將…再裝入，或是刷新重整的動作，在這裡就是指將錢裝入這張卡裡。
   在這裡還有一個簡報的小技巧，就是利用獎品吸引觀眾的注意力在你的簡報上，不過這只適合一般簡報，不適合嚴肅的簡報場合。

2. I can't help myself to talk a lot about the card.
   我情不自禁地談論這一張卡。
   I can't help myself 情不自禁，無法控制。照字面上看來，會很容易被認為是 "我幫不了我自己"，但其實指的是對自己的無能為力，可以指好的也可以指壞的情形。

3. Just my luck! Maybe today is not a perfect day for my presentation.
   真倒楣！或許我今天不宜做簡報。
   just my luck 真倒楣，真衰。這跟我們在倒楣時會自嘲說真幸運一樣，這裡是說反話。
   在簡報當中常會出現一些小問題，主講者如果能沈著的面對問題的話，會讓這場簡報大大加分。而在文中James利用會中出現的狀況，反過來利用，成為實例用以講解公司所提供的服務，除了讓人能清楚的了解產品之外，還會印象深刻。

Unit 30 開發專案

Dialog 1

A I have got the demographic report yesterday, and here's the slide. From the pie chart and the area chart above, we can see that there are very significant differences between our customers in New York and in Chicago. So maybe we will need to re-evaluate some of the content for our new project, especially emphasize the different promotional events in the different venues.

B What that's about?

A According to the demographic report, we find out that our New York customers are mostly from mid-level to upper-class income levels，and here's the summary of the demographic report on this slide. Most of them are university or postgraduates, married with no kids, white-collar workers…

C DINK?

我昨天拿到了人口統計報告，然後這有張投影片。從這一個派狀圖及上方的的區域圖，我們可以看出來我們在紐約及在芝加哥的顧客群有相當顯著的不同。所以或許我們需要重新評估我們新專案中的一些內容，特別是要著重在不同的地點用不同的促銷活動。

這怎麼說？

根據這份人口統計報告，我們發現我們紐約的顧客大多是中上層收入階級，這一張投影片上有這份人口統計報告的摘要。他們大部分是大學或是研究所畢業。已婚沒有孩子，白領階層…

頂客族嗎？

A Yep, that's right. And our customers in Chicago, on the contrary, are mostly mid to low income levels, single parents homes, and blue-collar workers. From this report, I think we are talking about two totally different target groups. So if we want to get the desired result from this project, and we have to come up with two completely different sales pitches to suit the needs of each groups.

對，沒有錯。然而我們在芝加哥的顧客，完全相反的，大多是中下收入，單親家庭，及藍領勞工。從這份報告中顯示，我認為我們是在討論兩個完全不同的目標族群。所以如果我們要達到這一個專案的預期效果的話，我們必須要制定兩個完全不同的銷售方式來配合各族群的需求。

B I have no idea there was that great of deviation between these two venues. So when can I get these two different sales promotion plans?

我不知道這兩個地點有這麼大的差別。所以我什麼時候能拿到這兩個不同的銷售宣傳計畫呢？

A We think we can still use the origin plan for the customers in New York. As for Chicago, my team and I will need two more days for a new plan.

我們認為針對在紐約的顧客我們可以沿用原來的計畫。至於芝加哥方面，新的計畫我和我的團隊需要再兩天的時間來完成。

Dialog 2

A   Ok, so let's move to the first part of my talk. This is the 2013 fiscal sales report, and you can find this overhead in page 3 of my handout. The blue line represents our sales from the year 2012, the red line is the sales in 2013. According to this line graph, it shows that in 2012, our sales were quite slow to start off with, but managed to make decent performance in the last 2 months of the year. And I remember we had a promotion event and offered 10% off for coffee drinks and 15% off for the merchandize at that time. And we all know that our sales dropped off dramatically since May, and similar situation happened in our competing companies as well. Many of them have reduced the price of their coffee to increase their sales…

B   Are you implying that we should reduce the price to increase our sales, same as our competitors?

Ok，所以讓我們來到我所要講的第一部份。這是2013會計年度的銷售報表，你可以在我發下的綱要中的第3頁看到這一張投影片。藍色的線代表我們在2012的銷售數字，紅線的部份是2013年的銷售。根據這一個曲線圖，顯示我們的銷量在2012年時從緩慢爬升開始，直到那年的最後兩個月有了相當不錯的表現。而我記得我們在那段時間有咖啡九折，商品八五折的活動優惠。而我們大家都知道從5月開始我們的銷量大幅下滑，同樣的情形也發生在我們的對手公司裡。他們大多以咖啡降價來增加他們的銷量…

那你是指我們應該和我們的對手一樣降價來增加銷量嗎？

A No. That's not the main idea of this new project that I'm going to propose, please bear with me until I finish my words. So we made a research on our customers, and we found out that because of the recession, so money is tight for everyone these days⋯

不。那不是我所要提的新專案的重點，請耐心等待我把話說完。所以我們做了顧客研究，我們發現因為經濟衰退的關係，所以這些日子大家的手頭都有點緊⋯

C That's true, my wife forbids me to spend more than $20 a day.

是事實，我老婆禁止我一天花超過$20。

A One of the reasons that our sales dropped down is that many of our customers don't want to spend money on the morning coffee, they prefer to brew coffee at home. I think we have the potential to get some home-brew coffee market shares by selling our premium coffee beans.

銷量下滑的原因之一是我們許多客人不想花錢買早上的咖啡，他們寧願在家自己煮。我認為我們有這個潛力能以販售我們的特級咖啡豆在在家煮咖啡的市場上來佔有一些比例。

B Hmm⋯ I love your idea, tell me more about this project.

嗯⋯我喜歡你們的主意，跟我多說一些與這個專案相關的。

精選單字及片語

1. demographic *adj.* 人口統計學的，人口統計的。
Demographic change is another reason of why the workforce is graying.
人口的變化是勞動力老化的另一個原因。

2. DINK 頂客族。DINK 是 "Double income no kids." 的簡寫，這是一種在 1950 年代起源於歐美國家的一種生活形態，其特徵為夫妻雙方各自都有工作，但沒有小孩。這種生活形態在 1980 年代之後逐漸的傳到亞洲地區。

3. deviation(s) *n.* 偏差，誤差。
A minimal error or deviation may result in wide divergence.
失之毫釐，謬以千里。

4. start off with 從…開始，用…開始。
Where shall we start off with?
我們要從哪兒開始呢？

5. dramatically *adv.* 戲劇性的，引人注目的。
The oil price has climbed dramatically in the last five years.
油價在過去五年來不斷的向上攀升。

6. main idea 重點，要旨，核心思想。
I couldn't grasp his main idea of his talk.
我無法抓住他話中的重點。

精選句子與延伸

1. From the pie chart and the area chart above, we can see that there are very significant differences between our customers in New York and in Chicago.
   從這一個派狀圖及上方的的區域圖，我們可以看出來我們在紐約及在芝加哥的顧客群有相當顯著的不同。
   pie chart 派狀圖，圓餅圖。
   area chart 區域圖，面積圖。
   在簡報當中，常會用到許多的圖表，用以讓觀眾能更加清楚看到差別，常用到的圖表還有：
   柱狀圖 bar graph
   條狀圖 column graph
   折線圖 line graph
   直方圖 histogram

2. So if we want to get the desired result from this project, and we have to come up with two completely different sales pitches to suit the needs of each groups.
   所以如果我們要達到這一個專案的預期效果的話，我們必須要制定兩個完全不同的銷售方式來配合各族群的需求。
   come up 提出。
   I hope you can come up with a better plan than that.
   我希望你們能提出比那個還好的計畫。
   sale pitch 銷售方式，推銷商品用語。
   Her sales pitch was smooth and convincing.
   她的銷售台詞流暢又有說服力。

3. Please bear with me until I finish my words.
   請耐心等待我把話說完。
   bear with somebody 忍耐，寬容某人，耐心等待某人。
   Please bear with me for a minute, and you'll see what I mean.
   請再耐心的等一下，你馬上就會明白我的意思了。

4. Money is tight for everyone these days.
   這些日子大家的手頭都有點緊
   money is tight 經濟拮据，手頭緊。這一個詞是由 "tight money"（銀根緊縮）衍生出來的，跟中文的說法相當類似。

Part Six

職場關係與溝通
Relationship at the Job career

（一對一）詢問工作上問題

Dialog 1

Hanzawa Mr. Lin, I know I mustn't take up your off-work hours, but this is really an emergency. Could you please work during the weekend to translate this document?

林先生，我知道我不應該佔用你的下班時間，但是這真的是一個緊急事件。能不能請你在週末時工作翻譯這份文件？

Lin But I have already got something to do on this weekend, I'm sorry. Besides, if I am not wrong, I remember that Shan is the translator mainly for your department. I think Shan will give you a hand if he has time.

但是我這個週末已經有事要做了，我很抱歉。除此之外，如果我沒弄錯的話，我記得Shan是負責你們部門的翻譯人員。我想Shan會願意幫你的忙，如果他有空的話。

Hanzawa I'm sorry about making this unreasonable requirement, but this document is for the Taiwan-based manufacturer, and need to be translated into traditional Chinese, most of all, by using Taiwanese terms and preferred usages. If you could help me out, I will double the pay for your working hours.

我很抱歉提出這個不合理的要求，但是這一份文件是要給一個台灣的製造商，需要翻譯成繁體中文，最重要的是要使用台灣的用語及習慣用法。如果你能幫我的話，我將依你工作的時數付雙倍的薪資。

Lin That is very generous of you. Can you tell me how many pages of that document?

你人真慷慨。你能告訴我這份文件有幾頁嗎？

Hanzawa	About 20 pages.	大約20頁吧。
Lin	Do you mind if I work at home?	你介意我在家裡工作嗎？
Hanzawa	No, not at all.	不，一點也不。
Lin	OK, I'll take it. I will probably need about 8 hours to work on it. How soon you really need it?	好，那我接這個案子。我大概需要8個小時來翻譯。你什麼時候需要這份文件？
Hanzawa	I will need it for the conference on Monday afternoon, is that possible for you to have it done by Sunday noon?	我星期一下午的會議中要用到這份文件，你有沒有可能在星期日中午前完成呢？
Lin	I will try my best. Like I told you, I've already got something to do on the weekend, so I will do the translation in my spare time. It should be okay for me to have it done by Sunday noon, and I will send it to you via email.	我會盡力試試看。像我告訴過你的，我這個週末有事要辦，所以我會在空閒時翻譯。我應該可以在星期天中午前完成，我會把它用email寄給你。
Hanzawa	Thank you for helping me out, and I promise I'll pay you back double.	謝謝你的幫忙，我承諾我將會加倍奉還。
Lin	You are welcome, just give me double pay, no need to double payback.	不客氣，只要給我雙倍薪水，加倍奉還就不用了。

Dialog 2

Paul	Oh my god, this stupid computer is down again. I think my computer must be jinxed and it's always breaking down. Dave, would you please come over here and take a look of my computer.	我的天啊，這台笨電腦又當了。我想我的電腦一定是被詛咒了才會一直壞掉。Dave，可以麻煩你過來看一下我的電腦嗎？
Dave	Okay, just give me a minute, let me finish my work in hand.	Okay，等我一下，讓我完成手邊的工作。
Paul	Sure, no problem, take your time.	當然，沒問題，不急。
Dave	Okay, let me run the virus scan on your computer first. It will take several minutes. (5 minutes later) It turns out that you have a lot of infected files in your computer. Good thing we don't have to format the hard disk or reinstall the operation system. Just clean up the viruses with the anti-virus software.	Okay，先讓我在你的電腦中執行病毒掃瞄。大約會花上幾分鐘的時間。（5分鐘後）結果是你的電腦中有很多病毒檔。幸好我們不需要將硬碟格式化或是重灌作業系統。只需要用防毒軟體將病毒清除。
Paul	I have been very careful when browsing online; I don't know why my computer can contract infections?	我上網瀏覽時都非常的小心，我不知道我的電腦怎麼會感染上病毒？

Dave	There are many ways for computer viruses to spread. Browsing the Internet is just one of them, opening email attachment is also a possible way to get infected. So you have to make sure that your anti-virus software is updated regularly. You didn't update the anti-virus software for quite a while, am I right?	電腦病毒的傳播有好幾種方式。上網瀏覽只是其中的一種,打開email的附件也是受到感染的一種可能的方式。所以你必須要確保定期的更新防毒軟體。你有好一陣子都沒有更新防毒軟體了,我說的對嗎?
Paul	Yes, you are right, I didn't update it for about 2 months. I didn't realize that would cause me trouble.	是,你說的沒錯,我有大約2個月沒有更新了。我並不知道這樣會為我帶來麻煩。
Dave	Now you know it.	現在你知道了。
Paul	Anything else I should be noted?	還有什麼我應該注意的嗎?
Dave	Please take good care of your computer, do not kick or hit it.	請好好愛惜你的電腦,不要踢它或是打它。
Paul	Oh, sorry about that, it won't happen again.	喔,對不起,不會再發生了。

💬 精選單字及片語

1. take up　佔去；開始從事。
   I am sorry to take up your time.
   不好意思，佔用了你的時間。
   When did you take up Spanish as your second foreign language?
   你們是從哪時候開始選修西班牙語作為第二外語的？

2. give a hand　幫助
   Would you please give me a hand with shifting those books?
   你可不可以幫我將那些書搬一下？

3. help out　幫忙，幫……擺脫困難。
   Is there any way for me to help out their families?
   是不是有什麼方法讓我可以幫助他們的家人？

4. jinxed　*adj.*　倒楣的，不祥的，帶來厄運的。
   This project is jinxed, but perhaps it's not without remedy.
   這個項目被搞砸了，但或許不是沒有補救的辦法。

5. infect　*vt.*　使受感染，使受影響。
   The new computer virus infected thousands of computers within a day.
   新的電腦病毒在僅僅一天的時間內就散布至數以千計台的電腦了。

6. take good care of　愛護，愛惜。
   Please take good care of public property.
   請愛惜公物。

🗨 精選句子與延伸

1. I'm sorry about making this unreasonable requirement.
   我很抱歉提出這個不合理的要求。
   ＝I know my request to you is quite unreasonable and I'm sorry about that.
   unreasonable requirement 不合理的要求。
   We have the right to refuse the unreasonable requirements from the company.
   我們有權拒絕公司提出的不合理要求。

2. Thank you for help me out, and I promise I'll pay you back double.
   謝謝你的幫忙，我承諾我將會加倍奉還。
   在最近流行的日劇當中，男主角說的「若人犯我，我必加倍奉還。」，英文媒體將
   其翻譯成 "If your enemies hurt you, take double the payback."。也可將我們一般
   常見的 "An eye for an eye, a tooth for a tooth."（以眼還眼，以牙還牙）改寫成
   "Two eyes for an eye, two teeth for a tooth."
   double 加倍，雙倍。
   tenfold 十倍。＝decuple
   If someone does me wrong, I'll take tenfold (decuple) the payback.
   人若犯我，十倍奉還。

3. Okay, just give me a minute, let me finish my work in hand.
   Okay，等我一下，讓我完成手邊的工作。
   ＝Wait a moment, let me finish the task at hand.
   in hand （工作）手邊正在進行的，待處理的。
   I am giving all I have to the project in hand.
   我盡我全力去做手頭上的這個項目。

4. Good thing we don't have to format the hard disk or reinstall the operation system.
   Just clean up the viruses with the anti-virus software.
   幸好我們不需要將硬碟格式化或是重灌作業系統。只需要用防毒軟體將病毒清除。
   good thing 還好，幸好。美國俚語，放在句首，在good thing後面接上一個完整的句
   子。
   Good thing we checked the train timetable.
   還好我們查了火車時刻表。

Unit 32 責備部門進度落後

Dialog 1

| Allen | Hey, Barclay, boss wants me to inform everyone that we will have a project status meeting on 10 am tomorrow. | 嘿，Barclay，老闆要我告訴大家，我們明天早上10點鐘要開專案進度會議。 |

Barclay　Geez, I want to bang in sick tomorrow.

天啊，我明天要打電話請病假。

Allen　What's wrong? Anything wrong with the project?

怎麼了？專案有什麼問題嗎？

Barclay　Frankly speaking, it's only 35% done, I am running a little bit behind.

老實說，專案才完成了百分之35，我的進度有些落後。

Allen　Oh, you should speed things up. Have you got any problem during the process?

喔，你應該要加快速度了。你在工作過程中是不是有遇到什麼困難呢？

Barclay　Yes, I have. You know, I am just a green hand in handling such things, not very quick at catching on to the work flow.

是的，我有。你知道，我在處理這類事情上只是個新手，在工作流程上還沒能這麼快上手。

Allen　I know, but I remember that we discussed this before you take over this project. I already told you that you have to cooperate with your colleagues. Ask them if you don't know how to do. So did you ask other colleagues for help?

我知道，但我記得關於這一點在你接手這項專案時我們就已經討論過了。我已經告訴過你應該和你的同事們合作。不知道怎麼做時就去問他們。所以你有沒有向其他同事尋求幫助呢？

Barclay	I tried, but they are always too busy to help me.	我試過，但他們總是忙到沒空幫我。
Allen	Alright, I think I know your problem. Have you ever helped others when they are in trouble? Most of them will give a hand back to someone who helped them.	好吧，我想我知道你的問題了。當別的同事有困難時，你有幫助過他們嗎？大部分的人在幫過他們的人有麻煩時會回幫一把。
Barclay	I did, but I don't seem to fit in with other colleagues. I feel so depressed.	我有，但我好像就是和其他同事們合不來。我感到十分沮喪。
Allen	Cheer up, I think you should make more connections with your colleagues and things will be much better. Most of them are really easy-going people, and it's speaking from my experience. Now, show me your work, I can give you some advice.	加油，我想你應該跟你的同事多接觸，情況會漸漸改善的。他們大部分都是很好相處的人，這是我的經驗談。現在，給我看看你做的，我可以給你一些建議。
Barclay	Thank you very much. Sorry, I need a few seconds to find out my weekly status.	非常謝謝你。對不起，我需要一下下的時間來找我的進度表。
Allen	That's ok. Barclay, I know this is not my business, but have you ever considered about to get your desk tidier? You have to tidy your documents away, otherwise you always waste too much time on finding your documents. I think it might be one of the reasons of why you are behind your schedule.	沒關係。Barclay，我知道這不關我的事，但是你有沒有考慮過要將桌上收乾淨呢？你必須將你的文件收好，要不然你總是浪費太多時間在尋找你的文件。我認為這可能是你進度落後的原因之一。

Barclay	Thanks for your advice, I'll get everything in order later on. Here's the weekly status.	謝謝你的建議,我待會兒會將所有東西排整齊的。這裡是每週進度表。
Allen	Hmm… Can you tell me why this part has fallen so far behind the schedule? It should be done 2 weeks ago.	嗯,可以告訴我這一個部分進度為什麼落後這麼多?這應該在兩週前就應該完成了。
Barclay	In this part, it requires technical support from other departments. It's very hard to coordinate people from different departments.	在這一部分,它需要其他部門技術上的支持。而要協調不同部門的人又很困難。
Allen	Did you figure out how to solve this problem?	那你想出解決的辦法了嗎?
Barclay	No, not yet.	還沒。
Allen	Darn! Barclay. If you told me 2 weeks ago, we would have done this part already. Didn't I tell you that you can ask Johnny if you have any problem with this project?	該死的!Barclay。如果你在2個星期前告訴我,我們早就已經完成這部分了。我有沒有告訴過你如果這個專案上有任何問題的話你可以去問Johnny?
Barclay	Yes, you did tell me that and I asked Johnny about this part, but he was too busy, and wanted me to solve this problem by myself.	有,你說過,我有問過Johnny有關這一個部分,但他太忙了,要我自己去解決。

Allen	Ok, I think I will have a serious talk with him. In this situation, you can talk to Julie, she can fix it for you. I will pass you some data for this project. I guess maybe you'll have to work overtime starting from today to meet the deadline of this project.	Ok，我想我會和他好好談一談。在這種情形，你可以跟Julie說，她可以幫你解決這個問題。我會把這個專案的相關資料傳給你。我猜想也許從今天起你必須加班才能在這個專案的期限內完成。
Barclay	I don't mind working overtime, only if I can finish the project on time.	我不介意加班，只要能準時完成這個專案就好。
Allen	Great, if you have any problem in your work, just let me know.	很好，如果你有任何問題的話，讓我知道。
Barclay	Thanks a lot, I promise I will work harder.	非常謝謝，我承諾我會更努力工作的。
Allen	No problem, and don't forget about making good connections with your colleagues, and teamwork is the key factor to the project's success.	沒問題，還有別忘了要和你同事建立良好的關係以及團隊合作是專案成功的關鍵因素。
Barclay	I will keep in mind.	我會銘記在心的。
Allen	One more thing, if you can't catch up and have no solution next time, be sure to tell me first. Then I can make some arrangements for the project, understand?	還有一點，如果你下次無法趕上進度並且沒有解決方法時，一定要先告訴我。這樣我才能為這項目作些安排，明白嗎？
Barclay	Yes, I undrestand, and I promise it won't happen again.	是的，我知道了，我答應不會再發生這樣的事了。

💬 精選單字及片語

1. inform *v.* 告知,通知
   I promise that I will keep you inform of the progress being made.
   我承諾一定會經常向你報告進度。

2. frankly *adv.* 坦白的,直率地,真誠地。frankly speaking 老實說,坦白說。
   Speak frankly, and don't beat about the bush.
   有話坦白說不要兜圈子。

3. speed up 加速
   Could you please speed up? I don't want to miss my flight.
   可以請你開快一點嗎?我不想錯過我的班機。

4. work flow 工作流程
   With so many increasing members, we have to consider about rearranging our work flow.
   增加了這麼多的會員,我們必須慎重考慮一下重整我們的工作流程。

5. coordinate *v.* 協調,整合
   We should coordinate what we will say to speak with one voice.
   我們應該先講好待會該說些什麼以保持口徑一致。

6. keep in mind 記住,記在心裡
   You must keep this lesson in mind.
   你要牢牢的記住這個教訓。

💬 精選句子與延伸

1. Geez, I want to bang in sick tomorrow.
   天啊，我明天要打電話請病假。
   ＝Gee whiz, I want to call in sick tomorrow.
   bang in sick 打電話請病假
   Influenza proliferated through the city, 5 more employees banged in sick today.
   流行性感冒在全城蔓延，今天又多了 5 個員工打電話來請病假。

2. I am just a green hand in handling such things, not very quick at catching on to the work flow.
   我在處理這類事情上只是個新手，在工作流程上還沒能這麼快上手。
   green hand 新手，生手，沒有經驗的人。
   Because he is just a green hand, I don't think we should be so critical of him.
   因為他只是個新手，我不認為我們應該對他這麼挑剔。

3. She can fix the problem for you.
   她可以幫你解決這個問題。
   在這個句子中的problem，代表的是 "coordinate people from different depart-ments" （協調各部門的人）這一個情形。
   也可以寫成 She is able to coordinate various departments to carry out the project.
   她能幫你協調各部門來執行這個專案。
   fix the problem 解決問題
   He thought he could fix the problem within two weeks.
   他以為他能在兩週內將這個問題解決。

4. I don't mind working overtime, only if I can finish the project on time.
   我不介意加班，只要能準時完成這個專案就好。
   only if 只要…就好
   Nothing will go wrong, only if we handle them with kid gloves.
   我們不會有事的，只要我們能小心行事就可以了。

工作份量過重

Maggic	Mr. Westland, is it all right for me to come in now?	Westland先生，我現在方便進來嗎？
Boss	Well, I am pretty busy, but… all right, come in. Please have a seat. OK, Maggie, tell me, what can I do for you?	嗯，我很忙，但是……好吧，進來吧。請坐。OK，Maggie，告訴我，我可以為妳做些什麼嗎？
Maggic	Hmm… I want to talk about my work…	嗯……我想跟你談一談我的工作……
Boss	That reminds me, did you finish the article that I returned to you the day before yesterday?	這提醒了我，妳完成了前天我退回給妳的那篇文章了嗎？
Maggic	Not yet, but…	還沒，但是……
Boss	Maggie, I am very disappointed at you. You know, I have been watching you for several weeks. And I found that you looked so busy but didn't finish any work.	Maggie，我對妳感到非常失望。妳知道嗎？我已經觀察妳好幾個星期了。我發現你總是看起來很忙碌，但卻沒有完成任何工作。

Maggic	That's not fair. I always get my work done ahead of schedule, but then you assigned me more tasks to do and assumed that I didn't finish my work. In fact, my workload is too heavy and sometimes I feel like I am burning out. My heavy workload has already infringed my personal life. I feel stressed and exhausted these days. I used to enjoy my job, but now I'm afraid of it.	這不公平。我總是提早完成我的工作，但跟著你就指派更多的工作給我，並認為我沒有完成工作。事實上，我的工作份量太重了，有時我覺得我都快要累垮了。我繁重的工作量已經侵犯了我的個人生活了。我這些日子感到壓力很大且精疲力盡。我以前很享受我的工作，但我現在卻感到害怕。
Boss	Well, why didn't you tell me before the problem become progressively worse?	在問題變得越來越嚴重之前妳怎麼都不跟我說呢？
Maggic	I did, but whenever I tried to tell you that I have too much work to cover, then you would be busy on your phone or computer or something else.	我說了，但當我試著告訴你我的工作太多了的時候，然後你就會忙著在講電話，用電腦或其他事情上面。
Boss	Oh, I apologize for that. I'm also under a lot of pressure recently. I didn't mean to do so.	喔，我感到很抱歉。我最近的壓力也挺大的。我並不是故意這樣做的。
Maggic	Yes, I do understand.	好的，我瞭解。
Boss	OK, I think we need to spend some time to go through your work schedule. Let's find out the solution.	好吧，我想我們需要花一點時間來看一下妳的工作行程表。讓我們來找解決的辦法。
Maggic	That will be great. Thank you so much, Mr. Westland.	那就太好了。非常的謝謝你，Westland先生。
Boss	No problem.	沒問題。

Dialog 2

Fion	Hi, Janice. How's everything going?	嗨，Janice。最近好不好啊？
Janice	Hi, Fion. Everything goes well, except for my new boss. And I am thinking about quitting.	嗨，Fion。一切都還好，除了我的新老闆之外。還有我正在考慮辭職的事。
Fion	Oh, what happened?	喔，發生了什麼事？
Janice	I think my new boss doesn't like me, and regards me as an imaginary enemy. Nothing can keep him from breathing down my neck. Do you remember the report on tax law that I mentioned to you last week.	我想我的新老闆不喜歡我，而且把我當成是假想敵。沒有什麼事能阻擋他緊盯著我不放。你還記得我上星期跟妳提過的那一個稅法的報告吧？
Fion	Yes, and I remember you said that you have 6 weeks to finish that report and you'll try your very best to impress your boss.	記得啊，我還記得妳說妳有6個星期的時間去完成那份報告，妳將竭盡妳所能來令妳的老闆刮目相看。
Janice	Not any more.	不再是了。
Fion	Why? Did he cancel it?	為什麼？他把這個報告取消了？
Janice	No, he moved the deadline up to April 20th.	不，他把期限提前到4月20日。
Fion	That means you have only less than 2 weeks away to do that report. Do you think you can finish it by then?	那意味著你只有不到2個星期的時間來做那份報告了。妳覺得妳能在那之前完成嗎？
Janice	I think I could if he didn't assign me another 2 projects.	我覺得我可以，如果他沒有指派另外兩個專案的話。

Fion	Oh, my dear. Your boss is too pushy.	喔，親愛的。妳的老闆太強人所難了。
Janice	I have been burning the candle at both ends recently. Look at my face, my eyes are black sockets, I have to wear much makeup to cover them.	我最近一直都是早出晚歸的長時間工作。看看我的臉，我的眼睛都成了兩個黑窟窿了，我必須化大濃妝來遮蓋。
Fion	Poor you. Is there anything I can do for you?	真可憐。我有什麼可以幫忙的嗎？
Janice	Well, I guess no one can help me but myself. But I am very glad to have you to talk to, and I feel much better now.	嗯，我猜除了我自己，沒人幫的上忙。但是我很高興有妳可以說說話，我現在覺得好多了。
Fion	I understand, and your pressure is unimaginable. Cheer up, don't let him beat you.	我了解，妳的壓力是無法想像的。加油，別讓他打敗妳。
Janice	Fion, it very nice to talk with you. But I really have to go, catch you later.	Fion，和妳談話很開心。但我必須離開了，待會兒見。
Fion	Good luck, Janice.	祝好運，Janice。
Janice	Thanks!	謝啦！

💬 精選單字及片語

1. workload(s) *n.* 工作量
   I am afraid I will collapse under the heavy workload.
   我怕我會因為工作量太重而累垮。

2. infringe *v.* 侵犯（某人的權益，權力，自由等）
   She refused to answer the question that infringed on her privacy.
   她拒絕回答侵犯她隱私的問題。

3. progressively *adv.* 日益增加地，逐步的。
   The amount of the loan from the bank was progressively decreased.
   從銀行得到的貸款金額越來越少。

4. move up 提前，提升
   There is room for another one if you move up in front a little bit.
   這裡還可再多容納一個人，如果你向前移一點的話。

5. pushy *adj* 強求的，固執己見
   Tempers will mount if you are too pushy at work.
   如果你工作中太過強勢的話將會「顧人怨」。

6. unimaginable *adj.* 無法想像的，難以想像的
   The great success would have been unimaginable two years ago.
   在兩年前完全無法想像會這麼成功。

精選句子與延伸

1. In fact, my workload is too heavy and sometimes I feel like I am burning out.
   事實上，我的工作份量太重了，有時我覺得我都快要累垮了。
   ＝Actually, my workload is too high, and makes me feel that I would collapse from exhaustion at any moment.
   burn out 耗盡精力，精疲力盡，消耗殆盡；燒光，燒毀。
   If you don't take care of yourself, and in this rate you will burn out before you are 30 years old.
   如果你不好好保重自己的話，照這樣的速度，你在不到 30 歲之前就會累垮的。
   The light bulb is burned out, can you fetch me a new one?
   這個燈泡已經燒壞了，你可以幫我拿一個新的來嗎？

2. I'm also under a lot of pressure recently.
   我最近的壓力也挺大的。
   ＝I am also under great strain lately.
   pressure(s) (n.) 壓力，精神壓力。
   You should bring some pressure on him.
   你應該對他施加點壓力。

3. Nothing can keep him from breathing down my neck.
   沒有什麼事能阻擋他緊盯著我不放。
   keep from 阻止，免於；隱瞞。
   The doctor guaranteed that his health will improve, only if he can keep from smoking for a month.
   醫生保證他的健康情況一定會好轉，只要他能一個月不吸煙
   breathe down someone's neck 對某人盯得特別緊，緊迫盯人，嚴密監視。
   I can't concentrate on my work with him breathing on my neck.
   他這樣的緊迫盯人讓我無法專心在工作上。

4. I have been burning the candle at both ends recently.
   我最近一直都是早出晚歸的長時間工作。
   burn the candle at both ends 蠟燭兩頭燒，因忙碌而晚睡早起，睡眠或是休息時間極短。
   No wonder she's ill, she has been burning the candle at both ends for a long time.
   她長期的不眠不休的工作，難怪她會病倒。

Unit 34 表現不如預期

Dialog 1

Boss	Jacob, could you please come to my office, I need to talk to you.	Jacob，可以麻煩你到我的辦公室嗎？我需要和你談談。
Jacob	Sure, boss. I will be there as soon as I finish this document.	當然，老闆。我盡快在做完這份文件後過去。
Boss	No, come here right now, I insist.	不，現在馬上進來。我堅決要求。
Jacob	All right.	好吧。
Boss	Jacob, please have a seat.	Jacob，請坐。
Jacob	Thank you. What's the matter?	謝謝你。有什麼事嗎？
Boss	We did a survey on your job performance.	我們對於你的工作表現作了份問卷調查。
Jacob	How did I do?	我的表現如何？
Boss	Not very well. Lots of complains. Most of them are about your inefficient work.	沒有很好。很多抱怨。大部分是跟你缺乏效率的工作有關。
Jacob	But I work very hard.	但我很努力的工作。

Boss	I know you work very hard, but not efficiently enough. Besides, you don't work well with your colleagues. You are a hotshot college graduate, we actually expected you can introduce better methods of management into this company. But I think I have to lower my expectation on you. You can't be a good executive unless you realize the importance of the good teamwork. I don't think your performance is quite in line with what we expect for our managements.	我知道你很努力的在工作，但是卻不夠有效率。除此之外，你和你的同事們無法好好一起工作。你是從名校畢業的大學生，我們實際上希望你能為本公司引進更好的管理方法。但我想我必須降低對你的期望。你無法成為一個好的管理人員，除非你能瞭解良好團隊精神的重要性。我不認為你的表現符合我們對於主管的要求。
Jacob	Please give me one more chance. I'll do my best, I promise. That will not always be the case.	請再給我一次機會，我會盡我所能，我保證。情況不會永遠是這樣的。
Boss	Well, I guess I can give you one more chance, and you better get started from keeping with your colleagues. I hope I have already made my point clear to you.	嗯，我猜想我可以再給你一次機會，你最好從和你的同事們好好的相處開始。我希望我已經向你清楚的表達了我的觀點
Jacob	Yes, I understand. Thank you for giving me another chance, you won't regret it.	是的，我明白了。謝謝你給我再一次的機會，我不會讓你後悔的。

Dialog 2

Johnny	Hey, Casey. I want to talk to you about our new financial advisor.	嘿，Casey。我想跟你談一下有關我們新的理財顧問。
Casey	Hmm… You mean Michael.	嗯，你是説Michael。
Johnny	Yes, Michael.	對，Michael。
Casey	Okay, sure. What's up?	好啊，沒問題。怎麼了？
Johnny	I don't think he is a good fit for our company.	我想他不太適合我們公司。
Casey	Okay, what makes you to say so? As I know, he has the formal qualifications and certificates for this position. And I thought you were satisfied with his overall performing, because you mentioned to me that you were impressed by his attitude, and he's already got some positive feedback from some of our regular customers.	Okay，你怎麼會這麼説呢？據我所知，他有這個職位所需的正式資格及認證。還有我以為你對於他的整體表現還蠻滿意的，因為你曾向我提過你很欣賞他的態度還有他已經獲得了我們有一些常客的正面反應。
Johnny	Yes, I did, but he has been underperforming since then. His attitude is still great, but not very reliable. He can be very productive, but he sometimes slacks off at work. Take yesterday for example, we had a department meeting in the morning, and he was almost an hour late.	是，我有提過，但之後他的表現就不如預期。他的態度還是很好，但有些靠不住。他可以非常有效率，但他有時會在工作時間摸魚。就拿昨天來説，我們在早上有個部門會議，但他卻遲到了快一個小時。
Casey	Well, I guess he must had a perfect good explanation for his lateness.	嗯，我猜他應該對他的遲到有一個好的解釋吧。

Johnny	That's not the only thing. He doesn't have a very good work ethic. You know I sometimes catch him on Facebook chatting with friends during the office hours.	並不只是這樣。他敬業態度不佳。你知道我有時候會抓到他在上班時間上臉書和朋友聊天。
Casey	Was there any guest wait for him in reception room?	那在接待室中有客人在等他嗎？
Johnny	Hmm… no, but…	嗯……沒有，但是……
Casey	Come on, Johnny, as if you don't check your Facebook at work. In my opinion, I think Michael is the right person for this position, he will fill the bill if you coach him. On the other hand, we have already invested a lot of time and money in his training, it will be a big loss for our company if we let him go.	拜託，Johnny，好像你上班時都不會上臉書查看一樣。我的意見是，我覺得Michael是這一個職位的適合人選，如果你能指導他的話，他將會非常稱職。另一方面來説，我們已經投入大把的時間及金錢在他的訓練上，如果我們讓他離開的話，對公司而言將會是一筆重大的損失。
Johnny	Okay, I see your point, I will talk to him.	好的，我知道了。我會和他談談的。
Casey	That's good.	很好。

💬 精選單字及片語

1. insist *v.* 堅持，強調。
   If you insist on leaving now, we have to declare the conference off.
   如果你堅持要離開的話，我們必須取消這次的會議。

2. inefficient *adj* 無效率的，效率不佳的。
   The inefficient operation costs the company a lot of money.
   效率不佳的運作方式花費了公司一大筆錢

3. in line with 跟…一致，符合。
   My project is in line with your opinions.
   我的專案是根據你的意見來制定的。

4. be a good fit for 合適；合身。
   Why are you a good fit for this job?
   你為什麼適合這個工作？

5. slack off 鬆懈，懈怠，放鬆。slack off at work 照字面上解釋為「在工作中懈怠」，也是我們一般常說的「上班摸魚」
   It is natural to slack off towards the end of a hard day's work.
   經過一整天的辛苦工作後，在快下班前時有所鬆懈是很正常的。

6. big loss 巨大的損失
   The manager charged off this big loss to his staff.
   經理將這個巨大的損失歸咎於他的下屬。

💬 精選句子與延伸

1. You are a hotshot college graduate, we actually expected you can introduce better methods of management into this company.
   你是從名校畢業的大學生，我們實際上希望你能為本公司引進更好的管理方法。
   hotshot college有名的大學，名牌大學。hotshot有「高手」、「成功人士」的意思。加上college就是我們一般常說的名校，名牌大學。
   graduate(s)(n.) 大學畢業生。

2. That will not always be the case.
   情況不會永遠是這樣的。
   本句為常用的美國俚語，用在覺得現在的狀況只是暫時的，並不會長久，還有轉圜的餘地的時候，就可以說 "That will not always be the case."。相反地，當覺得「情況就會是這樣了」的時候，我們則說 "That will be the case."。可以被視為是 "be the case" 這個片語的應用句型。
   be the case 是這種情況，如此。
   It does not look favorable to be the case.
   就這情形看起來並不樂觀。

3. Take yesterday for example, we had a department meeting in the morning, and he was almost an hour late.
   就拿昨天來說，我們在早上有個部門會議，但他卻遲到了快一個小時。
   ＝Take yesterday for instance, he was nearly an hour late for our department meeting in the morning.

4. Come on, Johnny, as if you don't check your Facebook at work.
   拜託，Johnny，好像你上班時都不會上臉書查看一樣。
   as if 好像，彷彿
   在完整的句子前加上 as if 這個片語，則整個句子的意思將完全相反，例如本句中說的是 you don't check your Facebook at work（你上班時都不會使用臉書），但加上 as if （好像），則是意味著「你有時在工作時是會去查看你的臉書的。」所以代表Casey知道Johnny在上班時是偶爾會上臉書查看。

Unit 35 （一對多）匯報工作狀況

Dialog 1

A　Hermione, I am running short of my business cards, would you please order some for me? I have to hand out my business cards in the event tomorrow afternoon.

Hermione，我的名片快要用完了，可以請妳幫我訂一些嗎？我需要在明天下午的活動發名片。

B　Henry, if you are going to pass out business cards tomorrow, don't you think you should check the amount of your cards earlier? I would say, maybe one week before that event. Luckily, I've already ordered some for you, here you go.

Henry，如果你明天要發名片的話，難道你不認為你應該早一點檢查你名片的數量嗎？我會說，也許在活動前一個星期吧。幸運的事，我已經幫你訂好了，喏，拿去。

A　Oh, thanks.

喔，謝啦。

C　Hermione, my printer broken down again, would you please send it for repair?

Hermione，我的印表機又壞了，你可不可以把它送修？

B　I've sent it for repair twice this month already, there's nothing wrong with your printer. All you have to do is to turn on the power switch.

我這一個月已經把它送修兩次了，你的印表機一點問題也沒有。你所需要做的事將電源開關打開。

C　Oh, there you go, it works.

喔，妳說的對，可以用了。

D   Excuse me. Hermione, I need the financial statements for the second quarter⋯

不好意思，Hermione，我需要第二季的財務報表⋯

B   Yes, Jason, and you need 20 copies of them for the meeting in the afternoon, here you go, am I right?

好的，Jason，還有你需要20份影本要在下午的會議中使用，都在這兒了，我做對了嗎？

D   Hey! You've got them all ready, thanks!

嘿！妳全都準備好了，謝啦！

B   Mr. Noah, you can't claim expenses with this kind of receipt, it will be rejected by the financial department. And there are a lot of documents piled up on your desk, so you must buckle down to office work today.

Noah先生，這一種收據是不能用來報帳的，這會被財務部門退回的。還有你桌上的文件堆積如山，所以你今天必須盡力處理辦公室的工作。

E   Ok, I will. Oh, Hermione, this office cannot function well without you.

Ok，我會的。這間辦公室沒有妳就無法正常運作。

B   Thank you for your compliment, but no is no. I must take a vacation from next week.

謝謝你的稱讚，但不行就是不行。我從下星期必須休假。

E   How did you know that I was going to talk about it?

妳怎麼知道我正要說的是這一件事呢？

B   I can read between the lines.

我聽的出你話中有話。

225

Dialog 2

A　Have you read the sales report for the third quarter? Who do you think is our biggest threat?

你有沒有看過第三季的銷售報表了？你認為誰是我們最大的威脅？

B　From those numbers, it seems like XYZ Company is our biggest competitor, and of course, the power of ABC Corporation and W Inc. can not be neglected, either.

從那些數字看來，XYZ公司是我們最大的對手，而且當然，ABC Corporation和W Inc.的實力也不容忽視。

A　I'll say! W Inc. is just a new kid on the block, I am impressed by that they get tremendous success in such a short time, and also worried about the intense competition at hand.

我同意！W Inc.只是個後起之秀，他們在這麼短的時間之內就能獲得這麼大的成功讓我印象深刻，而且也擔心即將到來的激烈競爭。

C　Here's the information about our competitors' market activities that you asked me to gather up from various sources last week.

這裡是你上星期交代我透過各種管道所收集到的我們的競爭公司的市場活動。

A　Thanks, Steve. About W Inc., what do you reckon?

謝了，Steve。關於W Inc.，你怎麼認為呢？

C　From the information I have got, W Inc. is a truly remarkable competitor, and I speculate that W Inc. will soon replace XYZ company and become our biggest threat, maybe on the next quarter.

從我所得到的資料中顯示，W Inc.是一個真正非同凡響的對手，我推測W Inc.將很快的會取代XYZ公司，並成為我們最大的威脅，或許是在下一季。

A   It's just what I thought. Joan, got any conclusion about the price?

正如我所想的。Joan，在價格的方面有任何結論嗎？

D   Sorry, chief. We can't achieve consensus with the manufacturing department. We are now trying to get more data to convince their head.

對不起，老大。我們和製造部門還未能達到共識。我們正在試著蒐集更多的資料來説服他們的上司。

A   That old fogey? Ok, if you've got any problem, just let me know. I will discuss with their head personally.

那一個老頑固？Ok，如果你有任何問題的話，就讓我知道。我會親自和他們的上司討論的。

D   Thanks, chief. One more thing about the production, we have already stepped up it.

謝了，老大。還有一件事是關於生產的，我們已經在加快生產了。

A   Great! Get a move on, everyone. I want to see the strategic marketing plan on my desk by next Monday noon. The competition never sleeps, and neither do we.

好極了！各位，動作快一點。我要在下星期一中午之前在我的桌上看到戰略行銷計畫。競爭永不停止，我們也是。

精選單字及片語

1. hand out　分發，傳遞。
Will you help me to hand out the materials for the meeting?
你可以幫我發一些開會用的資料嗎？

2. here you go　拿去吧，這是你的東西，你要的東西在這裡。除了在交付東西會說這一個片語之外，還可以用在鼓勵，稱讚上。例如下屬在策劃專案時，提出一個好的建議，這時就可以說 "Here you go."（做的好）。

3. there you go　你說的沒錯，你說的對。這個片語除了表示贊同對方之外，和 "here you go" 有相同的用法，可以在交付東西時，或是表示鼓勵上說。唯一不同的是 "there you go" 是用於事情完成後說，例如將東西已交到對方手上，交易已完成；或是下屬將專案完成，為表鼓勵時可以說 "there you go"。

4. threat(s) *n.*　威脅，恐嚇，凶兆。
The dark clouds brought the threat of rain.
烏雲是將要下雨的徵兆。

5. speculate *v.*　推測，猜測。
It would be pointless to speculate, because we know nothing about it.
妄加推測是毫無意義的，因為我們對這件事一無所知。

6. old fogey　老頑固，老古董。
Do not act like an old fogey, you must accept other's advice.
不要像個老頑固一樣，你必須接受別人的意見。

精選句子與延伸

1. Thank you for your compliment, but no is no.

謝謝你的稱讚，但不行就是不行。

和中文裡的用法相同，在英文裡也有加強語氣的用法，將自己要強調的事情在句首及句尾各放一個，中間加上be 動詞就是一種加強語氣的用法。例如同事正在喋喋不休的遊說你，而你說了 "That's enough, I'll think about it." （夠了，我會考慮的），但同事依然再接再厲的說下去，這時你就可以說 "Enough is enough." （我說夠了就是夠了），以加強的語氣來讓同事停止那個話題。其他常說的還有 "A win is a win." （贏就是贏）、"A no is a no." （不就是不），冠詞可加，可不加。

2. I can read between the lines.

我聽的出你話中有話。

read between lines 話中有話，弦外之音。這一個片語源自於戰爭時，雙方為了怕消息走漏，所以在信件上特別下了功夫，在信中寫的全是無關緊要的事情，而以特殊墨水在列與列之間寫上真正要傳達的事。之後便以 "read between the lines" 來表示瞭解對方的言外之意。

3. W Inc. is just a new kid on the block.

W Inc. 只是個後起之秀。

a new kid on the block 後起之秀，新來的菜鳥。照字面上的意思解釋為街上新搬來的孩子，用以形容最晚進入一個團體的人，而這裡指的是 W Inc. 可能是一家新的公司，也有可能是本來是從事其他的行業，而最近才跨足到這個領域。

4. I'll say!

我同意。

= I agree with you.

光看 I'll say，會很容易讓人情不自禁的想要解釋成 "我會說"，但其實這一句是表示 "我贊成" "可不是嗎" 的意思。是 "I will say the same thing" （我要說的是一樣的）。

Part Seven

業務絕對成交會話

Deal ! Absolutely Well-Done

拜訪客戶──初次見面寒暄

	Jason was holding a welcome board at the airport arrival to wait for his new client, Mr. Potter.	Jason拿著一張接機牌在機場入境大廳等候他的新客戶，Potter先生。
Jason	Excuse me, are you Mr. Potter?	不好意思，打擾了，請問你是Potter先生嗎？
Mr. Potter	Yes, I am.	是的，我就是。
Jason	How do you do, Mr. Potter. My name is Jason, the sales manager from Bestco Company.	你好，Potter先生，我的名字是Jason，是Bestco公司的銷售經理。
Mr. Potter	How do you do, Jason. I'm very glad to meet you.	你好，Jason，我非常高興能見到你。
Jason	Very glad to meet you, too. So how's the flight?	我也非常高興能見到你。所以旅途中一切都還好嗎？
Mr. Potter	Well, generally speaking, it was fine. But it's really a long distance from New York to Taipei.	嗯，整體而言還不錯。但是從紐約到台北真的是一場非常漫長的旅途。

| Jason | Yes, it is. I remember that when I first time traveled from Taipei to New York, I felt completely disoriented with the jet lag. But it seems like you don't have much trouble with jet lag, do you? | 沒錯，的確是如此。我還記得當我第一次從台北飛往紐約時，我整個人因為時差的關係而頭昏眼花的。但看起來時差對你而言好像影響並不大，是嗎？ |

| Mr. Potter | No, I don't. I don't have much trouble with jet lag, and I think that's because I'm traveling by plane very often. | 不，我沒有。時差對我的影響並不大，我想應該是我常搭飛機到各地的關係。 |

| Jason | Oh, I see. Let me help with your luggage. The hotel is already booked, let's go and check in first. You'll need some rest after such a long flight, and I will pick you up tomorrow to visit our factory and office. | 喔，我瞭解了。讓我幫你拿行李。飯店已經訂好了，讓我們先去辦理入住手續。在長途飛行之後，你將需要休息，我明天在過來接你參觀我們的工廠及辦公室。 |

| Mr. Potter | Great, thanks for the arrangement. | 好極了，謝謝你的安排。 |

| Jason | You are welcome, and this way please. | 不客氣，這邊請。 |

Dialog 2

Dennis Hart and Patrick Simmons first met and greeted in a conference.

Dennis Hart 和 Patrick Simmons在一場會議當中初次見面寒暄。

| Dennis Hart | Hello, I would like to introduce myself. My name is Dennis Hart from Bestco Company. | 哈囉，我作個自我介紹。我的名字是Dennis Hart，任職於Bestco公司。 |

Patrick	Very nice to meet you. I am Patrick Simmons from ABC International.	非常高興認識你。我是ABC國際的Patrick Simmons。
Dennis	Oh, you are from ABC International, our companies have established a cooperative partnership for a long time. This is my business card, may I have your business card, please?	喔，你在ABC國際上班，我們兩家公司長久以來都有建立合作關係。這是我的名片，能給我一張你的名片嗎？
Patrick	Yes, sure. Here's my business card. I work in the Marketing department. Dennis, I noticed that you work in the Sales department, so you must know Nelson Kim.	好的，當然可以。這裡是我的名片。我是在行銷部門工作的。Dennis，我看到你是在業務部門上班的，所以你應該認識Nelson Kim吧。
Dennis	Yes, sir. I do know Nelson, he is the top sales in our company. I'm so lucky to be in his team. He taught me a lot when I was a novice. He is a mentor to me.	是的，先生。我認識Nelson Kim，他是我們公司的頂尖業務。我非常幸運和他在同一隊上。在我還是個新手的時後，他教了我許多的東西。他是我的師傅。
Patrick	Don't call me sir, just call me Patrick. Several years ago, I got a chance to work with him, and now he is my best friend. He's the sort of man who would finish his job come hell or high water.	不用稱我先生，叫我Patrick就好。幾年前，我剛好有機會和他合作，現在他是我最好的朋友。他是那一種無論如何都會完成工作的類型。
Dennis	Yes, he certainly is.	是的，他的確是。
Patrick	Is this your first time to join this conference?	這是你第一次參加這個會議嗎？

Dennis	Yes, that's right.	是，沒錯。
Patrick	How do you find the conference?	你覺得這個會議如何呢？
Dennis	To be honest, I didn't quite catch them.	老實說，我不太懂他們說的。
Patrick	No worries, all you have to do here is to get to know other people in this conference. Try to build your business networking.	別擔心，你在這所要做的是去認識會議中其他的人。試著去建立你的事業人脈。
Dennis	Oh, I see, thanks for your advice.	喔，我懂了，謝謝你的建議。
Patrick	You are welcome, I think we'll have an cooperative opportunity in the near future.	不客氣，我想我們應該不久的將來就會有合作的機會。
Dennis	Wow, that will be great, I am looking forward to it.	哇，那就太棒了，我很期待。
Patrick	See you soon!	到時見！

💬 精選單字及片語

1. welcome board　接機牌，歡迎牌
   You should write the client's name, flight number and your company's name on the welcome board for picking up a client.
   在為客戶接機時，你應該在接機牌上寫客戶的名字，班機號碼及你公司的名稱。

2. disoriented *adj.* ＝disorientated 分不清方向或目標的，無判斷力的。在本文中解釋為因時差而造成的生理時鐘大亂所造成的頭暈眼花的現象。
   He became drunk and totally disoriented.
   他醉的一塌糊塗，完全搞不清楚東南西北。

3. jet lag　時差
   I couldn't fall asleep because of jet lag on the first might in Miami.
   在邁阿密的第一個晚上，我因為時差的緣故而無法入睡。

4. establish *vt.*　建立；開設；制定。
   He established close contact with the competitor behind my back.
   他背著我和競爭對手勾結。

5. come hell or high water　無論如何。美國俚語，這個片語可以用在句首，亦可放在句尾補述。使用時機是當要做一件事時，下定決心一定要達成，只許成功，不許失敗。類似我們所說的「上刀山，下油鍋」在所不辭的感覺。
   Come hell or high water I will get you to the examination hall on time.
   無論如何我都會準時的將你送到考場。

6. business networking　事業上的人脈，商業上的人脈。是屬於 social networking（社交人脈）的其中一種。
   Business networking is a key factor leading to business success.
   商業上的人脈是引領事業成功的關鍵因素。

精選句子與延伸

1. But it seems like you don't have much trouble with jet lag, do you?

   但看起來時差對你而言好像影響並不大，是嗎？

   句中的 "you don't have much trouble with jet lag, do you?" 是一個附加問句，類似於中文口語中常用的「對嗎？」「不是嗎？」，用以加強語氣。Jason在句中表達他認為Potter先生並不太因長途飛行而看起來氣色不佳等，再以附加問句更清楚表達他的想法。在附加問句中需注意時態與動詞的對稱，但有一個特殊用法當主詞為I，動詞為am的時後，在附加問句部分要用aren't I? 或是am I not?

   e.g. I am a good employee, aren't I? 我是一個好員工，不是嗎？

2. He taught me a lot when I was a novice.

   當我還是新手時他教了我許多的東西。

   ＝I learned a lot from Nelson when I was new to our company.

   novice(s) (n.) 初學者，新手。同義字有：beginner, tyro, newcomer etc.

   Please do have an eye on him, 'cause he is a novice.

   請一定要好好的關照他，因為他是個新人。

3. He is a mentor to me.

   他是我的師傅。

   ＝He is my mentor.

   mentor(s) (n.) （對初學者，新人等的）有經驗可信賴的人，顧問。

   在企業中，對於新員工的訓練，常會採用mentor program（工作導師計畫），以資深員工帶領新進人員的方式，藉由兩人的相處，讓新進人員更加瞭解工作內容，企業文化等。也是我們一般熟悉的在日本職場中的前輩、後輩制度，以及在歌唱選拔節目中的導師制度。

   Mentor is someone who imparts wisdom and share knowledge to a less experienced colleague.

   工作導師是傳授智慧及分享知識給資歷較淺同事的人。

Unit 37 拜訪客戶——關懷客戶近況

Secretary	General Manager's office, may I help you.	總經理辦公室，我能為您效勞嗎？
Frank	Hello, this is Frank Patterson calling from ABC Company, may I speak to Mr. Maurice, please?	哈囉，我是ABC公司的Frank Patterson，請問Maurice先生在嗎？
Secretary	Hold on a moment, please. I will switch you to the General Manager.	請稍候，我將為您轉接給總經理。
Frank	Thanks!	謝謝！
Mike	Hi, Frank, this is Mike speaking.	嗨，Frank，我是Mike。
Frank	Hi, Mike. Did you change your secretary?	嗨，Mike。你換新秘書啦？
Manager	No way, Sandy is my girl Friday, I won't let her go before my retirement. She's on vacation, and that's her assistant, Kyle.	門都沒有，Sandy是我忠心又幹練的秘書，在我退休之前都不會讓他離開的。她放假了，那是她的助理，Kyle。
Frank	Oh, I see. How's everything going?	喔，我知道了。一切都還好嗎？
Manager	It's a mess here. I can't find anything without Sandy.	這裡一團亂。沒有Sandy我什麼東西都找不到。
Frank	I totally understand your feeling.	我完全可以瞭解你的感覺。

Manager	Hey, what reminds you calling me today?	嘿，怎麼會想到打給我？
Frank	There's something I would like to talk over with you. Would sometime this week be convenient for you?	我有些事想要和你談一談。這個星期你有空嗎？
Manager	Hmm… I am not sure. I have to check my agenda first.	嗯……我不太確定。讓我先查一下工作日程表。
Frank	Of course.	當然。
Manager	Is that something momentous? You sound very serious.	是什麼嚴重的事嗎？你聽起來很嚴肅。
Frank	Well, take it easy, it's just a regular customer visit.	嗯，放輕鬆，只是例行的客戶拜訪。
Manager	Okay, let me see. Would it be all right on Wednesday morning?	Okay，讓我看一下。星期三早上可以嗎？
Frank	I have a meeting on Wednesday morning.	我星期三早上有一個會議。
Manager	Okay, how about Thursday? I am available from 11 a.m. to 2 p.m. on Thursday. Is it convenient for you?	Okay，那星期四呢？我星期四上午11點到下午2點之間有空，對你來說方便嗎？
Frank	Great, so I will be arriving at your office at 11 o'clock on Thursday morning.	好極了，那我會在星期四上午11點鐘到你的辦公室。
Manager	OK, see you then.	OK，下次見。

Dialog 2

Frank	Good morning, I am Frank Patterson from ABC Company, I have an appointment with Mr. Maurice.	早安,我是ABC公司的Frank Patterson,我和Maurice先生有約。
Receptionist	Welcome to Bestco. We have been expecting you, Mr. Patterson. Please have a seat. I'm sure Mr. Maurice's secretary will be here very soon.	歡迎光臨Bestco。我們正恭候您的光臨。Patterson先生,請坐。我肯定Marrice先生的秘書很快就會到這的。
Frank	Thank you.	謝謝你。
Receptionist	You are welcome.	不客氣。
Sandy	Mr. Patterson, I haven't seen you for a while. How are you?	Patterson先生,好一陣子沒見到您了,您好嗎?
Frank	Hi, Sandy. It's nice to see you. How's the vacation?	嗨,Sandy。真高興見到你。你的假期過得怎樣?
Sandy	It was nice. This way please, Mr. Maurice is expecting you.	很好。這裡請,Maurice先生正在等您。
Frank	Hi, Mike, my old pal, how have you been?	嗨,Mike,我的老朋友,最近過的好嗎?
Mike	Hey, Frank, not so bad and you look great.	嘿,Frank,還不錯,你看起來氣色很好。
Frank	Thanks. How's your business?	謝啦。最近生意如何?

Manager	Just checked with the operation team in the conference, and it seems everything's running smoothly. Frank, you said you have something to talk over with me, remember?	才剛在會議上和我的營運團隊確認過，看起來每件事都很順利。Frank，你說你有一件事要和我談一談，記得嗎？
Frank	Yes. Actually we are developing a new project, and I'm considering inviting you to work on it with us. But it's still a top secret in my company, so don't let the cat out of the bag.	當然記得。事實上我們正在籌畫一項新的項目，我考慮要邀你和我們一起做。但在我們公司裡，這個項目還是個最高機密，所以別洩漏秘密。
Manager	Wow, top secret, I'm so excited. No worries, your secret is safe with me.	哇，最高機密，我好激動。別擔心，我會守口如瓶的。
Frank	Of course, I know I can trust you. So you are the only one I want to work with on this new project.	當然，我知道我可以信賴你的。所以你是我唯一考慮要合作這個新項目的對象。
Manager	I have a question. Why this new project is confidential? Is that because this new project's unaccepted by the board of your company?	我有個問題。為什麼這個項目是列為機密？是不是因為你公司的董事會不通過這項專案？
Frank	Bingo! The board completely disregarded my recommendations.	賓果！董事會完全否決了我的提議。
Manager	Wow, that makes me feel more excited. Tell me all about the new project.	哇，那讓我感到更激動了。跟我說說這個項目吧。
Frank	Shall we go out and get some lunch, and we can talk about it in detail?	我們要不要出去一起用午餐，然後再討論細節呢？
Manager	Great!	好極了！

💬 精選單字及片語

1. girl Friday　忠誠，幹練的女秘書。這個片語是由魯賓遜漂流記中被魯賓遜取名為「Friday（星期五）」的忠僕而來的。他是對魯賓遜忠心耿耿，且非常能幹的得力助手，因此而被引用成形容忠心的得力助手。而 girl Friday，用我們常說的方式就是「女版星期五」。
   You really need a girl Friday, you can't do everything on your own.
   你真的需要一個忠心且能幹的女秘書，你不能做什麼事都自己來啊。

2. retirement(s) *n.*　退休
   I will devote myself to education after the retirement.
   退休後我將全心奉獻在教育上。

3. agenda　工作日程，手帳日誌。
   Let's draw up an agenda for our discussion.
   讓我們來擬定一個討論的日程表。

4. talk over　商討，商談。
   I have a very important thing to talk over with you.
   我有一件重要的是要和你商討一下。

5. confidential *adj.*　秘密的，機密的。
   She's the confidential secretary of Mr. Maurice.
   她是Maurice先生的機要秘書。

6. disregard *v.*　忽視，不顧。
   He disregarded his subordinate's advice.
   他忽視他下屬的忠告。

精選句子與延伸

1. I will switch you to the General Manager.
   我將為您轉接給總經理。
   ＝I will put you through to the General Manager.
   put through 轉接。一般電話的轉接使用的是 "put through" 這個片語。但在本句中轉接的對象是總經理，一般的高階主管大多會由秘書接聽電話並過濾後才轉給主管，所以這句中的轉接可以switch來表示。

2. Would sometime this week be convenient for you?
   這個星期你有空嗎？
   ＝When is convenient for you during this week?
   sometime(adv.)某時，改天，什麼時候。當放在名詞前時，作為形容詞使用，意思是「前任的」。
   Maybe we can go bungee jumping sometime.
   也許我們那天可以一起去高空彈跳。
   She is my sometime boss.
   她是我以前的老闆。

3. Don't let the cat out of the bag.
   別洩漏秘密。
   美國俚語。照字面的解釋為「別讓貓從袋子中出來」，將貓隱喻成秘密，請聽的人要守口如瓶，不要向其他人透露秘密。

4. No worries, your secret is safe with me.
   別擔心，我會守口如瓶的。
   ＝Don't worry, I will keep the secret.
   No worries為Don't worry的口語化說法。澳洲常用俚語，可作為別擔心或是沒問題使用，也常用對方表達感謝後，用no worries(worry) 來代替「不客氣」。

Unit 38 報價

Dialog 1

A　We are interested in all kinds of your goods, but for the first deal, we would like to order some rubber ducks in medium size, fans, and duck-shape balloons. Please quote us C.I.F. Taipei.

我們對貴公司所有的產品都很有興趣，但是第一次交易，我們想訂購中型橡皮鴨，扇子，及鴨型氣球。請以CIF台北報價給我們。

B　Would you please tell me the quantity you want to order, so that we can work out the insurance and freight charge.

你可以告訴我你所要訂購的數量嗎，這樣我們才算出所需的保險費及運送費用。

A　OK, we are going to place an order for 2,000 units of medium size rubber ducks, and 2,000 units of fans and 100 cartons of the duck shape balloons.

OK，我們要訂2000隻中號的橡皮鴨，2000支扇子及100箱的鴨型氣球。

B　OK, about the rubber duck, I would like to recommend you the small size rubber duck, that is very popular in the market, and if you order all 3 sizes, the price will be lower than you just order one certain size.

OK，關於橡皮鴨的部分，我想要跟你推薦小號的橡皮鴨，那個在市場上十分暢銷，如果你訂購全部3種尺寸的話，價錢會比你只訂一種尺寸的要低一些。

A　No, maybe next time.

不，也許下一次吧。

B　All right. Here are our F.O.B. price lists, and please allow me to inform you that all the prices are subject to our final confirmation.

好吧，這是我們的FOB價目表，還有請容我提醒你一下，所有的價格需以我方最後確認為準。

A　Yes, I do understand. Your price is quite reasonable, but I was wondering if we could get a discount. We usually get 2% or 3% discount from other suppliers.

好的，我瞭解。你們的價格還蠻合理的，但我想有沒有可能給我們折扣。我們通常從其他供應商那可以拿到百分之2-3的折扣。

B　Well, I'm afraid of that we cannot give you a discount for this time, because the quantity you want to order is not that much. Maybe you should consider my suggestion.

嗯，我恐怕這一次無法給你折扣，因為你們訂購的數量並不多。或許你應該考慮一下我的建議。

A　You mean to order rubber ducks in all 3 sizes?

你是說定3種不同尺寸的小鴨？

B　Yes. Maybe you can sell them as a set. I can give you 5% discount on this item if you purchase all 3 sizes.

對。也許你可以用整套販售的方式。如果你訂購3種不同尺寸的話，我可以在這個品項上給你百分之五的折扣。

A　Can I place an order for 1,000 units of medium size, and 500 units of both large and small size?

那我可以訂購1,000隻中號的，大的和小的各500隻嗎？

B　Hmm… all right, deal.

嗯……好吧，成交。

Dialog 2

Billy	Hi, Sophia. This is Billy Green at MP Ltd. How are you?	嗨，Sophia。我是MP Ltd。的 Billy Green。妳好嗎？
Sophia	Hi, Billy, I haven't heard from you for a long time. I'm good, thanking for asking, how about you?	嗨，Billy，我好久都沒有聽到你的消息了。我很好，謝謝關心，那你呢？
Billy	I'm surviving.	我還健在。
Sophia	Oh, seriously, are you okay?	喔，說真的，你還好吧？
Billy	I will be okay, if you give me some help.	如果妳能幫我些忙，我應該會好吧。
Sophia	Okay, Billy, what can I do for you?	好吧，Billy，我可以為你做些什麼呢？
Billy	Well, we are going to place our Christmas orders, and I was wondering if you could accept the order at the prices you quoted.	嗯，我們準備要下聖誕節的訂單，我在想妳是不是能以之前的報價來接單呢？
Sophia	I beg your pardon, but I don't remember that I have sent you any quotation recently.	請你原諒，但我不記得我最近有記任何的報價單給你啊。
Billy	No, you didn't. Oh, boy! I find it hard to speak out. Sophia, I am talking about the quotation that you emailed me a year ago.	不，你並沒有。喔，天啊，這真難啟齒。Sophia，我說的是妳一年前email 給我的報價單。
Sophia	Oh, I see. But I thought you had found a new supplier, so…	喔，我懂了。但我以為你們那時已經找到新的供貨商，所以……

Billy	Frankly speaking, my boss insisted on purchasing goods from the other supplier, I tried to convince him but to no avail. And that supplier was not that reliable and caused a lot of trouble for us. So my boss wanted me to ask you if we can get the lower price and discount as before.	坦白說，我老闆堅持要從那個供貨商那裡購買，我試著說服他但並不成功。那個供貨商不太可靠而且替我們製造的不少麻煩。所以我老闆要我問妳我們是不是能跟以前一樣拿到較低的價格及折扣。
Sophia	Well I can't promise you right now, I have to ask my boss first.	嗯，我現在不能答應你，我得先問過我的老闆。
Billy	Sure, of course.	當然。
Sophia	I have to remind you that as the wages and prices of materials have risen, so the price is a little bit higher than last year.	我必須提醒你工資及原料價格都上漲了，所以價錢方面比去年高了一些。
Billy	OK, I understand, can you give me a ballpark figure?	OK，我懂，可以給我一個大約的數據嗎？
Sophia	About 50 bucks per unit.	單價大約是50元左右。
Billy	Can you email me the quotation as soon as possible? And don't forget the discount.	妳可以盡快將報價單email給我嗎？還有別忘了折扣的事。
Sophia	Well, just because it's you, I'll do my utmost.	嗯，因為是你，我會盡力的。
Billy	Thank you so much, I owe you one. I'll buy you a dinner next time.	非常感謝，我欠妳一個人情。我下次請妳吃飯。

精選單字及片語

1. rubber duck 橡皮鴨。由於一般常見的橡皮鴨多為黃色，平底的造型，所以在台灣我們稱為「黃色小鴨」。
   We have a wide selection of rubber duck merchandise.
   我們有非常多的黃色小鴨周邊商品。

2. C.I.F. 到岸價格。為貨物成本 (Cost)，保險費 (Insurance) 及運送至買方港口的運費 (Freight) 的縮寫。
   F.O.B. 離岸價格。Free on Board 的縮寫。
   C.I.F. 及 F.O.B. 是常見的貿易條款，簡單來說 C.I.F. 就像是我們購買網拍的商品，由賣家將商品寄送至買家家中或是指定的地點，賣家在報價時，會將運費，商品保險費計入，費用由買家負擔，但聯絡快遞等的相關事項由賣家去接洽。而 F.O.B. 則像是面交，在指定地點，買家取貨後，相關的運費及責任由買家自行承擔。

3. ballpark figure 大概的數字，估計的數據。
   ballpark *adj.* 大致上的。作為名詞使用時，則是「棒球場」。
   Can you give me a ballpark figure of total sales of last month?
   妳能不能給我上個月總銷售金額的一個大概的數據？

💬 精選句子與延伸

1. Here are our F.O.B. price lists, and please allow me to inform you that all the prices are subject to our final confirmation.

   這是我們的 FOB 價目表，還有請容我提醒你一下，所有的價格需以我方最後確認為準。

   subject to 受…的約制，根據…的規定。這一個片語尤其是在商業英文中非常廣泛的被使用，可作為形容詞、副詞及動詞片語來使用。

   All applications must be subjected to careful scrutiny.

   所有的申請都必須經過仔細的審查。

2. I'm surviving.

   我還健在。

   ＝I am getting by.（我過的還好。）

   回答朋友詢問近況時，會以開玩笑的語氣來回答 "I am surviving/ I am alive."，來表示生活中雖有些小的不如意，但還能撐下去。

3. Oh, boy! I find it hard to speak out.

   喔，天啊，這真難啟齒。

   Oh, boy 這是常見的英文口頭禪，並不侷限於說話的對象是男是女，都可以說 Oh, boy! 或是 Oh, man! 類似於 Oh, my god. 的用法，也常用於自言自語中。還可以常聽到有女孩子會說 Oh, dear! 這就比較屬於女性的說法，一般男性請勿輕易嘗試。

Unit 39 詢價/議價

Dialog 1

Nancy　Hello, Pete. It is great to see you again. What can I do for you?

Pete　I have reviewed your quotation last night, and I think the price is a little bit higher than I expected.

Nancy　OK, would you please wait a moment? Let me take a quick look on it, see if I can give you a better price.

Pete　I will appreciate that very much.

Nancy　OK, I think I know what the problem is. I made this quotation according to the inquiry that your secretary emailed me the day before yesterday, and that's the best price I can offer. Some of your orders don't reach our minimum quantity per item, so the unit price will be 5% higher than the usual price.

Pete　Oh, I see. So, Nancy, please tell me what the minimum quantity of an order is?

Nancy　500 pieces per item.

哈囉，Pete。真高興又見到你。我有什麼能為你效勞的嗎？

我昨晚有看過你的報價單了，我覺得價錢比我預期中的高出了一些。

OK，可以麻煩請你一下嗎？讓我快速的瀏覽一遍，看我能不能給你好一點的價錢。

那我會非常感激。

OK，我想我知道問題出在哪了。我這份估價單是根據前天你的秘書email給我的詢價單來做的，而且我給你的價格十分的優惠。你有一些商品的下單數量並沒有達到最小訂購量的要求，所以其單價比原來的價格多了百分之5。

喔，我瞭解了。所以，Nancy，請告訴我你們的最小訂購量是多少？

每一個品項500件。

Pete	If we place a large order, can you give us a quantity discount?	如果我大量訂購的話，你可以給我大量購買的折扣嗎？
Nancy	Yes, sure. If you place more than 1000 pieces per item, and we will give you 10% discount.	可以啊，當然。如果你每一種商品訂購超過1000件的話，我們可以給你打9折。
Pete	1000 pieces for per item, I have to think about it.	每一項1000件，我必須考慮一下。
Nancy	No problem.	沒問題。
Pete	Nancy, you should know there are so many uncertain risks to introduce products into a new market, to limit the risk, I would like to test the waters first. Is that possible if I order 500 pieces per item, and you still give me the quantity discount for the first transaction between us?	Nancy，你應該知道將產品引進到一個新的市場時總有許多不能確定的風險，為了將低風險，我想先試試市場的反應。有沒有可能為了我們之間的第一次合作，我每種商品都訂購500件，而你還是給我大量折扣呢？
Nancy	All right, for the first transaction!	好吧，為了第一次合作！

Dialog 2

Lin	Hello, Mars Company, what can I do for you?	哈囉，Mars公司，我有什麼可以為您效勞的？
Collins	Hi, this is Sean Collins calling from ABC Company, may I speak to Mr. Lin, please?	嗨，我是ABC公司的Sean Collins，請問林先生在嗎？

Lin	Hi, Mr. Collins, this is Lin speaking.	嗨，Collins先生，我就是。
Collins	Hi, Mr. Lin, we have received your quotation by email, and you are very speedy.	嗨，林先生，我們已經收到你email過來的報價單了，你的動作真快。
Lin	That's my duty.	這是我應該做的。
Collins	I would like to get the ball rolling by talking about the price.	那我就直接和你討論價錢的問題了。
Lin	Yes, please, I would be glad to answer any questions you may have.	好的，請，我很樂意回答你所有的問題。
Collins	OK, first, I have to admit that your product is really great, and it's more eye-catching than others.	好的，首先，我必須承認你們的產品非常棒，比其他家的產品都要更吸睛。
Lin	Thanks, that is a great compliment.	謝謝，我深感榮幸。
Collins	But I have a concern about the price you quote.	但我對你報的價錢有些疑慮。
Lin	Mr. Collins, I think you know that our product has a steady demand in the global market, and the quality is definitely excellent. The price I quote is reasonable. And of course, if you can place a larger order, then I will give you a discount on it.	Collins先生，我想你應該知道我們的產品在全球市場上有穩定的需求量，品質極佳。我的報價也很合理。當然，如果你能大量訂購的話。我能給你折扣。
Collins	I'd like to have a 10% discount.	我想要的是百分之10的折扣。

Lin	Gee, that's not possible. Our research costs are very high, and I don't know how we can cover the expenses with your offer. To speak frankly, this price will leave us no profit to speak of.	哎，這是不可能的。我們的研究費用很高，你出的價格都不夠去攤平那些費用。老實說，這個價錢對我們來說毫無利潤可言。
Collins	But what if we said we want to place more than 20,000 pieces in the next 3 months, and we guarantee that we will have a great number of orders at least for one year.	但如果我們在接下來的三個月會訂購至少20,000件呢？而且我們保證會大量採購至少一年。
Lin	I have to think over your offer.	我得仔細考慮你的出價。
Collins	Sure, no problem.	當然，沒問題。
Lin	Ok, you sold me on your guarantee, but you have to guarantee that on paper, then I think we can take your offer.	好吧，你用你的保證說服了我，但你必須以書面形式保證，那我想我們可以接受你的議價。
Collins	Great, I will prepare the agreement, and I'll see you next time.	好極了，我會準備協議書，那我們下次見。

💬 精選單字及片語

1. quotation(s) *n.* 估價單，行情；引文，引用語。
   Would you please give me a quotation for the car?
   你能不能給我一張汽車的估價單？

2. inquiry(inquiries) *n.* 詢價單，詢問；調查。
   We appreciate your inquiry of August 20 about our goods.
   感謝您在8月20日對我們產品的詢價單。

3. quantity discount 大量購買的折扣，大量折扣。
   We intend to place regular large orders, and would like to know what quantity discount you allow.
   本公司將定期的大量訂購，並希望知道貴公司能給的大量折扣為多少。

4. get the ball rolling 使開始，開始著手。
   Let's get the ball rolling on this plan.
   讓我們從這個計畫開始著手吧。

5. sell someone on 以…說服某人。
   He sold me on his sincerity.
   他用他的誠意說服了我。

6. on paper 以書面形式。
   It is a perfect scheme on paper, but will it work in practice?
   書面上的計畫看起來很不錯，但實際上的可行度呢？

💬 精選句子與延伸

1. Please tell me what the minimum quantity of an order is?
    請告訴我你們的最小訂購量是多少？
    ＝Please let me know the minimum quantity for each order.
    minimum quantity 最小訂購量。
    What is the minimum quantity of an order for your goods?
    訂購貴公司的商品最小的訂購量是多少呢？

2. Nancy, you should know there are so many uncertain risks to introduce products into a new market, to limit the risk, I would like to test the waters first.
    Nancy，你應該知道將產品引進到一個新的市場時總有許多不能確定的風險，為了將低風險，我想先試試市場的反應。
    introduce into 引進
    We have to introduce this new idea into our business.
    我們必須將這一個新觀念帶入我們的事業。
    test the waters 測試市場反應。這個片語也是我們常說的「試（市場）水溫」。

3. That's my duty.
    這是我應該做的。
    ＝That is my pigeon.
    be someone's pigeon 是某人的事，職責。這個片語多用於說英式英文的國家，pigeon是由pidgin這個字而來。pidgin是在19世紀初期時，英文的business在中國的訛音字，現在也有「洋涇濱英文」的意思。

4. Thanks, that is a great compliment.
    謝謝，我深感榮幸。
    compliment指的是稱讚，恭維，本句的字面翻譯為「那是一個很好的稱讚」，但在中文裡，我們很少用這樣的說法，所以用「深感榮幸」比較貼近我們的語法。

Unit 40 討論新專案

Dialog 1

Mike	Now you can tell me more about your new secret project.	現在你可以跟我多聊聊你的神秘新專案了吧。
Frank	Yeah, I would glad to. You are my fat cat.	當然,我很樂意。你可是我的金主。
Mike	It's my honor.	是我的榮幸。
Frank	Okay, let me tell you this, I think you should know that the reason why we are ahead of our rivals, because our products have advance technology.	Okay,讓我告訴你,我想你應該知道我們一直能領先我們的競爭對手的原因是因為我們的產品採用的是先進的技術。
Mike	Yes, I do know that, and…	對,我知道,然後……
Frank	Let me finish my story. Several months ago, our team had a major breakthrough in our advanced technology.	讓我說完。幾個月前,我們的團隊在我們的先進技術上有重大的突破。
Mike	What kind of breakthrough you are talking about?	你說的是怎樣的突破?
Frank	Basically, it's in the design. I will show you. Here is our patented design.	基本上,是在設計上面的。我讓你看看。這是我們的已申請了專利的設計圖。

Mike	Wow, you acted so fast, you already got the patent on this design.	哇，你動作真快，你已經取得設計的專利了。
Frank	Yes, I got this just before I met you in your office, and it's still hot.	對，在去你的辦公室見你前才拿到的，還熱的呢。
Mike	So why this new project's unaccepted by the board since you already got the patent?	既然你已經拿到專利，那這個新專案怎麼會不被董事會通過呢？
Frank	We'll need a large amount of capital before launching into formal manufacture. Besides, our board considered that we are already in the vanguard with our existing technology, no need to pour money into research and development.	在正式生產之前，我們需要大筆的資金。除此之外，我們的董事會認為我們現有的技術已經是在領導的地位了，不需要在研究發展上頭投入大把金錢。
Mike	I disagree with them. Investment in the research and development is always necessary.	我不同意他們的看法。在研究發展上的投資總是需要的。
Frank	Same here.	我也是這樣想的。
Mike	How do you reckon up the new project?	那你怎麼看這一個新專案？
Frank	It will be profitable. We need about 5 months to launch the new product. And then we will corner the market for at least 5 years with this new technology.	它是有利潤的。我們需要大約5個月的時間來推出這項新產品。然後有這項新技術將能讓我們獨占市場最少5年。
Mike	Okay, I'm in.	Okay，我參加。
Frank	Welcome aboard!	歡迎加入！

Dialog 2

Ryan	Hello, Scarlette, this is Ryan from XYZ Group. How's everything going?	哈囉，Scarlette，我是XYZ集團的Ryan。一切都好嗎？
Scarlette	Oh, terrible, it's a mess here. I was drowned in work.	喔，糟透了，這裡一團亂。我快要被工作給淹沒了。
Ryan	You shouldn't be so hard on yourself.	妳不應該給自己這麼大的壓力。
Scarlette	Thanks for being so understanding, so I can get more time for the new project?	謝謝你這麼諒解，所以在新專案上我能有多一些的時間囉？
Ryan	Haha, I'm so sorry. I can't do that, we still need to finish the new project on time.	哈哈，我很抱歉。我沒辦法做到，我們還是要如期做完新專案。
Scarlette	OK, I knew it. All joking apart, what can I do for you?	OK，我就知道。說正經的，我能為你做些什麼嗎？
Ryan	Well, I would like to discuss with you and your team about the new project sometime next week. Do you have time to meet?	嗯，我想和妳及妳的團隊在下星期某個時間討論一下新專案的事。你們有空嗎？
Scarlette	Well, I'm not sure, let me check my calendar.	嗯，我不太確定，讓我查一下我的日程表。
Ryan	Sure, no problem.	當然，沒問題。
Scarlette	Hmm… I am free on Monday afternoon from 2p.m. to 3 p.m., is it convenient for you?	嗯……我在星期一下午2點到3點有空，這時間對你來說方便嗎？
Ryan	Nope, I have a meeting at that time.	不行，我那個時候要開會。

Scarlette	Uh... How about Friday afternoon? My team and I have a meeting about the new project at half past one in the afternoon. I think you can join us, if you don't mind.	喔……那星期五下午呢？我的團隊和我在下午1點半時要開會討論新專案的事。我想你可以參加，如果你不介意的話。
Ryan	No, not at all. It's Okay with me, and I would like to show you some related charts, so is there a projector in the meeting room?	不會，一點也不。那時間我可以參加，還有我想要給你們看一下相關的數據圖，所以在會議室中有投影機嗎？
Scarlette	Yes, there is one, but it's a little bit old, so you better bring your own laptop or flash drive.	有，有一個，不過有點舊，所以你最好帶你的筆記型電腦或是隨身碟來。
Ryan	OK, I got it. I will be arriving at your office around 1 pm, because I have to discuss with you about the new project in private. It's about the reshuffle.	OK，收到。我會在下午1點左右到妳的辦公室，因為我想要私底下和妳討論一下新專案的事。是有關人事異動的。
Scarlette	Well, why don't we make an appointment for lunch?	嗯，那要不我們約在午餐時間？
Ryan	That would be terrific.	那再好也不過了。
Scarlette	OK, I'll see you on next Friday at a quarter past 12. I'll make a reservation, and text you the address of the restaurant.	OK，那我跟你約在下星期五12點15分見。我會先預約，然後傳簡訊給你餐廳的地址。
Ryan	OK, see you then.	OK，那下次見。

💬 精選單字及片語

1. fat cat　大亨，有錢的人。一般是指肥貓，但有時是指在政治活動中金援的大亨。
   The boss of that edible oil factory is a fat cat businessman.
   那一家食用油工廠的老闆是一個有錢有勢的生意人。

2. ahead of　在…之前
   We worked hard to finish our job ahead of schedule.
   我們努力的工作，在預定的時間前將工作完成。

3. vanguard(s) *n.*　先鋒，領導者。
   They are in the vanguard of technological advance.
   他們技術進步上具有領導性的地位。

4. drown *v.*　淹沒；淹死。
   I tried to recollect things and drowned myself in them.
   我試著回想過去的事，並沈浸在其中。

5. reshuffle(s) *n.*　改組；重新洗牌。用於公司行政事務上，則大多是指人事上的異動。
   The new CEO decided to reshuffle the top management of the company.
   新上任的執行長決定重新改組公司的管理高層。

6. text *v.*　傳簡訊。text 原本只做名詞使用，是指課文、原文等，在發明了行動電話的簡訊功能之後，才有了動詞的新用法。而一般常見的 text message 可解釋成名詞「簡訊」及動詞「傳簡訊」。
   It is not allowed to text during the meeting.
   在會議中是不准傳簡訊的。

精選句子與延伸

1. Same here.
   我也是這樣想的。
   ＝Me, too.
   當說到「我也是」的時候，應該不自覺的就會說出 "me, too"，而這裡的 "same here" 則是比較有老外味道的說法，而讓我想到以前唸書時當有人提出建議，而第二人附議說 "me, too" 時，總會有第 3 個人說 "me three"，接下來就沒完沒了。

2. Okay, I'm in. Welcome aboard!
   Okay，我參加。歡迎加入。
   I'm in.＝Include me. 算我一份。而 "Welcome aboard"，通常是被用在歡迎上船，上飛機，及上車的旅客；用在要一起工作的夥伴上，則有我們中文裡「同舟共濟」的感覺。

3. You shouldn't be so hard on yourself.
   妳不應該給自己這麼大的壓力。
   也可解釋成「你不要對自己這麼嚴格」，通常是當對方表示自己的壓力太大，用於安慰對方，讓對方感覺好些，是美國俚語。

4. My team and I have a meeting about the new project at half past one in the afternoon.
   我的團隊和我在下午 1 點半時要開會討論新專案的事。
   除了一般幾點幾分的講法，在英文中時間的敘述，還會常用到half及quarter，分別代表 30 分鐘及 15 分鐘，例如 3 點 45 分，我們會說 "a quarter to 4"（還有 15 分鐘就 4 點了）。也有再幾分鐘就幾點，例 "2 to 5"（再 2 分鐘就 5 點了）或是幾點過幾分，例 "2 past 5"（5 點 2 分了）。

產品介紹

Dialog 1

Kimi Hi, Mr. Johnson, very nice to meet you, my name is Kimi.

Mr. Johnson Hi, Kimi. Very nice to meet you, too. Let's talk turkey. Lately I have found that my company morale is at an all time low. What can your firm do to help my business back on track?

Kimi You definitely made a right move by choosing us. Here's our brochure, our primary business and counseling services we can provide are all detailed in this brochure. In this case, I'll suggest the intensive interactive human resources workshops for your company. Our firm will customize, create and conduct the workshops to raise staff morale.

Jenny Well, that sounds great, anything else?

嗨，Johnson先生，非常高興見到你，我的名字是Kimi。

嗨，Kimi。我也非常高興能見到妳。我有話就直說了。最近我發現我們公司的士氣空前的低落。你們公司可以做些什麼來幫助我的公司重上軌道呢？

選擇我們絕對是你最正確的選擇。這裡是我們的介紹手冊，在手冊當中有詳細的列出我們主要的業務及我們所提供的咨詢服務。在這種情形下，我會建議貴公司應該要有密集互動的人力資源研討學習會。我們的公司將會以客製化的方式，策劃，及安排研討學習會來提升員工的士氣。

嗯，聽起來還不錯，還有其他的嗎？

Kimi	Before conducting the workshop, you may invest in more plants, according to our experience, one of the most cost-effect ways of raising staff morale is by placing more potted plants in the office.	在實施研討學習會之前，你可以花些錢購買植物，根據我們的經驗，在辦公室中擺放更多的盆栽有助於提升員工士氣，是一種符合成本效益的方法。
Jenny	That's easy. If the staff morale can be improved simply by placing more plants, why should I need the workshop?	這很簡單。如果員工士氣能簡單的僅僅靠擺放多一些植物就能改善的話，那我為什麼還需要研討學習會呢？
Kimi	That's not the best way for the long-term development, Mr. Johnson. Nothing comes out of a can.	Johnson先生，這並不是一個對於長期發展的最好的方法。世上沒有現成的簡單解決方法。
Jenny	Yeah, you are right. It seems that my employees are having trouble to work as a team, and not to mention dreadful mistakes in work.	好吧，妳是對的。因為看起來我的員工在團隊合作上有很大的問題，在工作上的嚴重過失就更不用說。
Kimi	Well, I think you can count on us, we have years of experience tailoring workshop for the companies just like yours.	好，我認為你是可以信賴我們的，我們有多年的經驗專門為像你這樣的公司量身定做研討學習會。
Jenny	My heart is lightened already since I have confided my trouble to you.	在我和妳說了我的問題之後，我心中的大石頭終於可以放下了。
Kimi	That's what we're here for. We are at your service anytime.	那就是我們公司的宗旨。我們隨時都準備為你服務。

Dialog 2

Salesman	Excuse me, ma'am, do you have a minute? I would like to give you a demonstration of our latest and best selling product. The whole new Easie Mop.	不好意思，女士，請問妳有時間嗎？我想要為妳展示一下我們最新，最熱賣的商品。全新的超好拖。
Candice	Yeah, I guess I have a few minutes. Is that a mop?	好，我想我有一點時間。那是拖把嗎？
Salesman	Yes, it is. But it is much than an ordinary mop. Let me show you. As you can see here, the Easie Mop has a 360 degree swivel yarn disc and it allows you to clean hard-to-reach area thoroughly, such as the corners, narrow spaces. And it's also a multi-purpose cleaning solution, you can use it to clean glass windows, cabinet tops, fans, air cons and etc. It is suitable for wet or dry cleaning, and ideal for various surfaces and floors, and it also can be used in car wash and polish.	對，沒錯。但它並不只是隻普通的拖把。讓我展示給妳看。妳可以看到，這個超好拖有一個可以360度旋轉的布盤，可以讓妳徹底的清潔一般不容易清到的地方，像是角落，窄小的空間。而且它還可以作為多功能的清潔工具，妳可以用它來擦玻璃窗，櫃子的上方，電風扇，冷氣機等等。它可以乾濕兩用，適用於各式各樣的表面及地板，甚至還可以用在洗車及打蠟上。
Candice	Wow, that sounds great. What's that pail for?	哇，聽起來真棒。那個水桶是做什麼用的？

Salesman	This pedal pail is included in the Easie Mop set. You know what, one of the cleaning chores I hate most was mopping the floor. My hands got wet and dirty when wringing the mop head. Not to mention the winter. With the pedal pail, you don't have to wring the mop by your hands any more, just simply step on the pedal to spin the mop clean and dry.

這個腳踏式水桶是包含在超好拖的組合中的。妳知道嗎，我以前最討厭做的清潔工作中就是拖地。在擰拖把頭時會弄髒及弄濕我的手。在冬天時就更不用說了。有了這一個腳踏式水桶，妳就再也不用用妳的手來擰拖把了，只要輕輕鬆鬆的踏這個踏板就能將拖把旋轉乾淨及脫水。

Candice	That's good, I don't like mopping either. I think I might want a set. How much for a set?

很不錯，我也不喜歡拖地。我想我要一組。一組多少錢呢？

Salesman	Here comes the most important part, the Easie Mop set is affordable and economical. We are doing a special promotion of the Easie Mop set this month, you can have the Easie Mop and the pedal pail with 5 yarn discs for just NT$990.

我們說到重點了，這個超好拖組經濟又實惠。我們這個月有在做超好拖組合的特別優惠，妳可以得到這一個超好拖，腳踏式水桶還有5個布盤只要990元。

Candice	OK, I'll get a set, please.

OK，麻煩請給我一組。

精選單字及片語

1. morale *n.* 士氣。
The layoff news chilled the morale of the employees.
裁員的消息造成員工的士氣低落。

2. dreadful *adj.* 糟糕的，可怕的。
The way they treat their staff is dreadful.
他們對待員工的方式非常的糟糕。

3. tailor *v.* 調整使適應，為…定做。tailor-made *adj.* 量身定做的，特製的。
She seems tailor-made for this job.
她看起來非常適合這份工作。

4. demonstration(s) *n.* 示範；示威遊行。
Please allow me to give you a demonstration.
請容許我為您示範。
The demonstration erupted into violence.
示威遊行中傳出暴動。

5. pail(s) *n.* 桶子。
Education is not the filling of a pail, but the lighting of the fire.
教育不是灌滿一桶水，而是點燃一把火。

6. wring *v.* 絞，擰，扭乾。
Can you wring juice from a tangerine with only one hand?
你可以只用一隻手將橘子榨出汁來嗎？

💬 精選句子與延伸

1. Let's talk turkey.

   我有話就直說了。

   talk turkey 照字面的解釋是談論火雞，真正的意思是「打開天窗說亮話」，是美國俚語。據說是在美國殖民時期，有一個白人和一個印地安人去打獵，打到了 3 隻鳥及 2 隻火雞，白人客氣的說 "You take 3 birds, and I only take 2."（你拿 3 隻鳥，我只拿 2 隻。）印地安人便回他 "Stop talking birds, talk turkey"（別談鳥的事，來談談火雞吧。），之後便被引伸為坦白說，有話直說的意思。

2. Nothing comes out of a can.

   世上沒有現成的簡單解決方法。

   "nothing comes out of a can" 沒有什麼事是會直接從罐子中出來的。不管如何，還是要有開罐的動作，用以指「事情沒有那麼簡單，要花一些功夫來解決」。

3. I would like to give you a demonstration of our latest and best selling product.

   我想要為妳展示一下我們最新，最熱賣的商品。

   ＝I want to show you our latest and the most popular product.

   best selling 最暢銷的，最紅的。

   This is the best selling item in this line.

   在同類產品當中，這一款式最暢銷的。

4. You know what, one of the cleaning chores I hate most was mopping the floor.

   妳知道嗎，我以前最討厭做的清潔工作中就是拖地。

   you know what 常可在口語中聽到這一句，是「你知道嗎？」的意思＝ "do you know?"，也可以說 "guess what"。

   chore(s) (n.) 家務；瑣事；苦差事，討厭的工作。

   It's such a chore to mop in the winter.

   在冬天拖地是一件苦差事。

Unit 42 商品售後服務

Dialog 1

A　Excuse me.

不好意思。

B　Good afternoon, ma'am. May I help you?

午安，女士。有什麼我能效勞的嗎？

A　Yes, please. The thing is that I bought this skirt here several days ago, and I found the saleslady got me the wrong size.

有的，要麻煩妳。事情是這樣的我幾天前在這裡買了一件裙子，然後我發現售貨小姐給了我錯誤的尺寸。

B　Ok, no problem, we can exchange one for you immediately, what size would you like?

好的，沒有問題，我們可以馬上為您做更換，您要的尺寸是多大呢？

A　I want the size L.

我要L尺碼的。

B　But this skirt is size L. Have you tried it on for size before purchasing?

但這一件裙子是L尺寸的。您在購買前有先試穿合適的尺寸嗎？

A　Yes, I have tried the size L on and that was fit. But this one is too small for me.

有，我有試穿L尺寸的，而且那一件很合適。但這一件對我來說太小了。

B　Ok, would you please wait for a moment? I'll handle that for you. Please have a seat, and would you like to have coffee or tea?

好的，那可以麻煩您稍待一會嗎？我來為您處理。這裡請坐，您要不要來杯咖啡或是茶呢？

A   That's ok.

B   Ma'am, I think I know what the problem is. This skirt is mislabeled, it should be the size S. I'm very sorry to be causing you so much trouble.

A   That's okay.

B   I'll change you a new one immediately. Please wait for a moment.

A   Thanks.

B   I am terribly sorry, ma'am. We now only have one size L, but it's blue.

A   I don't like blue.

B   I will get a transfer from the allocation of other shops. It will take about 3 days. Is that convenient for you, ma'am? Or, I can send the skirt by express to your place.

A   In fact, I will leave the country tomorrow. I would really prefer a refund.

B   No problem, ma'am. Please give me your receipt, and I'll process the return for you.

不用了。

女士，我想我知道問題出在哪裡了。這一件裙子的尺碼標錯了，這應該是S尺寸的。我非常抱歉造成您的困擾。

沒關係。

我立刻為您更換一件新的。請稍等一下。

謝謝。

我感到十分的抱歉，女士。我們現在只剩下一件L尺碼的，但是藍色的。

我不喜歡藍色。

我將為您從其他的店調貨。大概需要3天的時間。這對您來說方便嗎，女士？或是我可以為您用快遞寄出這一件裙子到您的府上。

事實上，我明天就要離開這個國家了。我希望退款。

沒有問題，女士。請給我您的收據，我將幫您辦理退貨。

Dialog 2

Mr. Furton	Excuse me, Mr. Holmes, I would like to talk to you about quality of 300 cartons of cigarboxes.	不好意思，Holmes先生，我想和你談有關那300箱雪茄盒的品質問題。
Mr. Holmes	Yes, sure. Is there anything wrong?	好的，當然。有什麼問題嗎？
Mr. Furton	They reached us about a week ago, and they were examined immediately after arrival. We found that about 30% of them were moldy, we can not accept them in this state, and they are not qualified for sale.	它們在約一個星期前到貨，在抵達之後立刻進行檢驗。我們發現大概有30%的都發霉了，我們無法接受這樣的狀態，這樣的品質不能販售。
Mr. Holmes	But we haven't got any complaint of this kind before. Our cigarboxes have a worldwide reputation for good quality. Would you mind showing me the evidence you've got?	但我們從來沒有遇到這類型的抱怨。我們的雪茄盒的好品質是享譽全球。你介意給我看一下你們的證據嗎？
Mr. Furton	No, not at all. Here's the survey report by an authoritative laboratory, whose testimony is definitely reliable.	不，一點也不。這裡是一個權威實驗室的檢驗報告，他們的證詞是絕對可靠的。
Mr. Holmes	Ok, let me have a look. Did your surveyors mention anything about the damage?	Ok，讓我看一下。你們的檢驗人員有提到任何相關的損傷嗎？

Mr. Furton	Here is the statement. It said that there's no damage in the carton at the time of survey. So the reason of the damage might be that cigarboxes were not completely dried before shipping.	這裡是相關的陳述。有提到在檢驗時，木箱是完整無缺的。所以有可能是因為雪茄盒在出貨前並沒有完全的乾燥。
Mr. Holmes	Well, as you know, our products had been adequately tested before being put on the market. We had the inspection certificate of this consignment which issued by the Commodity Inspection Bureau, it said the goods were well dehydrated, and up to standard for export. Besides, you bought the goods F.O.B. and on shipping quality, not on landed quality, therefore we can't accept your claim for compensation for loss incurred in transit. In my opinion, your claim should be refered to the insurance company.	嗯，如你所知，我們的產品在上市前都有通過完整的檢驗。我們還有商品檢驗局所核發的這一批貨物的檢驗證明。上面說，貨物是良好防潮的，達到出貨的標準。除此之外。你們是以離岸價格購入這批貨品，是以裝船品質，而不是到岸品質為準，因此我們無法接受你對於運輸中所產生的損失的賠償要求。我認為，你應該向保險公司求償。
Mr. Furton	I have already contacted with the underwriter, but they refused to accept the liability.	我已經和保險公司聯絡過了，但他們拒絕承擔責任。
Mr. Holmes	So I guess you didn't insure against the damage by sweating.	所以我猜你們並沒有保受潮險。
Mr. Furton	Yes, you are right. Live and learn, it's a lesson to us.	沒錯，你說對了。真的是活到老，學到老，這對我們來說是個教訓。

271

💬 精選單字及片語

1. try on 試穿;使受審。
   I tried on the pants, but they were too tight.
   我試穿了這件褲子,但它太緊了。
   She was tried on charges of spying for foreigners.
   她被指控為外國人從事間諜活動而受審。

2. mislabel *v.* 貼錯標籤(不僅指商品,也可用於指人或事因為刻板印象而被錯貼標籤)。
   This product was accidentally mislabeled as 50% off.
   這個產品不小心被錯標成5折。

3. allocation(s) *n.* 配額。
   Sugar is under allocation during the war time.
   糖在戰爭時期是採配給的。

4. moldy *adj.* 發霉的。
   We regret to inform you that the goods arrive in a moldy condition.
   我們遺憾的告知貴公司,貨物抵達時已呈現發霉狀態。

5. authoritative *adj.* 權威的,官方的。
   As an authoritative magazine, we strive to conduct exclusive reports.
   身為權威性雜誌,我們力求傳遞獨家報導。

6. underwriter(s) *n.* 保險業者,保險公司。
   Insurance contract is conclude by the policy-holder and the underwriter.
   保險合約是由被保險人及保險公司共同訂立的。

精選句子與延伸

1. That's okay.

   不用了。

   = No, thanks.

   當回答 "that's okay" 的時候，帶有 "沒關係"， "無所謂" 的意思，跟只回答 "Okay" 是相反的意思，所以在詢問對方要不要喝東西或是做什麼事的時候，對方如果回答 "that's ok"，那就代表 "我這樣就好，甭操心招呼" 的意思。

2. I think I know what the problem is.

   我想我知道問題出在哪裡了。

   本句是將一個問句併入一個句子中，被稱為是間接問句。在這一種句型當中，需特別注意的是問句中動詞或是助動詞的位置需擺放在主詞的後面，例如本句中的問句應該是 "what is the problem"，在併入句子後，is 改放置在 the problem 的後面，在英文書寫上需特別注意，而口語上則沒有這麼多限制。

3. Live and learn, it's a lesson to us.

   真的是活到老，學到老，這對我們來說是個教訓。

   live and learn 是一個片語，常被翻成 "活到老，學到老"，這個片語是指因為經驗而獲得知識，碰上了才知道，通常帶有驚訝的感覺。與 "活到老，學到老" 的意思相同，但在前面加上 "真是" 或是寫成 "真是活一天，學一天"，比較貼切英文中的口吻。

   lesson 在這裡作為 "教訓" 來解釋。本句的中文翻譯也可以寫作 "對我們而言是寶貴的一課"。

跟單/追單

Jenny	Mr. Myer, shall we talk about the packing?	Myer先生，我們可以談一談包裝的事嗎？
Mr. Myer	Yes, of course, I am sure that you've already received the packaging specification of the product.	好啊，當然可以。我確信妳應該已經收到商品的包裝規格了。
Jenny	Yes, I've received the email from your secretary last night, and here's the sample of packing.	是的，我昨晚就已經收到你的秘書傳過來的email了，這裡是包裝的樣品。
Manager	Wow, you are so speedy.	哇，你的動作真快。
Jenny	I thought you might be here today to inspect the production line, so I got everything ready beforehand.	我想你今天可能會來這裡視察生產線，所以我事先將所有東西先準備好。
Manager	Great, show me the sample, please.	很好，請讓我看看樣品。
Jenny	Here's the sample. As you can see, we have made a lot of improvement in packing to meets your requirement.	這裡是樣品。正如你所看到的，我們在包裝上面做很多改進來達到你的要求。
Manager	Quite nice. Look at this beautiful design and the bright color, it looks great, but…it seems like lack something, don't you think so?	很不錯。看看這個漂亮的設計及明亮的顏色，它看起來還不錯，但是……看起來好像少了點什麼，妳覺得呢？

Jenny	Same here. May I suggest adding a little eye candy design to the packing? For example, your company's new logo.	我也有同樣的感覺。我可不可建議在這個包裝上加上一個搶眼些的設計。例如,你們公司的新標誌。
Manager	I like your idea, let's do it. A well-designed package helps sell the goods, so the products must not only be excellent in quality, but also attractive in appearance.	我喜歡妳的主意,我們就這樣做吧。一個設計精緻的包裝有助於商品的銷售,所以除了產品本身的品質要卓越之外,在外觀上也要引人注目。
Jenny	Yes, I understand. It is our policy to render the best service and product, and fully meet customer needs and expectations. We will make your products not only appeal to the eye but also to the purse.	是的,我瞭解。我們公司的宗旨是要為我們的客戶提供最棒的產品及服務,全面滿足顧客的需求及期望。我們會讓你的產品除了能吸引目光之外,還能吸引錢包。
Manager	If so, that'll be wonderful!	如果能這樣的話,那就太好了!

Dialog 2

| Kidman | Hello, Mr. Taylor. This is Jamie Kidman calling ABC Corp. | 哈囉,Taylor先生。我是ABC公司的Jamie Kidman。 |
| Taylor | Hi, Ms. Kidman. What can I do for you? | 嗨,Kidman小姐。我有什麼能為你效勞的嗎? |

Kidman	The thing is like this, we have not received your order since last April, and my manager has asked me for many times. We would like to find out what the trouble has been. Was our service not satisfactory to you or did we do something wrong? And I was wondering if you could tell me the reason.	事情是這樣的，我們從四月開始就沒有接到你們的訂單了，我的經理已經問過我好幾次了。我們想要知道是不是有什麼問題。是你們對我們的服務不夠滿意還是我們做錯了什麼事嗎？我想知道你是否能告訴我原因呢？
Taylor	Well, Ms. Kidman, actually I am not quite sure about the reason. This decision is straight from the top, and I have no right to against them.	嗯，Kidman小姐，事實上我並不太確定原因。這是上面的人所做的決定，我沒有權力去反對。
Kidman	Please, Mr. Taylor. We really don't want to lose this business. I might get fired if I can't get this business back.	拜託，Taylor先生。我們真的不想失去這一筆生意。我可能會被開除如果我無法重新獲得這筆生意的話。
Taylor	Hmm… As I know, our boss is very old-fashioned, and always order goods from a selected group of suppliers. So we don't change our suppliers easily. He expects absolute the best price possible. A little bird told me that several months ago, my boss found out one of our competitors got an even better price from your company.	嗯……據我所知，我們老闆是一個念舊的人，總是會和固定的供應商訂購商品。所以我們並不輕易的更換供應商。他希望他拿到的絕對是最好的價錢。有人跟我說在幾個月前，我老闆發現我們的競爭公司從你們公司拿到了更低的價錢。

Kidman	But that's not possible. We always consider your company as our most valuable client, and I always quote you the best price.	但那是不可能的。你們公司被認為是我們最重視的客戶，而且我總是報給你們最好的價格。
Taylor	Yes, I know. But I suggest you ask your manager to figure this situation out.	是啊，我知道。但我建議妳去問問妳的經理，了解一下情況。
Kidman	Does the information come from a reliable source?	消息來源可靠嗎？
Taylor	Yes, and it's true, I heard it straight from the horse's mouth!	可靠，而且是真的。這消息絕對是可靠的！
Kidman	Mr. Taylor, thank you very much, I owe you a favor.	Taylor先生，非常謝謝你，我欠你一個人情。
Taylor	No problem.	不客氣。

💬 精選單字及片語

1. specification(s) *n.* 規格，詳細敘述，說明書。
   Do you have a product of this specification?
   你有沒有這一種規格的產品？

2. eye candy 吸引目光；花俏的事物；賞心悅目的俊男美女。由於花俏的事物或是俊男美女等在刻板印象中總會有華而不實評價，所以有時 eye candy 也會被人用以指稱華而不實的事物。
   Oh, my gosh, look at the sunset, its eye candy.
   喔，我的天啊，看看那夕陽，它的光彩奪目。

3. render *v.* 提供（服務）；給予（幫助）。
   She needed him to hear her out and render advice.
   她需要他把她的話聽完並提出意見。

4. this one's straight from the top 這是直接由上頭交代的。在這裡的 top 指的可以是父母，老師，或是老闆等。可以藉此表達這一件事的重要性，也可以表示這個決定跟自己無關。

5. the best price 最好的價錢。也可以解釋成最低的價錢，取決於對方是買家或是賣家，對於買家而言，價錢當然是越低越好，而對於賣家，則是越高越好。
   This is the best price I can offer.
   這是我可以報的最低的價錢。（對買家說）

6. reliable *adj.* 可靠的，確實的。
   She may be slow but she's absolutely reliable.
   她或許有些遲鈍，但她絕對是最可靠的。

精選句子與延伸

1. We will make your products not only appeal to the eye but also to the purse.
   我們會讓你的產品除了能吸引目光之外，還能吸引錢包。
   ＝We'll make your goods appeal to the eye as well as to the purse.
   在句子中説的除了對「眼」有吸引力，還對「錢包」有吸引力，指的除了能吸引消費者的目光還能讓他們掏出錢包來購買商品。
   appeal to 對…有吸引力的。
   We need to appeal to a wider range of customers.
   我們需要吸引更廣泛的客戶群。

2. And I was wondering if you could tell me the reason.
   我想知道你是否能告訴我原因呢？
   wonder 的用法有三種，分別為 I wonder；I am wondering；I was wondering，其中最常使用的是 I was wondering，時態雖然是過去進行式，但其時間點卻可被認為是現在，使用過去式來表示帶有保守及慎重的態度，對所請求的事情並不抱持著對方一定會答應的希望，被認為是較有禮貌的説法，因其態度及語氣較不強硬。也可與I wonder互換使用，但語氣上稍有差異。而 I'm wondering 則適用於強調在當下要做出決定及選擇的情況。例如 I'm wondering what to have for lunch; there's nothing in the fridge.（我在想午餐要吃什麼，冰箱裡沒有東西了。）
   wonder 後面可以接 whether/if，但不要接 that，wonder that 帶有驚訝的意思，是比較老式且已不常使用的英文用法。

3. Yes, and it's true, I heard it straight from the horse's mouth!
   可靠，而且是真的。這消息絕對是正確的！
   在本文中，用了兩種不同的消息來源，一個是鳥 (a little bird told me)，另一個是馬。而兩者的差異是在 "a little bird told me" 是由消息靈通人士指出的，而 "straight from the horse's mouth" 通常則是與事件相關者或是當事人説的。事情的真實度則是「馬」説得最正確，「鳥」則帶有聽説的成分。

Unit 44 確認交期

Dialog 1

Colby	Hey, David, since we have already settled the terms of payment. I want to know is it possible to effect the shipment on October?	嘿，David，既然我們已經都談好了付款的條件。我想要知道是不是能在10月份的時候裝運呢？
David	I'm afraid not.	恐怕不行。
Colby	So according to your estimate, when is the earliest shipment we can expect?	那根據你的預估，最早什麼時候能夠發貨呢？
David	I think, maybe by the early November.	我想，大約是在11月上旬。
Colby	Oh, no, that's too late. David, could you do something to advance your time of the shipment?	喔，不，這樣太晚了。David，你有沒有辦法早一點發貨呢？
David	I will try my best, but I can't guarantee anything. The fact is all our factories are fully engaged at this moment, and some of our clients are even placing orders for delivery in the beginning of next year.	我會盡我最大的努力，但我沒辦法保證任何事。事實上我們所有的工廠目前的生產任務都已排滿，我們有些客戶甚至已在訂明年初發的貨了。

Colby	Come on, David. We have cooperated with each other nicely all these years. You know, we always want to get a drop on our competitors by placing our goods on the market first. Otherwise, our market share and sales will plunge. Besides, after the shipment, that will take about 3 to 4 weeks altogether for our goods to reach our retailers, at that time, I don't think we can be in time for the selling season. Is there any way to get round the factories for the earlier delivery?	拜託，David。我們這些年一直都合作得很好。你知道。我們總是想搶先我們的對手一步將商品上市。要不然我們的市場佔有率及銷售量就會驟跌。除此之外，發貨之後，總共要花約到3到4星期的時間送到我們的零售商手上，到那個時候，我不認為我們趕得上銷售的季節。有沒有辦法說服那些工廠早一點發貨呢？
David	All right, Colby. I will contact with our factories, and see what we can do. But please allow me to say so, you should place the order earlier. at least two months ago. Did you forget and wait until the last minute?	好吧，Colby。我會聯絡我們的工廠，看我們能做些什麼。但請允許我這樣說，你應該早一點訂貨的，最少在兩個月之前。你是不是忘記了，直到最後一刻才訂？
Colby	As a matter of fact, yes, I did. So you have to help me this time, please.	事實上，對，我忘了。所以你這一次一定要幫幫我，拜託。
David	Well, I will check the production schedule of the factory, and try my best to advance the shipment by the end of October. You also have to start preparing all relevant documents concerning the shipment.	嗯，我將會查一下工廠的生產進度，盡我所能的將發貨時間提前到10月底。你也必須開始著手準備這批貨運的相關文件。

Colby	David thanks for your help. I am really appreciated. You have done me a big favor. I owe you once.	David，謝謝你的幫忙。我真的非常的感謝。你幫了我一個大忙。我欠你一個人情。
David	No, you owe me not only once, you have already owed me many times. When will you buy me a dinner or a drink?	不，你不只欠我一次而已，你已經欠了我好多次。你什麼時候才要請我吃飯或是喝酒呢？
Colby	How about tonight?	今晚如何？
David	Great, from now on, I'm not going to eat anything. I want to go pig out tonight.	好極了，從現在開始，我就不吃東西了。我今晚要大吃一頓。

Dialog 2

Tracy	XYZ Company, Tracy speaking. May I help you?	XYZ公司，我是Tracy，有什麼能為你效勞的？
Emily	Hi, Tracy. This is Emily calling from ABC Corp.	嗨，Tracy。我是ABC公司的Emily。
Tracy	Hi, Emily. Did you get my email?	嗨，Emily。有收到我的email嗎？
Emily	Yes, I've received your email, and I want to talk about the date of shipment with you.	有，我已經收到妳的email了，而且我想和妳討論一下有關發貨的時間。
Tracy	Ok, Sure. no problem. So what's that about?	Ok，當然，沒問題。所以是有關哪部分呢？

Emily	In your email, you mentioned about the shipment will be arranged by the middle of July, and I'm afraid that will be too late for us. As the season in Taiwan for this commodity starts from July, so I want to know is that possible for you to reschedule the shipment to the middle of June?	在妳的email中，妳提到發貨的時間會被安排在7月中旬，但我恐怕這個時間對我們而言太晚了。在台灣，對這一樣商品的需求季節是從7月開始，所以我想要知道妳有沒有可能可以重新安排發貨時間至6月中旬呢？
Tracy	Hold a second please. Let me check the schedule first. I'm sorry, Emily, I'm afraid it won't be ready until the late June, and I can promise you that the shipment will be made no later than the beginning of July.	請等一下，讓我先查一下進度安排。我很抱歉，Emily，恐怕要一直到6月底之前才能出貨，我能向妳保證發貨的時間不會遲於7月初。
Emily	All right, and I also want to know how long it will take for the shipment?	好吧，我還想知道貨物運送的時間大約會是多久呢？
Tracy	It will take about two days for the domestic shipping here. And the freight will take about 2 weeks on the open ocean, and will arrive in Kaohsiung. The domestic shipping in Taiwan will be your responsibility.	在這裡的國內運輸大約要2天的時間，然後在遠洋上的航行時間大約需要2個星期，然後抵達高雄。那在台灣的國內運輸的部分將會事由你們負責。
Emily	Okay, we will handle that, but what about the Customs? Should we prepare anything or pay tariff on our goods?	好的，我們會負責那部分的，那有關海關的部分呢？我們應該要準備什麼東西或是支付關稅嗎？

Tracy	Nope, our company will have that all worked out.	不用，我們公司會將所有事情都安排妥當的。
Emily	Oh, one more thing, we will open our L/C in the middle of June.	喔，還有一件事，我們會在6月中旬開立信用狀的。
Tracy	That will be great. If there's any chance to advance the shipment, I will let you know.	那就太好了。如果有能夠提前出貨的機會，我會讓妳知道的。
Emily	Tracy, thank you for your help.	Tracy，謝謝妳的幫忙。
Tracy	That's my pleasure.	是我的榮幸。

精選單字及片語

1. settle *v.* 安排，解決。
   We should settle the business on hand first.
   我們應該先解決手邊的事情。

2. effect the shipment 發貨，裝船，交貨。
   Is it possible to effect the shipment immediately?
   有沒有可能立刻裝船交貨呢？

3. get the drop on 搶先一步，佔上風。這個片語大約是出現在 1850 年代的美國西部，用在我們在電視或是電影上常見的西部槍戰上，形容對決時先以槍瞄準對方的那一個人。這時圍觀的人就會說 "He gets the drop on his opponent." （他搶先一步以槍對準了他的對手）。後來被引用到商業及政治界，用來形容先發制人或是比對手搶先一步。

   The candidate got the drop on his opponent by announcing first.
   這位候選人搶先他的對手一步宣布參選。

4. domestic *adj.* 國內的。
   The new policy will advantage the reduction of the domestic unemployment.
   新的政策將能有助於減少國內的失業人口。

5. L/C 信用狀（letter of credit）。

We will arrange the shipment as soon as your L/C arrives.

在收到你的信用狀之後，我們將立刻為你安排出貨。

💬 精選句子與延伸

1. Is there any way to get round the factories for the earlier delivery?

   有沒有辦法說服那些工廠早一點發貨呢？

   get round 說服；迴避；（消息）傳開；走動，旅行。get round 在本句中是作為「說服」來解釋，與我們台語中所說的「搓圓仔」有異曲同工之妙。在英文中也還可說 "talk round"，也有說服某人的意思。

   I tried to get her round.

   我試著說服她。

   A smart lawyer might find a way of getting round that clause.

   一個優秀的律師可能能找到規避那項條款的方法。

2. I want to know is that possible for you to reschedule the shipment to the middle of June?

   我想要知道妳有沒有可能可以重新安排發貨時間至 6 月中旬呢？

   我們一般常說的月初，月中及月底，在英文中有幾種說法，在這裡以 6 月為例

   6月初（上旬）- early June, the beginning of June.

   6月中（中旬）- mid-June, the middle of June.

   6月底（下旬）- late June, the end of June.

Unit 45 展場交談——新客戶

Dialog 1

Nancy	Good afternoon, sir. My name is Nancy, I am the manager of the sales department.	午安，先生。我的名字是 Nancy，我是銷售部門的經理。
Pete	Good afternoon, here's my business card. I am Pete, the import manager of ABC Corp. Very nice to meet you, Nancy.	午安，是我的名片。我是 Pete，ABC股份有限公司的進口部經理。非常高興見到妳，Nancy。
Nancy	Very nice to meet you, too. Mr. …	我也非常高興見到你，…先生。
Pete	Just call me Pete.	叫我Pete就好。
Nancy	OK, Pete, please sit down.	OK，Pete，請坐。
Pete	Thank you.	謝謝妳。
Nancy	Would you like to have coffee or tea?	你要不要來杯咖啡或是茶呢？
Pete	I would prefer coffee, please.	麻煩請給我杯咖啡。
Nancy	No problem. Is this your first trip to the Fair?	沒問題。這是你第一次參加這個會展嗎？
Pete	Yes, this is my first time to be here.	是的，這是我第一次參加。

Nancy	Wow, you are lucky, because I think this time is the best Fair ever. The business scope has been broaden, and there are so many varieties of items and styles that you can choose.	哇，那你很幸運，因為我覺得這次的會展是有史以來最棒的一次。展場內的商業經營範圍擴大了，所以有非常多種的品項及風格可供選擇。
Pete	Yes, this Fair is definitely great. I have already placed several orders not only for the company but also for myself.	沒錯，這個會展的確很棒。我不單單只是替公司還為了自己，已經下了好幾張訂單。
Nancy	Great, looks like you have enjoyed this Fair. Pete, could you please tell me if you find anything interesting in our products?	太好了，看起來你很喜歡這次的會展。Pete，可不可以請你告訴我是否有對我們公司的產品感到興趣呢？
Pete	Yes, in fact, I am especially interested in your products.	好的，事實上，我最感興趣的是貴公司的產品。
Nancy	I am so glad to hear that. What style are you particularly in the market for?	聽你這樣說我感到很高興。你所物色的是什麼風格呢？
Pete	I am looking for something fashionable and casual for young women, especially with high quality and reasonable price. We will purchase large quantities of selected items.	我想找的是時尚兼具休閒，適合年輕女性，特別是品質要好，價格合理。我們將會對選中的品項大量採購。
Nancy	Oh I see. I know what you're exactly looking for. This way, please. I'll show you our products.	我明白了。我知道你所要找的是什麼了。這裡請，我將帶你看我們的產品。

Dialog 2

Angic	Good afternoon, ma'am.	午安，女士。
Belinda	Good afternoon.	午安。
Angic	Welcome to our display. These are some of our company's products, and you may want to take a look. Please take your time, and if you have any question about our product, just let me know.	歡迎光臨我們的展示區。這裡有我們公司的一些產品，妳應該會想要看一下。請慢慢來，如果妳對於我們的產品有什麼疑問的話，請告訴我。
Belinda	Yes, I will and thanks.	好的，我會的，謝謝。
Angic	You are welcome.	不客氣。
Belinda	Excuse me.	不好意思。
Angic	Yes, ma'am.	是的，女士。
Belinda	I want to know which one is the latest product of your company.	我想要知道你們公司最新的產品是哪一個？
Angic	Let me show you the whole series. This way please, ma'am. We have some special promotions on these latest products, and only in this Fair.	讓我帶妳看一整個系列。這裡請，女士。我們最新的產品有在做特別的促銷活動，只有在這個會展上才有。
Belinda	Wow, that sounds very attractive.	哇，聽起來真吸引人。
Angic	It surely does. As you can see here, our ranges of patented products are designed to be stylish. Ma'am, would you please tell me what item you are particularly interested in?	它的確是。就像妳在這裡所看到的，我們的專利產品都有非常時尚的設計。女士，是不是可以告訴我哪一種產品是妳特別有興趣的呢？

Belinda	I am most interested in the facial cleansing device.	我最感興趣的是臉的清潔設備。
Angic	That is the most popular product in the market.	這是市場上最熱銷的產品。
Belinda	Yes, I know.	是的，我知道。
Angic	Have you ever used it?	那妳有用過嗎？
Belinda	Yes, I bought one several months ago. And I found my face skin is smoother, and my complexion is radiant and luminous.	有，我在幾個月前有購入一隻。接著我就發現我臉部肌膚更光滑了，我的膚色光彩有亮澤。
Angic	We always say to our customers "We promise to transform your skin.", and we mean it. Here are our latest products, and you may want to have a try. In the mean while, could you please leave us your contact information, so that we can provide you the latest information in time?	我們總是對我們的顧客說「我們保證會改善你的肌膚」我們是認真的。這裡是我們最新的產品，妳應該會想試用一下。同時，是否可以留給我們妳的聯絡方式，我們將能為妳提供最新的資訊？
Belinda	Sure, here's my business card.	當然可以，這是我的名片。
Angic	Thank you, and here's my card, you can contact us anytime.	謝謝，這是我的名片，妳可以隨時聯絡我們。
Belinda	Okay.	好的。
Angic	Thank you for your visiting and have a nice day.	謝謝妳今天的光臨，祝妳有個愉快的一天。

💬 精選單字及片語

1. import *v.* 進口
I want to import these products into Taiwan.
我要將這些商品進口至台灣。

2. fair(s) *n.* 商品展覽會，博覽會。我們一般習慣稱展覽為 "exhibition"，展覽會為 "fair" 或是 "trade fair"。這兩種用法，看起來好像沒什麼分別，但在英文中，"exhibition" 是將東西陳列出來，「僅」供參觀，而 "fair" 指的是參展商，和參觀的人可在會場中買賣，我們常見的旅展，電腦展及書展等，在展覽中是可以購買商品的，所以應以 "fair" 來稱這類的展覽。
I bought a lot books in the book fair.
我在書展中買了很多書。

3. business scope 營業範圍，經營範圍。
Our company has a wide business scope, including the manufacturing and sales of all kinds of textiles.
我們公司的經營範圍非常廣泛，包括各類紡織品的生產及銷售。

4. ma'am 女士，小姐，夫人。常見的還有 madam 及 madame。madam 一般可用於稱呼年紀較長，且不知姓名的女性，而 madame 是法文，用來稱呼知道姓名的女士為「…夫人」。在美國及加拿大常會以 ma'am 稱呼不知道姓名的女士或小姐，有部分女性不喜被稱呼為 madam，因在英文中也會稱那些從事仲介賣淫行業的女性為 madam。所以在稱呼上必須小心的選擇。

5. complexion *n.* 面容，氣色
She has a pretty complexion.
她的長相清秀。

6. luminous *adj.* 發光的，明亮的。
There was a luminous UFO flying over Hong Kong last month.
上個月有一個發光的幽浮飛過香港上空。

精選句子與延伸

1. Because I think this time is the best Fair ever.
   因為我覺得這次的會展是有史以來最棒的一次。
   the best ever 有史以來最棒的，至今最好的。
   This is the best movie that I have ever seen.
   這是我看過最好看的電影。

2. What style are you particularly in the market for?
   你所物色的是什麼風格呢？
   be in the market for 想買，積極物色（有足夠能力及金錢購買的狀況下）。美國俚語。
   We are in the market for a 5-bedroom house.
   我們想買一幢有 5 個房間的房子。

3. Could you please leave us your contact information, so that we can provide you the latest information in time?
   是否可以留給我們妳的聯絡方式，我們將能為妳提供最新的資訊？
   could 是 can 的過去式，但在本句中不是過去式，而是一種比較有禮貌，比較客氣的說法。can 及 could 都有請求允許的意思，但在對於關係較生疏或是長輩，客戶時，建議使用 could 為比較有禮貌的說法。

展場交談──同業拜訪/寒暄/市場狀況討論

Dialog 1

Muriel	Good Morning, I am your neighbor, my name is Muriel and I am from ABC Corp.	早安,我是你們的鄰居,我叫 Muriel,是ABC Corp。的員工。
Kelvin	Hi, Muriel, I am Kelvin, and this is Matt, we work for XYZ Company. Very nice to meet you.	嗨,Muriel,我是Kelvin,這是 Matt,我們替XYZ公司工作。非常高興認識妳。
Matt	Hi, Muriel. Let's exchange business cards, shall we? Here's my name card, great to see you.	嗨,Muriel。讓我們來交換名片,可以嗎?這是我的名片,非常高興見到妳。
Muriel	Me, too. Here's my card, and I'll give you guys a discount on our products if you collect ten of these.	我也是。這是我的名片,如果集滿十張的話,我會給你們折扣買我們的商品。
Kelvin	Sorry, I am all out of cards.	不好意思,我名片用完了。
Muriel	That's too bad, you'll need your business cards all day long, and the card is the key element for you to get orders.	真糟糕,你一整天都需要名片的,名片可是你拿到訂單的關鍵要素。
Kelvin	I know, my colleague's on his way to the Fair from our company, and he'll bring me a box of my cards.	我知道,我同事正在從公司來展場的途中,他會幫我帶一盒名片過來的。

Muriel	Lucky you!	你真幸運！
Matt	Muriel, is this your first time to participate in the Fair?	Muriel，這是妳第一次來博覽會嗎？
Muriel	Yes, and I am so nervous, because I didn't get any order yesterday.	是啊，而且我非常緊張，因為我昨天沒有拿到半張訂單。
Kelvin	That's very normal, those buyers usually place orders on the last day of the Fair.	這非常正常，那些買家通常會在會展的最後一天才下訂單。
Muriel	Really? Some of them looked like very interested in our products, but they just took the brochures and my cards then went to another booth.	真的嗎？他們有些人看起來對我們的產品非常有興趣，但他們只拿了宣傳手冊及我的名片就到下一個展位去了。
Matt	Don't worry, they will probably come back to you and place orders on the last day.	別擔心，他們大概會在最後一天時回來找妳下訂單的。
Muriel	Thanks for your pep talk.	謝謝你的鼓勵。
Matt	Any time.	不用客氣。
Kelvin	We gotta go, Muriel, talk to you soon.	我們得走了，Muriel，之後再聊。
Muriel	See you soon.	待會見。

Dialog 2

Vick	Hi, I am Vick, I am in booth 29…	嗨,我是Vick,我是29號展位的……
Paul	Booth 29? ABC Corp, right?	29號展位?ABC Corp。,對嗎?
Vick	Yes, that's right.	對,沒錯。
Paul	Hi, I am Paul. I am the executive assistant of the Fair Organizing Committee.	嗨,我是Paul。我是博覽會組織委員會的行政助理。
Vick	So that explains it. So you remember every company's booth number?	原來如此。所以你記得每一家公司的展位編號?
Paul	Yes, most of them. Vick, I think you are looking for something, right? May I help you?	對,大部分。Vick,我想你好像在找什麼東西,對嗎?我可以幫得上忙嗎?
Vick	Yes, in fact I am looking for the information center. I would like to have the layout of the exhibition hall and the brochure.	對,事實上我正在找服務中心。我想拿一份展覽館的佈置圖,及宣傳手冊。
Paul	I do have the brochure with me, you can have this one if you like. But I don't have the layout of the exhibition hall.	我剛好有一份宣傳手冊,如果你要的話可以拿去。但我沒有展覽館的佈置圖。
Vick	Thank you very much. Paul, would you please tell me where the Fair Forum Hall is?	非常謝謝你,Paul,那可不可以請你告訴我博覽會論壇廳在哪?

Paul	What a coincidence! I am on my way to the Fair Forum Hall as well, it's on the 4th floor, west corridor, please follow me.	真巧！我也正要去博覽會論壇廳，它在西邊迴廊的四樓，請跟我來。
Vick	You save my day. Thanks, Paul.	你幫了我個大忙。謝謝你，Paul。
Paul	My pleasure. Vick, are you going to join the Forum?	我的榮幸。Vick，你是不是要參加論壇？
Vick	Yes. My boss wanted to join the Forum, but he's too busy, so he sent me here to join the Forum, I have to take some notes for him.	對，原本是我老闆要參加的，但他太忙了，所以他派我來參加論壇，我必須替他記些筆記。
Paul	The main topic of this conference is about the Global Challenges in Economics. It's not that interesting but very useful.	今天會議的主題是有關全球經濟挑戰。不太有趣但非常有用。
Vick	How long will it last?	大概會多久啊？
Paul	About 2 hours. Here we are.	大約2個小時。我們到了。
Vick	Paul, thank you for your help.	Paul，感謝你的幫忙。
Paul	It's my pleasure.	這是我的榮幸。

💬 精選單字及片語

1. exchange *v.* 交換
   I would like to exchange a few words with you in private.
   我想私底下和你交換點意見。

2. booth(s) *n.* 展位，攤位，售貨棚。
   Let's walk around to each booth.
   讓我們四處走走去看看每個展位。

3. element(s) *n.* 要素，元素。
   Any investment involves the element of risk.
   任何一項投資都有一定的風險。

4. executive assistant 行政助理
   She works as an executive assistant in the marketing department.
   她在行銷部的職位是行政助理。

5. committee(s) *n.* 委員會。
   I will communicate your opinions to the members of the committee.
   我將會把你的意見傳達給委員會成員。

6. layout(s) *n.* 佈置圖，佈局，安排。
   Their booth has a good layout.
   他們的展位規劃得很好。

精選句子與延伸

1. Thanks for your pep talk.
   謝謝你的鼓勵。
   pep talk 鼓勵的話，打氣加油。美國俚語。pep 做動詞時意思為「給…打氣，激勵」，名詞則是「活力，精力」。
   The coach gave his team a pep talk before the game.
   教練在賽前對他的隊伍說了一些加油打氣的話。

2. We gotta go, Muriel, talk to you soon.
   我們得走了，Muriel，之後再聊。
   在日常會話當中，常會在談話結束前以 "Talk to you later" 或是 "See you soon" 來作為結束。代表的是 "see you" 或是 "good-bye" 再見的意思。並不是如字面上的翻譯為稍後再聊的意思，比較像我們常說的「下次見面再聊」的意思。

3. So that explains it.
   原來如此。
   美國俚語，用於在覺得困惑，但突然出現答案時。如本文中 Vick 覺得 Paul 能依展位號碼說出他的公司名稱時而感到不解，但 Paul 解釋後便恍然大悟。也可以說 "So that explains everything."。

4. You save my day.
   你幫了我個大忙。
   照字面上的解釋是「你拯救了我的一天」，save the day 這個片語是用於原本預期是壞的結果，但卻出現好的結果，有轉敗為勝的含意。在本文中，Paul 帶著 Vick 找到舉行論壇的地方，而 Vick 說了這一句話，我們可以推測 Vick 可能原本認為會趕不上論壇，因 Paul 的介入而順利達成老闆交付的任務。

Part Eight

上班後

Behind the work

Unit 47 提出辭呈/被挖角

Dialog 1

A Jenny,I have to tell you something! Promise me this is between you and me.

Jenny Sure,my lips are sealed, What is that?

A I got a call from the headhunter from XX Company saying they would like me to work for them.

Jenny For real?It is an international corp. Many people would kill for this job.

A I know,but Boss has always been kind to me,I am in a dilemma.Do you have any suggestions?

Jenny What do they offer?

A Honestly,It is pretty decent!They offer a decent benefit package and a 20% raise of my salary.

Jenny Well, I can't make the decision for you,but i would go if i were you.

Jenny，跟你説一件事，你保證不能説出去。

好啊，我一定幫你保密，是什麼事？

前幾天XX公司的人事資源部經理打電話給我，説要挖我過去他們公司。

真的假的？那是國際級的大公司耶！是個好機會。

是阿，但是老闆對我很照顧，現在我覺得很兩難。你有什麼建議嗎？

他們開出來的條件怎麼樣呢？

老實説，很不錯，薪水比現在高20%，福利也很不錯。

這樣啊！我不能幫你做決定，但如果我是你的話，我想我會去！

(一個禮拜後) one week later

| A | Boss, can I talk to you? | 老闆，我可以和你談談嗎？ |

| Boss | Oh sure,I have a meeting at 4, Can we wrap up by then? | 喔，可以啊！不過我四點有個會議，你可以在那之前結束嗎？ |

| A | I think so!It is hard to say... | 我想可以！但這有點難啟齒... |

| Boss | If you are here for the project,Our company has a budget cutback,It is not a good time. | 如果你是為了上次那個提案，公司刪減了一些預算，現在不是好時機。 |

| A | Oh,no!!It's that I know we have to give one month's notice if we decide to resign.I will hand in the resignation letter next week. | 喔，不是的！是這樣的，我知道公司員工要辭職得提前一個月通知.我下禮拜會呈上辭職信。 |

| Boss | I beg your pardon? | 你說什麼？ |

| A | Thank you for your encouragements during the past several years.Due to my personal affairs I have to resign.It has been a great honor working with you,sir. | 謝謝公司這些年來的鼓勵，但是因為一些私人因素，所以不得不辭去這裡的職務，和您共事是我莫大的榮幸。 |

| Boss | Well,seems like you have made up your mind.I wish you all the best. | 好的，看來你已經決定了。祝你的未來一切順利。 |

Dialog 2

(knock knock)敲門聲

Ben	Hi, Boss, Can I talk to you?	Hi老闆，我可以和你談談嗎？
Boss	You can but you may not! Ben, seriously, I am pretty busy right here.	你可以，但我不想，Ben，我現在真的很忙
Ben	Okay, I'll just leave my resignation letter on your desk tomorrow then.	好吧，那我明天就直接把我的辭職信放你桌上
Boss	Excuse me, are you saying that you are resigning?	什麼？你說你要辭職嗎？
Ben	Yes, XX Company has made a pretty decent offer. There is no reason for me to let the chance go.	對阿，ＸＸ公司給我很棒的條件，我沒理由放棄這麼好的機會
Boss	Well, you do know that according to the company's regulations, you have to give a one month's notice, right?	那好，你應該知道根據公司規定，辭職的話你要在一個月之前告知吧？
Ben	Yes, that's why I need to talk to you now.	我知道阿，所以我才現在來找你談
Boss	All right, what's that all about? Ben, please take a seat, and I would like to have a serious talk with you.	這究竟是怎麼一回事？Ben，請坐下，我想認真和你談一談。
Ben	So now you have time to talk to me, hem?	所以你現在有時間和我談了，是吧？

Boss	Hmm··· you know, I was quite busy, and now I think I can manage that, and should take time from my weighty duties to talk about your resignation with you.	嗯，你知道的，我剛剛很忙，而現在我想我應付的過來，及應該在百忙中抽空和你談一下有關你要辭職的事。
Ben	Boss, I think you really have to learn to keep your temper under control.	老闆，我認為你必須要學著控制你的脾氣。
Boss	Oh, well. Ok, I will, maybe I can go to the anger management class, so you're not going to quit now, right?	喔，嗯。Ok，我會的，也許我可以去上那種憤怒管理的課，所以你不辭職了，是吧。
Ben	Sorry, boss, I still want to quit. I've run out of steam, and I think I need a different environment. Besides, my wife and I have already decided that we'll move back to Los Angeles a year later.	對不起，老闆，我還是要走。我已經失去動力了，我認為我需要一個不同的環境。除此之外，我太太和我已經決定一年後要搬回洛杉磯了。
Boss	And XX Company has promised you the allocation?	那XX公司已經答應你調職的條件？
Ben	Yes, that's right.	是的，沒錯。
Boss	Would you be happier with higher pay here? I'm sure something can be worked out.	那如果給你高一點的薪水在這會讓你快樂些嗎？我想事情還是有轉圜的餘地。
Ben	I'm afraid not. Boss, you should know that I always want to move back to Los Angeles because of my parents.	恐怕不行。老闆，你應該知道因為我父母的關係我一直都想搬回洛杉磯。
Boss	Okay then, I'd like to say I've really enjoyed working with you, and good luck to your new job.	好吧，我想說你共事我非常的開心，還有祝你的新工作順利。

💬 精選單字及片語

1. Headhunter　替公司物色人才的人
   A good headhunter can find the best and most suitable people for his company.
   一個好的人力搜尋人員可以為公司找到最適合的人才。

2. kill for this job.　意指極力爭取這個工作
   Many girls would kill for working for fashion magazines.
   很多女生會為了在時尚雜誌工作搶破頭。

3. in a dilemma.　進退兩難
   I am in a dilemma of telling the truth or covering for my co-worker.
   我在説出實話和掩護我同事之間進退兩難。

4. benefit package　工作福利
   I got a job with a pretty good benefit package in SONY.
   我在SONY得到一個福利很不錯的工作。

5. wrap up　結束，完成
   I should be wrapping up by now; I spent too much time talking with the sales person.
   要不是我和那個業務聊太久了，工作早就該結束了。

6. decent　合宜的，還不錯的
   Their spokesman is a nice decent gentleman.
   他們的發言人是個還不錯的紳士。

精選句子與延伸

1. **My lips are sealed.**
   我一定幫你保密。
   字面上的意思為我的嘴唇是封住的，以比喻法的方式表明"不會將秘密或是八卦告訴其他人"。

2. **But I would go if I were you.**
   但如果我是你的話，我想我會去！
   在這個句子當中，if 條件句為過去式，結果句為語氣助動詞 would ＋原形動詞 go，代表的是與現在事實相反的 if 假設句。由於這一個假設句是建立在與現在事實不符的情況下，所以這個結果當然也是不成立的，是一個"純假設"的句子。在這裡要注意的是，在與現在事實不符的條件句中使用的 be 動詞不管是第幾人稱，一律都使用 were。

3. **You can but you may not!**
   你可以，但我不想！
   也可以解釋為"你能，但你不被允許"。這是一句常被學校老師或是父母用以教導孩子來分別 can 與 may 的不同。can 一般被認為是指能力上，而 may 則是指是否得到允許。在第 2 段的對話中，Ben 詢問老闆 "Can I talk to you?"，這在一般的對話當中是沒有問題的，但很明顯的是老闆當時因為很忙所以心情煩躁，於是玩起了文字遊戲，回答 Ben "你可以（有說話的能力），但我不想！（但你不被允許）"。

4. **I've run out of steam.**
   我已經失去動力了。
   用蒸汽機的蒸氣用完來比喻人失去了動力。在美國或是澳洲，也可以說是 "run out of gas"。
   I worked really well for two months of the project then I suddenly run out of steam.
   我兩個月的時間在專案上的表現非常的好，然後我突然失去了動力。

Unit 48 開除某人

Dialog 1

A　Have you heard about the budget cutback?It seems the company is going to lay off some employees.

你有聽說了有關縮減預算的事嗎？看起來公司準備要裁員了。

B　Seriously?I have never heard about it.

真的嗎？我不知道有這件事。

A　Some people in marketing department have been let go.I think this is not just a rumor.Maybe the manager will make an announcement in today's meeting.

行銷部已經有一些人被解雇了，所以我想這應該不是謠言。也許主管會在今天的會議上宣布這件事

B　I hope I'm not on the list, I just bought a house and have a family to support. I can't imagine that what will happen if I lose my job.

我希望我沒有在名單上，我才剛買了房子還要支撐一個家庭。我無法想像會發生什麼事如果我沒了工作的話。

A　Don't worry, I think you will be fine. After all you are an experienced hand and win the salesman of the month frequently. I don't think you are on the list. As for me, I don't have much confidence on myself. Frankly speaking, it makes me break out in a cold sweat.

別擔心，我想你會沒事的。畢竟你是個熟手，而且常常拿到每月的銷售冠軍。我不認為你會在名單上。倒是我，我就沒這麼有信心了。老實說，這消息把我給嚇出了一身冷汗。

(Phone is ringing)

C   Ben,Boss wants to see you.

Ben   Oh my goodness,this can't be good. Wish me luck.

A   Ben, I will cross my fingers for you. Good luck, Ben.

Boss   Ben, I've reviewed the performance of last month.Your team is far behind average.

Ben   Yes, I know!Because of the recession, People can't afford buying luxury cars.

Boss   It's true,I understand.But under this circumstance we will have to let some people go.

Ben   AmI fired,sir?

Boss   Oh,No,relax! You are a senior and valuable employee in this company;we need you to hang in there with us.As for your new coming member Lola,it's another story.

Ben   Lola? She just passed her probation. She needs time to get on the track.

Boss   I am afraid we don't have enough time waiting for her.Ben,she is getting the pink slip by Friday.

(電話鈴響)

班，老闆請你到他辦公室

喔，天哪，這不會是好事，祝我好運吧

Ben，我會幫你祈禱的。祝你好運，Ben。

班，我看過了你們團隊上個月的業績表現，好像有點不如預期。

是的，我知道！因為最近的大環境影響，買車的人真的減少很多。

沒錯，我了解！但在這種情況下，我們不得不刪減一些人力。

我被解雇了嗎，長官？

喔，別緊張！你已經是公司的資深員工，表現一直都很好。我們需要你留下來一起努力！但是，你新進的手下的蘿拉，就是另外一回事了。

蘿拉？他才剛過試用期，還需要一點時間來上軌道。

我們恐怕沒有時間等他了！班，我們禮拜五之前就會解僱她了。

Dialog 2

A This is my last day in GTC, thank you all for your support and for your confidence in me in the past 10 years. I will keep myself strong.

這是我待在GTC的最後一天，謝謝你們大家在過去10年對我的支持及信任。我會堅強的。

B Chief, I don't understand, you did very well here. Why you have to quit?

老大，我不懂，你在這裡做得很好。為什麼要辭職呢？

A I already explain that a million times. My wife got a very good job in Shanghai. She's been a force behind me for so many years. Now it's my turn to pay her back.

我已經解釋過無數次了。我的太太在上海找到一份很好的工作，她這麼多年來一直都在我的背後支持我，現在輪到我來回報她了。

C Oh, chief, you are such a nice guy.

喔，老大，你真是個好男人。

D No, he's not. That's not the real reason for his resignation. Mr. Marni, here's your marching orders.

不，他不是。那不是他離職的真正原因。Marni先生，這裡是你的解雇通知書。

A I totally don't understand what you are talking about, Ms. Swan. My resignation has been accepted two weeks ago.

我完全不懂妳在說些什麼，Swan小姐。我的辭職信在2個星期前就已經批准了。

D Your resignation has been rejected after we found out enough evidence to accuse you of leaking trade secrets.

你的辭職信在我們找到足夠的證據能以洩漏商業機密為由起訴你之後就被駁回了。

A No, that's impossible.

不，這是不可能的。

D   Homer sometimes nods. We have already called the police. Here they are.

智者千慮，必有一失。我們已經報警了。他們到了。

E   Mr. Marni, you are under arrest for leaking trade secrets. You have the right to remain silent. Anything you say can and will be used against you in a court of law. Ms. Swan, we will need your help in the investigation.

Marni先生，你因洩漏商業機密而被逮捕。你有權保持緘默。但你所說的一切將會成為呈堂證供。Swan小姐，我們在調查中需要妳的協助。

D   No problem, I will let my legal team to handle that. I have some words for my employees, may I?

沒問題，我會讓我的律師團隊處理的。我有些話要對我的員工說，可以嗎？

E   Sure, please.

當然可以，請。

D   My dear colleagues, sorry to disrupting this party. I'm afraid I have to announce that the party is over. But I promise all of you, we'll have another party to celebrate the bright future of our company.

我親愛的同仁們，抱歉擾亂了這個派對。我恐怕必須宣布派對結束。但我承諾你們大家，我們將會有另一個派對來慶祝公司光明的未來。

精選單字及片語

1. rumor(s) *n.* 謠言，傳聞
   The rumor of the new CEO goes rampant.
   關於新任CEO的謠言甚囂塵上。

2. recession(s) *n.* （工商業的）衰退價格上的暴跌
   Our firm went through the bad time in the recession.
   我們公司在經濟衰退時期歷經了千辛萬難。

3. hang in there 撐住，堅持下去，不要放棄
   Hang in there, after passing the probation you will be officially hired.
   堅持下去，撐過試用期你就會被正式任用了。

4. resignation 辭職
   His resignation precipitated a leadership crisis.
   他的辭職引發了領導階層的危機。

5. marching orders 解雇通知書。照字面上的意思，我們還可以將它解釋為 "逐客令"，除了這一個片語及在 Dialogue 1 中出現的 "pink slip"，我們還可以說 "walking papers"，要注意的事，除了 "pink slip" 是單數之外，其他兩個都是以複數型態表示。
   I got my marching orders last week.
   我上星期收到了解雇通知書。

6. Homer sometimes nods. 智者千慮，必有一失。Homer 是希臘最偉大的詩人，而 nods 在這裡是當 "發睏，打瞌睡" 解釋，這一句諺語有 "即使是 Homer 的經典範本，但也偶有瑕疵" 的含意，也可解釋為 "百密一疏"。

💬 精選句子與延伸

1. Have you heard about the budget cutback?It seems the company is going to lay off some employees.
   你有聽説了有關縮減預算的事嗎？看起來公司準備要裁員了。
   budget cutback 縮編預算，預算刪減。
   I am afraid that we have to skip this year's Christmas party because of the budget cutback.
   因為預算刪減，今年我們恐怕不能舉辦聖誕派對了。
   lay off 解雇
   If you don't want get laid off, you'd better work harder.
   如果你不想被裁員，那就更努力工作吧。

2. She is getting the pink slip by Friday.
   我們禮拜五之前就會解僱她了。
   = She will be pink slipped by Friday.
   pink slip 解雇通知書。字面上可解釋為粉紅小紙條，這個片語最早出現在 20 世紀初時，會在將被解雇員工的週薪信封中（在歐美國家大多是領週薪的）放入粉紅色的紙條，據說粉紅色較為柔和，能讓被解雇的員工心靈小小的被撫慰一番。

3. I already explain that a million times.
   我已經解釋過無數次了。
   million times 百萬次。在這一句當中，藉由數字的誇大來加強語氣，聽起來是不是比 several times 強很多的感覺呢？

4. You are under arrest for leaking trade secrets.
   你因洩漏商業機密而被逮捕。
   我想這一句，大家一定都耳熟能詳，這應該在電視或是電影中聽過 "a million times" 了吧。最常聽到的是 "You are under arrest."（你被逮捕了），如果在後面加上原因的話，可以接上 "for" 再加上原因。
   leaking trade secrets 洩漏商業機密。

轉職談待遇

Manager	Tammy, would you please come to my office? I have some words for you.	Tammy，可以請妳來我的辦公室嗎？我有話對妳說。
Tammy	Yes, sir. I will be there in a moment.	好的，先生。我一會兒就過去。
Manager	Please have a seat. Tammy, I want to talk you something good, so relax, don't worry.	請坐。Tammy，我要和妳談的是好事，所以放輕鬆，不要擔心。
Tammy	Phew, I was worried about…	啊，我還在擔心…
Manager	I want let you go?	我要讓妳離職嗎？
Tammy	Yes, my best friend got the sack yesterday, because compare with her colleagues, she's a newbie in the office.	對，我最好的朋友昨天被辭掉了，因為和她的同事相比，她是辦公室裡的菜鳥。
Manager	Don't worry about that, our company runs well this year. Ok, let's cut the waffle straight to the point. Tammy, I've been watching you and paying attention to you over the last quarter. I'm very impressed that you've done tremendous job in tackling some difficult accounts. I want to let you know that we'll have performance reviews this month, and after that I'm recommending you a promotion.	不用擔心，我們公司今年情況不錯。OK，不談其它的直接切入正題。Tammy，我一直在觀察妳，上一季時一直在注意妳的表現。妳在處理一些棘手的帳目時表現非常好讓我印象深刻。我要讓妳知道我們這一個月會有績效評估，在這之後，我會力薦妳升職。

312

Tammy	I'm… hmm… kind of speechless. Thank you, sir. But I don't know there were any positions opening up in our department.	我…嗯…有些說不出話來。謝謝你，先生。但我不知道我們部門還有空缺。
Manager	No, it's not going to be in our department. I've recommended you for an interdepartmental transfer. There's a supervisory spot opening up in financial department. But, because of the work content in financial will be quite different from in our department, so you'll get 40K per month for the first 3 months.	不，不會在我們部門裡。我推薦妳轉任到其它部門。在財務部有一個管理階層的位置。但是，因為在財務部的工作內容和在我們部門會相當的不同，所以妳前3個月的月薪是4萬元。
Tammy	Sort of like on probation?	像是在試用期一樣？
Manager	Yes, that's right.	對，沒錯。
Tammy	Will my salary be raised after 3 months?	那我3個月後會加薪嗎？
Manager	Yes, and I'll suggest HR to offer you 50K, if you perform as well as in our department.	會，我會建議人事部給妳5萬元，如果妳的表現和在我們部門時一樣好的話。
Tammy	Thank you, sir. I won't disappoint you. I give you my word.	謝謝你，先生。我不會讓你失望的。我保證。
Manager	Great, then I'm turning your name for that position.	好極了，那我就提名你接那一個職位了。
Tammy	Thank you very much, sir.	非常感謝你，先生。

Dialog 2

Brooke	Hey, Zoe, can I have a minute?	嘿，Zoe，妳有時間嗎？
Zoe	Sure, what's up? Any new gossip?	當然，怎麼了？有新的八卦？
Brooke	Yes, actually I have a new piece of gossip to tell you.	對，事實上我有個新八卦要告訴妳。
Zoe	Wow, I'm excited. What's that about?	哇，我好激動。是有關什麼的？
Brooke	I want to tell you that I've put in notice. This is my last week in this company.	我要告訴妳我辭職了。這是我最後一個星期在這家公司上班。
Zoe	Why?	為什麼？
Brooke	Many reasons. You know, my new boss doesn't like me, and he always makes me feel stressful. Another reason is that I've got a better offer from another company.	許多原因。妳知道的，我的新老闆不喜歡我，他總是讓我感到壓力很大。另一個原因是我被另一家公司以更好的條件給錄用了。
Zoe	Oh, that's great! Congratulations! I'll miss you, we have spent so many unforgettable days together.	喔，那太好了！恭喜！我會想妳的，我們一起度過這麼多難忘的時光。
Brooke	Oh, don't be sentimental. We can get together sometimes.	喔，別這麼感性。我們有時可以聚一聚。
Zoe	Sure. What's your new position? How about the salary?	當然。新的職位是什麼？薪水方面呢？
Brooke	Senior director of marketing. In addition to a nice pay rise, it has some nice perks, such as a company car, one month paid vacation and a suite downtown.	行銷部高級主管。除了薪水增加之外，還有一些額外的補貼，像是一輛公司車，一個月帶薪假期，還有一間在市中心的套房。

Zoe	That sounds great. How about the future development?	聽起來棒透了。那未來的發展性呢？
Brooke	It is an international company, I will have a lot of chances to travel around and meet new people. It'll be very helpful to broaden my global perspective and my career.	是一間國際性的公司。我將有許多的機會能到世界各地，及認識新的人。對於擴展我的國際觀及對我的事業都非常有幫助。
Zoe	It's a great opportunity indeed. I bet that you had no difficulty when making this decision.	這的確是一個很好的機會。我猜妳在做選擇時一點困難也沒有。
Brooke	Let's stay in touch, okay? I want you to know how things going.	讓我們保持聯絡，好嗎？我要妳知道事情的進展。
Zoe	Of course, I want you to tell me everything.	當然，我要妳告訴我所有的事。
Brooke	No problem.	沒問題。
Zoe	I gotta go, I'll call you.	我得走了，我再打電話給妳啊。

💬 精選單字及片語

1. phew *int.* 啊！唷！唉！感嘆詞，通常會表現在感到累，炎熱或是放心。常會看到有人在說 phew 的時候會誇張的做一個在頭上抹一把汗的動作，以表示安心。

2. get the sack 解雇，開除，辭退。與 get fired 相比，這個片語比較偏英式的說法。sack 是麻袋，這個片語的典故是出自於工匠在被辭退時，會以麻袋裝自己的工具打包帶走。
   Joe got the sack when they found out that he's lie about his qualifications.
   Joe被開除了，因為他們發現他偽造學歷。

3. interdepartmental *adj.* 跨部門的，各部之間的。
   I recognized the importance of controls and interdepartmental communication.
   我意識到控制及部門之間溝通的重要性。

4. gossip(s) *n.* 八卦，流言，閒聊。
   A new piece of gossip came into the office.
   有新的八卦傳到辦公室。

5. perk(s) *n.* 津貼，額外補助（口語化的說法），正式的說法為 perquisite。
   What perks do you get from this job?
   這份工作你可以拿到什麼樣的額外津貼呢？

6. global perspective 國際觀。
   You have to obviously have a global perspective.
   你顯然必須要有國際觀。

💬 精選句子與延伸

1. Ok, let's cut the waffle straight to the point.

   OK，不談其它的直接切入正題。

   waffle(s) (n.) 胡扯，廢話。waffle 一般是指鬆餅，但在言談及文章上的 waffle 則是指不必要的內容，與正題無關的，除名詞的用法之外，也可當動詞使用。所以在對話中，如果對方說 "cut the waffle" 則是指 "不說廢話了"。

   He waffled on for hours.

   他廢話了好幾個小時。

2. I give you my word.

   我保證。

   = I promise.

   word 在這裡當 "諾言" 解釋，單數型態。

   He broke his word.

   他違背了他的承諾。

3. I want to tell you that I've put in notice.

   我要告訴妳我辭職了。

   I've put in notice. 這是一句 have+p.p.現在完成式的句子，put 的過去式及過去分詞都是 put，代表已將 notice 送出，已完成動作。put in notice 在這裡只是指已提出通知，Zoe 應是從以前的談話或是 Brooke 給她的訊息中得知辭職的事，如果要確切的說是辭職申請的話，可說是 two weeks notice，因為一般公司規定辭職需事先在 2 個星期前提出。

   Make sure you know your employers resignation process before putting in your two week notice.

   在提出辭職信之前，要確認你了解雇主的辭職流程。

轉職談工作內容

A	Do you mind talking about what you did in your former company?	你好，你介意先談一下你在之前公司工作的內容嗎？
B	Of course not, the majority of my work was making marketing strategies.	當然不介意。我主要是負責行銷策略的部分。
A	Okay, I see! Well, if you work here, that would be a little more than just making plans.	喔，這樣啊，但是在我們這，可能不只是制定策略這麼輕鬆了。
B	I know, that's also why I am attractive to this opening. I've been wanting to do more in executing my theories tasks.	我了解，這也是我被這個工作吸引的原因，我一直希望可以更接近執行面。
A	Great, we do flexible working hours here, but you may have to work late a lot, would that bother you?	很好，我們實施彈性工時，但可能需要常常加班，這會對你造成困擾嗎？
B	I don't think so. But do we have to work on weekends?	我想不會，但是周末的時間會需要工作嗎？
A	It depends. Why?	看情況，怎麼了嗎？
B	I take a course in XX University and have to go to school every weekend.	我在XX大學修了一堂課，需要每個週末上課。

A   You do work hard, don't you? You are exactly what we are looking for, No worries, I'll let your supervisor know.

你真的很努力，對吧？正是我們公司需要的人才，別擔心，我會先讓你的主管知道這個情況。

B   That would be great, thank you for understanding.

那就太好了，謝謝您的體諒。

A   Do you have any questions else? About your work or the company?

對於工作內容或公司，你還有什麼問題嗎？

B   Not at this moment. I will finish reading the office brochure tonight, I am sure I will learn more afterwards.

目前沒有，但我今晚回去會仔細把辦公室手冊讀完，我確定我讀完後能學到很多東西。

A   Oh, one more thing, we have assigned you your very own assistant. She will help you settle in and keep up your future schedule.

對了，還有一件事，我們會安排一個你私人的助理給你，她會協助你進入狀況並安排你的行程。

B   I appreciate it. This is better than I ever expected.

謝謝，這比我預想中的還要好。

Dialog 2

Raymond	Excuse me, my name is Raymond Howard.	不好意思，我的名字是Raymond Howard。
Cedric	Welcome aboard, Raymond. I am Cedric Jenner. I am expecting you.	歡迎報到，Raymon。我是 Cedric Jenner。我正在等你。
Raymond	Hi, very nice to meet you, Mr. Jenner.	嗨，非常高興認識你，Jenner 先生。
Cedric	Just call me Cedric, let me show you your cubicle, here it is.	叫我Cedric，讓我帶你到的小隔 間，這裡就是了。
Raymond	Thank you Cedric. I think I'll enjoy working with you.	謝謝你Cedric。我想我會喜歡和 你一起工作的。
Cedric	So will I. Ok, Raymond, do you have any questions about the company or your duties?	我也是。Ok，Raymond，你有 沒有任何關於公司或是你的工作 職責的問題要問呢？
Raymond	Yes, I do have tons of questions. Let me start with a rumor. I've heard that this company is very strict to its staff, is that true?	有，我有一大堆的問題。讓我先 從謠言開始。我聽說公司對員工 十分的嚴厲，是真的嗎？
Cedric	Not exactly. So long as you follow all regulations, just like in the other companies.	並不盡然。只要你能守規定，就 像是在其他的公司一樣。
Raymond	Oh, I see. I've heard the rumor from my former colleague, and he almost made me believe that. On the interview, my interviewer informed me that I'll need to travel a lot, is that true?	喔，我懂了。我從我以前的同事 那裡聽到這一個傳聞，他幾乎要 讓我相信這事了。在我的面試 上，，我的面試官告訴我我將要 常常出差，是真的嗎？

Cedric	Yes, it's true. You and I will have to be dealing with overseas companies and flying to the other side of the world from time to time.	是，沒錯。你和我將負責與外國公司的業務，需要不時的飛到世界的另一頭。
Raymond	That will be great. I will resign myself to your guidance.	那就太好了。我將會遵從你的指示的。
Cedric	Don't be so modest, Raymond. From what I have heard, you are excellently fit for this position, and we really need your experience in this field. I hope we can help each other in our work.	不要這麼謙虛，Raymond。從我所聽到的，你是這個職位的最佳人選，我們非常需要你在這個領域的經驗。我希望我們在工作上能互相幫忙。
Raymond	Sure, because we are partners.	當然，因為我們是夥伴。
Cedric	Thank you, partner. Oh, I have to remind you one thing that we sometimes have to get our work done under super strict deadlines. You have to learn to enjoy pressure in this company.	謝啦，夥伴。喔，我提醒你一件事，我們時常要在非常緊迫的期限內完成工作。在這間公司裡你必須學著享受壓力。
Raymond	Ok, thanks for the advice. I've found swimming an excellent way to relieve my work-related stress.	Ok，謝謝忠告。我發現游泳十分適合抒解我工作上的壓力。
Cedric	Wow, same as me. I think we have a many things in common. It's a great beginning for our partnership.	哇，和我一樣。我想我們有許多相同的地方。這對我們的夥伴關係是個好的開始。

精選單字及片語

1. flexible working hours　彈性工時
   I don't have to get into work at 9 like most of people, we do flexible working hours in our office.
   我不需要像大部分的人一樣九點上班，我們公司實施彈性工時

2. afterwards *adv.*　然後，以後，之後。
   Afterwards, he was sorry for what he had said.
   之後他對他所說過的話感到後悔。

3. settle in　安頓，適應新環境
   I still need time to settle in my new job.
   我還是需要時間適應我的新工作

4. cubicle　辦公室的隔間，小房間。
   I love to decorate my cubicle with photos of my families and friends.
   我喜歡用我家人及朋友的照片來裝飾我的辦公室隔間。

5. from time to time　不時，偶爾。
   He fired a series of questions at me from time to time.
   他不時的對我提出一系列的問題。

6. resign to　使順從，託付給。
   You shouldn't resign to your fate.
   你不應該向命運屈服。

精選句子與延伸

1. I know, that's also why I am attractive to this opening. I've been wanting to do more in executing my tasks.
   我了解，這也是我被這個工作吸引的原因，我一直希望可以更接近執行面
   opening(s) (n.) 空缺的職位。
   She gave me a tip about a job opening at her friend's travel agent.
   她建議我在她朋友的旅行社中有一個空缺。
   I've been wanting… have been + Ving 現在完成進行式，用來表示到說話的這一刻還在持續的進行。

2. Yes, I do have tons of questions.
   有，我有一大堆的問題。
   tons of 一大堆。多到要以噸計，用以表示非常的多，是一種數量上的誇飾，用以加強語氣。
   I drink tons of coffee everyday to keep myself awake!
   我每天都喝一大堆咖啡來保持清醒。

3. Oh, I have to remind you one thing that we sometimes have to get our work done under super strict deadlines.
   喔，我提醒你一件事，我們時常要在非常緊迫的期限內完成工作。
   under strict deadlines 在緊迫的期限內，這個句子中用 super 代替 very，是一種非正式但常聽到的說法，不能用於書寫上。

好書報報－生活系列

愛情之酒甜而苦。兩人喝，是甘露；
三人喝，是酸醋；隨便喝，要中毒。

精選出偶像劇必定出現的**80**個情境，
每個情境－必備單字、劇情會話訓練班、30秒會話教室
讓你跟著偶像劇的腳步學生活英語會話的劇情，
輕鬆自然地學會英語!

作者：伍羚芝
定價：新台幣349元
規格：344頁 / 18K / 雙色印刷

全書中英對照，介紹東西方節慶的典故，
幫助你的英語學習－學得好、學得深入!

用英語來學節慶分為兩大部分－東方節慶&西方節慶

每個節慶共**7**個學習項目：
節慶源由－簡易版、精彩完整版＋實用單字、閱讀測驗、
習俗放大鏡、實用會話、常用單句這麼說、互動單元...

作者：Melanie Venekamp、陳欣慧、倍斯特編輯團隊
定價：新台幣299元
規格：304頁 / 18K / 雙色印刷

用現有的環境與資源，為自己的小寶貝
創造一個雙語學習環境；讓孩子贏在起跑點上!

我家寶貝愛英文，是一本從媽咪懷孕、嬰兒期到幼兒期，
會常用到的單字、對話，必備例句，
並設計單元延伸的互動小遊戲以及童謠，
增進親子關係，也讓家長與孩子一同學習的參考書!

作者：Mark Venekamp & Claire Chang
定價：新台幣329元
規格：296頁 / 18K / 雙色印刷 / MP3

好書報報

心理學研究顯示，一個習慣養成，至少必須重複21次！
全書規劃30天學習進度表，搭配學習，
不知不覺養成學習英語的好習慣！

▲ 圖解學習英文文法 三效合一！
◎刺激大腦記憶◎快速掌握學習大綱◎複習迅速

▲ 英文文法學習元素一次到位！
◎20個必懂觀念 ◎30個必學句型 ◎40個必閃陷阱

▲ 流行有趣的英語！
◎「那裡有正妹！」
◎「今天我們去看變形金剛3吧！」

作者：朱懿婷
定價：新台幣349元
規格：364頁 / 18K / 雙色印刷

要說出流利的英文，就是需要常常開口勇敢說！

國外打工兼職很流行，如何找尋機會？
怎麼做完整的英文自我介紹，成功promote自己？
獨自出國打工，職場基礎英語對話該怎麼說？
不同國家、不同領域要知道那些common sense？
保險健康的考量要更注意，各國制度大不同？

6大主題 30個單元 120組情境式對話 30篇補給站！
九大學習特色：
■主題豐富多元 ■多種情境演練 ■激發聯想延伸
■增強單字記憶 ■片語邏輯組合 ■例句靈活套用
■塊狀編排歸納 ■舒適閱讀視覺 ■吸收效果加倍

作者：Claire Chang & Melanie Venecamp
定價：新台幣469元
規格：560頁 / 18K / 雙色印刷

上班族一開口就會的英語溝通術

作　　者／倍斯特編輯部

封面設計／King Chen

內頁構成／菩薩蠻有限公司

發 行 人／周瑞德

企劃編輯／倍斯特編輯部

特約編輯／陳欣慧

印　　製／世和印製企業有限公司

初　　版／2013 年 12 月

定　　價／新台幣 329 元

出　　版／倍斯特出版事業有限公司

電　　話／（02）2351-2007

傳　　真／（02）2351-0887

地　　址／100 台北市中正區福州街 1 號 10 樓之 2

E m a i l ／best.books.service@gmail.com

總 經 銷／商流文化事業有限公司

地　　址／新北市中和區中正路752號7樓

電　　話／（02）2228-8841

傳　　真／（02）2228-6939

國家圖書館出版品預行編目(CIP)資料

上班族英語高校溝通術 / 倍斯特編輯部著. — 初
版. — 臺北市： 倍斯特, 2013. 12
　　面； 公分
　　ISBN 978-986-89739-7-8(平裝)

　1. 英語 2. 職場 2. 讀本

805.18　　　　　　　　　　　102024455